THE
PARTY
ON LAUREL
STREET

BOOKS BY RUTH HEALD

THE
PARTY
ON LAUREL
STREET

RUTH HEALD

Bookouture

Published by Bookouture in 2023

An imprint of Storyfire Ltd.
Carmelite House
50 Victoria Embankment
London EC4Y 0DZ

www.bookouture.com

ISBN: 978-1-83790-514-0
eBook ISBN: 978-1-83790-513-3

PROLOGUE

TWENTY-FIVE YEARS AGO

I'm here, because they're coming. Tonight. To these woods. The three girls.

I heard them plan their midnight feast, listened to their childish ideas.

They'd been jealous of the adults, having their own New Year's Eve party. Drinking and dancing and having fun. They'd been told they were too young, that they couldn't stay up.

So they've planned to sneak out, to meet in the woods. One will bring chocolate, one will bring crisps and one will bring Haribo. They'll sit in the woods and eat their wares, then tell ghost stories and dance.

The noise of the party drifts over the fields and into the woods. If I can hear it then the two of them who live in the street can hear it too. They'll be in their beds listening, waiting for the moment to sneak out. I look at my watch: 11.45 p.m. It's soon. They plan to sneak out at midnight, on the notes of 'Auld Lang Syne', while people hug and laugh and kiss and celebrate.

. . .

I hear footsteps. The first girl. I remain still, silent. I can see that her coat is too thin, that she's not wearing gloves. I rub my own gloved hands together, imagining her frozen fingers. But she is too excited to feel the cold. A white plastic bag swings back and forth in her hand as she runs to the clearing. The crisps. I can see there are two huge packets, sticking out of the top of the bag. She'll be pleased with herself. She's done well.

She has a rucksack on her shoulders. A dirty-red colour, an old one she used to take to school a few years ago, before her mother made her replace it with a new one. A second girl appears now, the one from the council flats in the village. She always seems so wired, always on edge, fuelled by adrenaline. She hugs her friend and shows off her chocolate. There are only two small bars, and her friend looks disappointed.

When the third girl comes, she is jittery. Her eyes keep darting round as if she senses me watching. She hasn't thought to dress in her day clothes like the others. Instead she is wearing pyjamas under her coat and she shivers. I can tell she wants to go home. I want to reach out to her, to take her.

But I don't. I leave them alone to get on with their feast. I'll stay nearby, close enough to hear their chatter, to know they are still there.

After the little party finishes, there is no one but me to hear their screams. No one but me sees two of them running back through the woods as if someone is chasing them, their legs pumping frantically as they stumble over tree roots.

Two girls have left the woods. There is one girl remaining. And I must find her.

ONE

NOW

Monday 2nd January

Mel's headlights rolled over the small white sign protruding from the overgrown hedge.

Laurel Street.

The road sign was deliberately discreet. You could only spot it if you knew where to look. The people on the street didn't like strangers intruding on their lives.

Mel felt nostalgia wash over her. She was coming home. The place where she'd grown up, changed from a child into a woman. The place where her grandmother had provided her with respite from her neglectful mother. And the place where her best friend disappeared, aged ten. She gripped the steering wheel harder, overcome by a mix of emotions. When she was living in London she'd longed for the fresh air of the countryside, and the feeling of community in the street. But the shadow of Erin's disappearance would always hang over it.

Mel glanced in her mirror to check on Lily sleeping in her

car seat in the back, mouth open, eyes closed, her mop of dark brown hair a carbon copy of her husband Luke's. They'd celebrated her first birthday just before Christmas, and Mel could hardly believe her maternity leave had come to an end already.

'We're here,' she whispered, checking behind her in her mirror, her fifteen-year-old purple Fiat Punto rattling as she turned into the small road. Luke was following in his van, all their worldly possessions loaded into the back.

The narrow private street had a 5mph speed limit, and Mel drove slowly past rolling fields, aware of the speed bumps that were designed to ruin the suspension of any cars that broke the rule. Ahead of her she could see the two neat rows of cottages that led to the huge Gothic mansion where Erin had lived with her mother, Tamsin. Years ago, this had been a country estate, with the manor house at its centre. Tamsin was the last descendant of the original owner and now its only occupant.

She thought of her friends in London, how their mouths had dropped open when she'd shown them pictures of the estate, and the cottage she'd be moving into. Her friend Gabbie's Instagram account showed the street in all its picture-postcard perfection: horses in green rolling fields, the rows of quaint cottages, wildflowers growing next to the wooden swing that hung from a branch of the old oak tree on the little green. Gabbie had been Mel's best friend as a teenager. She'd moved back to the street six months before with her husband, into the house next to Tamsin's, the second-biggest house on the street, redeveloped and extended beyond recognition from the maid's cottage it had once been.

A howl of wind came from nowhere, and Lily stirred in the back and then woke up with a muffled sob, which quickly turned into a scream. Mel knew she must be hungry after the two-hour journey.

'Nearly there,' Mel said softly, slowing the car to a crawl

and turning in her seat to squeeze her daughter's leg. 'Our new home.'

There was a sudden rapping next to Mel's head and Mel spun back round in shock, pushing her foot down hard on the brake. A face appeared at the car window. A man with long dark hair and a thick beard. She froze for a moment, terrified, her feelings from childhood suddenly engulfing her. After Erin disappeared, the children on the street had been told again and again to watch out for strange men.

She took deep breaths, reminding herself that she was no longer that child. She was an adult moving to her dream home and she had nothing to fear.

The man knocked again. 'You weren't looking where you were going!' he shouted through the window. 'You could have hit me.'

Instinctively, Mel turned away from him, not making eye contact. She put the car into gear and drove on. When she glanced in the mirror, she saw the man was walking a brown Labrador. He was almost invisible in the dark in his bulky winter coat. He must be a local, one of the neighbours. She kicked herself for driving off like that, for being so rude.

Shaking, she kept driving, reaching the line of cottages that used to serve as homes for the workers on the estate. Mel's grandmother's house was the third one on the right, backing on to fields that led down to the woods. It was her house now. She would make a life for her family here.

Mel pulled up onto the driveway slowly, taking the turn between the two pillars carefully. In the van behind her Luke pressed his horn lightly. She glanced in her rear-view mirror and saw his wide grin splitting his face. He meant the honking as a joke – he was always teasing her about her driving – but Mel winced. The noise was bound to annoy the neighbours. She half expected the man with the Labrador to come rushing back to tell them off.

Mel eased herself out of the car, stiff from driving. Behind her, Luke jumped out of the van.

He put his arm round her as they took in the homely cottage with the overgrown garden. 'It's wonderful here,' he said simply. 'We're so lucky.'

Then he went round the back of Mel's Fiat and got Lily out of her car seat, hugging her close to him in the cold night air. As Mel looked at the house, a rush of memories of her gran made her vision blur. She remembered her bent over the flowerbeds pulling up the weeds; her smiling as she opened the door to Mel. The fact that Mel would never see her again hit her like a ton of bricks.

Luke seemed to sense her distress. 'It must be hard coming back without your grandmother here,' he said softly, holding Lily tightly as he absorbed Mel into a family embrace.

Mel nodded. 'Let's go inside,' she said.

Luke smiled. 'I'd carry you over the threshold if I didn't already have Lily,' he said.

'It's OK,' Mel said. 'I'm a bit heavier than I was when we first moved into our place in London.' Mel felt self-conscious about the baby weight she'd put on, but life had seemed too busy and full-on for her to be able to shift it.

'You're still absolutely stunning,' Luke said, with a cheeky grin. He took her hand as they reached the front door.

Mel unlocked it and as they stepped inside, a musty smell engulfed them, but it was too cold to open the windows. Mel reached for the thermostat and turned it up. She heard the clunk of the central heating coming on and let out her breath, relieved. At least the boiler was still working. Luke had been over to the house a few times the previous week to make sure everything was ready for them to move in.

'Right then,' Luke said. 'I'll go and get the rest of the things out of the van.' He handed Lily to Mel and ambled out.

Lily started to grumble, and Mel reached into her bag for

her training cup of water, which was nearly empty. She was about to go to the kitchen at the back of the house to fill it up, when she paused.

She could hear voices coming from the kitchen. Men's voices, talking quietly. She shivered as she thought back to her childhood, wandering through the woods with her friends, the glimpse of a man following them, Erin's later disappearance. Was there someone in their kitchen?

Luke came in with a pile of boxes, and put them in the middle of the living room floor in front of her.

'Shh,' she whispered. 'Can you hear that?'

He nodded slowly, and she could see his body tensing as he glanced round the room. His gaze settled on a heavy metal doorstop in the shape of a cat and he lifted it easily.

Clutching it in his hands he crept over to the door to the kitchen. Mel watched, fear caught in her throat, afraid of who might be behind the door, afraid of what Luke might do to them.

'Hello?' Mel called out, her voice timid.

Luke frowned and pushed open the heavy kitchen door. It swung back and banged against the wall.

Mel let Luke go through the door first, and then, seeing there was no one there, stepped through behind him, still holding Lily. The strip-light flickered above the kitchen counter and Mel saw the source of the noise. A small radio was playing Radio 4. She shivered. Had Luke left the radio on the last time he was here?

A figure rose from behind the kitchen island and Mel gasped.

She saw Luke lift the metal doorstop, and then stop.

The woman's eyes widened and then her face split into a huge smile. 'Mel!' she said. 'I didn't hear you come in! I had the radio on and I was concentrating, sorting out your fridge.'

'Gabbie!' Mel said, her fear quickly turning to excitement as she grinned back at her friend. Mel wrapped her arms around her, feeling her small frame underneath her fitted green gilet. 'I'm so pleased to see you!'

'Me too,' Gabbie said, holding her a bit longer than necessary. Mel smelt slightly stale alcohol on her breath.

'Good to see you again, Gabbie,' Luke said, stepping forward and giving her a light peck on the cheek. 'Thanks for sorting out the fridge... but you really didn't have to.'

'Oh, I just wanted to make sure you had supplies for the morning. Bread, milk, cheese. I had a spare key that your grandmother had given Tamsin, so I let myself in. I hope I didn't scare you.'

'No, of course not,' Mel said, glancing at Luke, who had put down the cat doorstop.

'So this is Lily,' Gabbie said, reaching out and gently stroking her chubby cheek. 'She's so gorgeous. You're both so lucky.'

'Thanks,' Mel said, with a smile.

Lily started to whine again. 'She's hungry.' Mel shifted Lily's position against her chest.

'Of course. I'll let you get on.' Gabbie's face adjusted shape, and she smiled. 'I've put champagne in the fridge to welcome you to the house. I had to clean it out a bit, that's why I was crouched down like that.'

'Thanks,' said Luke. 'That's very kind.'

'No problem,' Gabbie said, smiling at Luke. 'It's nice to see you finally moving in, after all the work you put in last week.' Gabbie pushed her blonde hair back behind her ear.

Mel smiled and squeezed Luke's arm. Luke hadn't mentioned running into Gabbie when he'd been working on the house last week. 'We wanted to make sure it was safe for Lily,' Mel said. 'I don't think the electrics had been checked for at least forty years.'

'Well, I'd better be off,' Gabbie said. 'You should both come round to ours for dinner and drinks one day. Stuart would love to see you, too.'

'That sounds great,' Mel said, smiling, grateful to Gabbie for making her feel so at home, so quickly. She and Gabbie had lost touch over the years, but it seemed like it would be easy to settle back into their friendship, as if neither of them had ever left.

Mel showed her out. 'See you soon!' she shouted as she disappeared down the street.

After Gabbie left, Luke gave Lily her water, and she sat next to them on the sofa.

'I can't believe we thought Gabbie was an intruder,' he said, his face flushed.

'I know!' Mel grinned. 'At least you didn't hit her with that doorstop.'

'I just picked it up to protect you and Lily. I'd never have used it.'

Mel leant her head into the soft wool of his jumper. 'I know,' she said, contentedly. She was glad he'd been there. With him by her side, the fear that she'd lived with for nearly her whole life seemed more manageable. She turned her head and looked into his eyes. 'I feel safe with you.'

He smiled down at her, revealing the dimples in his cheeks that made him look so much younger than he was. 'You *are* safe with me,' he said, as he stroked her hair. 'Let's unpack the rest of the van. Before the evening gets away from us. And then we can get out the champagne that Gabbie bought and toast our new home.'

TWO

The next day, after a long day of unpacking and debating paint colours for the living room, Mel and Luke took Lily for a walk down Laurel Street in the pushchair. It was already dark, and the sky was cloudless, the stars sparkling in the sky. Lily marvelled at the Christmas lights and trees which were still up in the windows of some of the cottages on the street.

'We need to go soon,' Luke said, looking at his watch.

Mel nodded. It was the day she dreaded every year, when Tamsin held the annual memorial for Erin at the village church.

'Do you want to walk?' Luke asked.

'No,' Mel said quickly. 'It's much easier to drive.' The walk to the church was through the woods behind the cottages. The woods where Erin had gone missing twenty-five years before. Mel had been so familiar with those woods as a child; she'd loved watching the squirrels and mice that had scrambled through the undergrowth, and the sense of peace she'd felt under the canopy of tree branches. When she'd lived in the village with her mother, they'd walked through regularly to visit her gran and Erin. But after Erin disappeared, Mel had never been back.

On the drive to the village, they saw a family walking together in woolly hats and thick coats: a mother and father, two children and two grandparents. Mel felt a twist of longing in her heart and thought of her grandmother, who had always gone to the memorial with her until she became too frail. Neither she nor Luke had close family anymore and they'd spent Christmas just the three of them. Mel had felt full of delight watching Lily opening her presents, but she couldn't help wishing they'd had family to share it with.

They passed the school that Mel, Erin and Gabbie had gone to together, the school where Mel herself would be teaching next week. She knew she had been lucky to find a job nearby. One of the teachers had retired early due to poor health, and she was taking over the year two class.

When her grandmother had died Mel hadn't been sure she wanted to come back to Laurel Street. Her happiest memories were from the time she lived with her gran, after her mother had become too unwell to look after her. But the street would always remind her of Erin, of the huge loss that hung over them all. She'd inherited her grandmother's house jointly with her mother, but her mother wanted to stay where she was in Spain. They'd talked about selling the house and splitting the proceeds, but when Mel and Luke's landlord in London had said he was increasing the rent on their one-bedroom flat, it seemed obvious they should move to Laurel Street.

As they pulled into the church car park, Mel took a deep breath to calm herself. Mel had been to the memorial every year, even when she'd moved far away. She hadn't wanted to go to the first one, but her grandmother had made her, forcing her into the church and then to light a candle. She'd only been eleven, and at that time there'd still been hope that Erin would somehow be found alive somewhere, or would just reappear one day back at Tamsin's house. But hope had faded with each passing year.

As Mel attached Lily to her chest in a sling, she saw several people she knew from the street standing in the churchyard: Gabbie and Stuart, Gabbie's parents, Tamsin, and a few others she recognised from further down the road. The numbers had dwindled over the years. Some of the residents had died or moved on, and had been replaced with people who had never known Erin. But no one who'd lived on the street at that time would ever forget her.

Luke squeezed Mel's hand as they followed the others into the church. They each lit a prayer candle and placed it in the candle rack, then went to sit down for the service. 'Are you OK?' Luke whispered in her ear before it began.

'I think so,' she said. It was good to have him by her side. For several years, after her grandmother had become ill, she'd come alone.

After the hymns and prayers, Tamsin spoke about her loss, her voice cracking with every word. Mel ran her hands through Lily's thick hair, unable to imagine the pain of losing a child.

Mel couldn't wait until the memorial finished and she could escape to the pub with Luke. The memories were always so painful, and the pub felt like a refuge. Her gran had used to take her there every year after the service, telling her she was a brave girl and buying her fish and chips.

In the pub, exactly three years ago, she'd met Luke. Mel was feeling drained after the church service. Her grandmother had been living in a home by then, so she was on her own. She'd recently split up with a man she'd assumed she had a future with, and had felt like her life was going nowhere. She'd been teaching at a primary school in London and she loved spending every day with the kids, but it had dawned on her that she was running out of time to meet someone to have her own. She hadn't wanted to come to the memorial, but she'd felt she had to. When Tamsin had spoken about Erin's life stopping aged ten, about all the things Erin might have done, Mel had felt an overwhelming sense of guilt for not making the most of hers.

Afterwards, she hadn't wanted to go back to her lonely flat in London. She'd wandered over to the pub to treat herself to a drink and a meal on her own. Somehow she thought it would be less lonely eating in a crowd of people than by herself at her flat. She'd been wrong, and the couples sitting at the nearby tables had only made her feel more miserable. Until Luke came along.

He'd come over to her table and asked if she wanted company. He was younger than her, still in his twenties, and she'd been surprised by how forward he was. He talked easily about everything and nothing, and she'd been charmed by his Scottish accent. He'd only moved down from Scotland a few weeks before and he was staying in a room above the pub, doing some building work in a house up the road. There'd been nothing left for him up in Scotland after his mother had died, and he wanted to try his luck in England like so many of his friends had.

They'd talked for hours, as Mel ate and Luke drank. She'd told him about the memorial service, about Erin, and he'd listened intently. It was good to talk to a stranger about it all. He'd made her feel at ease as he told her about his life in Scotland and his handyman business. He'd told her how his surname, Singh, and his thick dark hair came from his Indian mother. He hardly remembered his father, just like Mel didn't know hers, and for a moment she thought they had so much in common, before she stopped herself getting too excited about such a normal thing. And yet, as the night wore on the conversation quickly got deeper, and they talked about how they both longed for the close-knit nuclear family they hadn't had themselves.

When the bell for last orders rang and Mel said she had to go, Luke suggested she should stay. It was late for her to drive back, and he could see she was tired. He reached across the table and took her hand. She squeezed his hand back and looked searchingly into his eyes, as he leant across the table and kissed her deeply. She lost herself in the kiss, completely unaware of the other patrons in the pub.

'Do you want to come up for a cup of tea?' he said.

'A tea?' she said, laughing. 'Isn't coffee usually the euphemism?'

'Yeah, sorry,' he said. 'But I've used all the instant coffee. I only have tea.'

They'd both laughed then, as if it was the most hilarious thing that had ever been said, and she'd followed him up to his room, and watched him turn the key in the lock.

She had a moment when she thought she should turn back, that it was too risky to go to this room above a pub with this stranger, but the moment passed. She wasn't even drunk; she'd thought she was going to drive back, so she'd only had one glass of wine. No, this was what she wanted, Luke was what she wanted.

'You can sleep on the bed, if you like,' Luke said. 'I'll sleep on the floor.'

She smiled at him, reaching up and running her hands through his dark hair, then slipping them under the buttons of his dark blue shirt.

'I don't want that,' she'd said.

And then he'd lifted her up and carried her over to the bed.

After that night they'd never looked back. When Luke finished his work on the house in the village, he'd moved into Mel's flat in London and started a handyman business there. A year later they were married, and a year after that they had Lily.

THREE

Standing outside the church making small talk was always the most exhausting part of the memorial. Everyone was tired from Christmas and it was freezing cold, but Mel couldn't leave Tamsin there to face it alone. She put Lily's woolly hat on her head and stood on the dark pathway between the ancient gravestones. The others chatted about what a wonderful child Erin had been, how loved she'd been, what she might be doing if she was alive today. She'd always wanted to be a doctor. Mel nodded along, but the truth was she couldn't remember much about Erin anymore. Her best friend, the girl she'd done everything with as a child, had become lost in a sea of meaningless clichés. She tried to remember the fun times, the laughter, the dares they used to do, the tricks they played. But she couldn't even let herself think of that. Not without feeling the overwhelming guilt. That she was still here. And Erin had disappeared.

A bright light caught her eye. A TV camera had been set up in the corner of the churchyard. It was a long time since Erin's case had been covered by the news, but there must have been more interest because of the twenty-fifth anniversary. A reporter was walking round, looking for people to interview. Mel saw her approach Gabbie, who was swaying slightly. Gabbie nodded and walked with her to a suitable spot. Mel wondered if she should stop her. But she didn't. Any publicity for the case was good publicity. She left her to it, watching from a distance, despite the nervous knot in her stomach.

'Shall we go?' Luke said quietly. 'Have you spoken to everyone you need to?'

'Yes,' said Mel, glancing round the small group. She saw Tamsin on her own. 'I'll just go and say goodbye to Tamsin.'

'OK,' Luke said.

Mel walked the couple of steps over to Tamsin and put her hand on her arm. 'Thanks for organising this,' she said. 'It's good to remember Erin.'

Tamsin looked at her with irritation, sweeping back her long, fiery, auburn hair as it blew across her face. 'How could a mother not do this?' she asked. 'I think of her every day.'

'I know you do,' Mel said. 'I do too.' The white lie couldn't hurt.

'And I'm sure she's still out there,' Tamsin said. 'I know she is. I can feel it in my bones.'

Mel nodded and glanced back at Luke. When Mel had been a child, she had convinced herself that Erin had run away and would eventually return. Erin had often talked of how she hated her stepfather, how she wanted to escape. But as the years had passed, Mel had started to agree with the others on the street; it was most likely that Erin wasn't alive anymore. She put her arms around Tamsin, then pulled away. 'You take care,' she said.

Tamsin reached out and clutched her arm, and Mel could see tears in her eyes. When Mel was a teenager, she had been the one to go round and comfort her, to listen to her stories about Erin. Mel had been struggling with the loss, too. She'd had therapy paid for by her grandmother, but she'd found it easier to talk to Tamsin. Something about listening to Tamsin had felt right. When she had been younger Tamsin had been a bit like a mother to her, and Mel had felt she'd owed her that kindness.

'Mel,' Tamsin said. 'What are you doing now? Do you and Luke want to come back to mine? I'd love to see Lily. She's growing up so quickly.'

Mel looked into Tamsin's eyes, and could see how much she didn't want to go back to her house alone. Mel felt a surge of pity for her. Tamsin had split up with her husband shortly after Erin disappeared and had been on her own ever since. She needed Mel. Mel thought of the pub dinner she'd planned with Luke, but then dismissed that idea.

'Of course,' she said to Tamsin. 'We'd love to come back to yours for a bit.'

They parked their car next to the green and Mel carried Lily past the wooden swing. In front of the manor house, an indignant open-mouthed gargoyle sat on top of a dry circular fountain. Tamsin let them into the house in silence.

'I only use the upstairs now,' she said, as she started up the wide staircase. It was years since Mel had been inside. She and Erin had used to climb in and out through the basement window as often as they'd used the front door. When Erin had been alive Tamsin had been planning to convert the lower floors into flats, but it had never happened. Now the lower floors were left empty.

'Wow,' said Luke, running his hand over the ornate banister as they went up the wide staircase. He looked up at the paintings of Tamsin's ancestors that stared back down at them from the walls. 'This place is amazing.'

'It's been in my family for over a century,' Tamsin said, and

Mel remembered the first time she'd come here to play with Erin, how overwhelmed she'd been. At that time, she'd been living with her mother in a two-bed council flat in the village the other side of the woods where the memorial had been held. She'd met Erin at the village school, where she would soon be teaching.

They got to the top floor of the house, and Tamsin showed them inside.

'Let me show you my studio,' she said. Tamsin had always been an artist, but now she had knocked down the walls of the top floor and made the front half into a huge open-plan artist's studio.

There were paintings and sketches everywhere, half-finished on easels and in piles leaning against the walls.

'It's wonderful in here,' Mel said, adjusting Lily's position in her arms. She was relieved that Tamsin was still painting, still finding some joy in life.

'I'm lucky. From my window I can see the whole landscape spread before me. Laurel Street and beyond. I can see the tiny shifts every day as the seasons change.'

Luke took Lily from Mel and set her down on the floor, following her closely as she crawled around the studio.

Mel looked at the closest picture, marvelling at the detail. It was the view from the window on the left, over Gabbie's house. Her huge cottage was in the foreground, along with the dilapidated pool house and the new stables. Behind the buildings the rolling fields led down to the woods beyond.

'It really captures Laurel Street,' she said.

Tamsin smiled. 'I've lived here all my life. I know every nook and cranny.'

There was a small balcony to her left, full of overflowing pot plants, and Mel pulled the catch on the full-length single-glazed window and stepped out into the drizzle. The balcony below her feet was stable, but the tiles were slippery from the rain.

The waist-height railing was rusty and when she rested her hand on it, it gave under the pressure, tilting alarmingly. She took a quick step back, her heart pounding. What if she'd leant on it when she was holding Lily?

'Sorry, the railing's a little unstable,' Tamsin said. 'I should have warned you.'

'It's OK,' Mel said, standing back from the edge. From here she could see right inside Gabbie's house. Gabbie was standing by the mirror in the bedroom, brushing her hair. Then, as if sensing Mel watching, she glanced up and quickly drew the curtains.

Tamsin took her arm and led her back inside. 'This is the picture I'm working on at the moment,' she said, pointing to a canvas.

Mel looked at the painting. A wood in the moonlight. Three children playing in the dark beneath the trees, their bright coats smudges against the dark night. Mel, Gabbie, Erin. It was the night Erin disappeared.

'Was it like that?' Tamsin asked. 'That night – the three of you playing together?'

'I think so,' Mel said. 'At least, that's what I remember.'

Tamsin sighed heavily. 'It's so hard not knowing what happened to her. Most of the time I'm so certain she's alive...' She paused and swallowed back tears. 'But sometimes I can't ignore what everyone else thinks. That Joe took her.'

Mel shivered at his name. Joe had been the maintenance man for the estate, and had previously worked for Tamsin in her home, where he'd become close to Erin, almost like a father figure. They'd spend time together just the two of them in his storage hut in the woods. At the time Mel hadn't realised how odd it was for a thirty-year-old man to befriend a ten-year-old child.

'I can't believe I trusted him,' Tamsin said. 'I let him work in my house, play with my daughter. Could it have been me who introduced her to her murderer?'

Mel put her arm round Tamsin as her body shook. 'No one knows what happened to her,' she said. 'Erin could still be out there somewhere.' But even as she said it, Mel felt guilty. It wasn't what she believed anymore.

'I was looking through all the old newspaper articles before the memorial,' Tamsin said. 'I'd forgotten how convinced everyone was that Joe killed her. I think at the time I just wanted to ignore the evidence, believe she was alive.'

Mel could see the internal battle raging in Tamsin written all over her face. She desperately wanted to believe Erin was still alive, but as time went by it was getting harder and harder to hang onto hope. Mel remembered reading the newspaper articles about Joe at her mother's kitchen table. For weeks, the paper had been obsessed with him. The headlines were etched into her brain.

TROUBLED LONER ARRESTED FOR MURDER

CONCERNED LOCALS RAISED SUSPICIONS ABOUT JOE MURRAY MONTHS AGO, BUT POLICE DID NOTHING

DID JOE MURRAY FLASH AT YOUNG GIRLS IN THE WOODS JUST WEEKS BEFORE HIS ARREST?

'The press were so interested in Erin,' Mel said. 'Everyone just wanted to find her.'

'Do you think they were right about Joe?'

'I don't know,' Mel repeated.

Mel could recall how Joe always seemed to be around wherever she and her friends were. After Erin disappeared, it had turned out that a couple of residents in the street had already spoken to Joe about the time he spent with Erin, and warned him off. And there were rumours about a flasher in the woods. The police had arrested Joe immediately when Erin disappeared and they had interrogated him for days. But there had never been enough evidence to charge him.

FOUR

'That was intense,' Luke said, as Mel unlocked the door of their cottage an hour later. Mel hadn't wanted to leave Tamsin until she was sure she was OK, and would be able to get through the night on her own.

'It's always like that here at this time of the year. It's emotional for everyone. But the street isn't like that normally.' She frowned. She'd sounded more flippant than she intended.

'I can understand how something like that leaves a scar on the community,' Luke said.

'Yeah. It doesn't help that Erin's never been found. There's always an idea in people's minds that she might still be out there.'

'What do you think?' Luke asked.

'I don't know,' Mel said, thinking of Joe, of the fear she'd lived with throughout her teenage years that he might come back. Even if he hadn't hurt Erin, the thought of the way he'd watched them made her body tense.

Mel fed Lily and then took her up to bed, reading to her until she fell asleep. Mel's new job at the school was starting on Monday and she needed to prepare. At the village school, she'd be one of just seven teachers, unlike in the sprawling inner-city London primary school she'd previously taught at. She settled down beside Luke on the sofa with her computer. The school had sent her pages and pages of information and policies, which she'd saved on her desktop. She opened up her timetable and started to prepare lesson plans for the first week's English lessons.

'Looks like you've got a lot to do,' Luke said.

'I feel so unprepared. There hasn't been much time, what with the move.'

He kissed her on the cheek. 'I'm sure you'll be great,' he said. 'Kids love you. Now, what would you have had to eat if we'd managed to go to the pub like we'd planned?'

'Umm, I don't know. Probably a burger.'

'Right then, I'm going to nip down to the supermarket and pick us up some burgers and chips to cook in the oven. We'll have burgers à la Luke.'

'À la Luke?' Mel laughed.

'Yep, a speciality of mine. Burger with ketchup and cheese, too. It will blow your mind.'

'Sounds delicious,' Mel said.

Mel managed to finish the first lesson plan while Luke was out and then they ate together, with a single glass of wine each. She felt a wave of exhaustion rush over her. Although it was the anniversary of her and Luke meeting, Erin's disappearance would always overshadow it.

'I'm glad today's over,' she said. 'I find this time of year so difficult.'

'I can't imagine what it's like to lose a friend when you're that young.'

'We should watch the local news. Gabbie's interview might be on it.' Mel had tried to avoid thinking about what Gabbie might have said in the interview, whether it would upset Tamsin. Historically it had always been Tamsin who'd spoken to the press. And Mel had seen that Gabbie had been drunk, swaying slightly in front of the microphone.

It was past ten already, so they switched on the TV and watched the national news while they waited for the local news. There was a long segment on the redundancies in the local fire brigade, then something about a stabbing in a town centre. Mel realised with relief that Gabbie was unlikely to be on, that the memorial might not be covered at all. But then, just before the weather, the news anchor started showing a picture of a smiling schoolgirl from the 1990s. Erin. The newsreader spoke about how it was twenty-five years since the disappearance, then cut to the interview with Gabbie.

'So, Gabbie, you were one of the two girls with Erin in the woods that night?'

Gabbie nodded. 'Yes, me and my friend Mel. We're both living locally again now. And we've never forgotten Erin.'

Mel tensed up. Why was Gabbie mentioning her name? When they'd been children they had remained anonymous, their names kept out of the papers.

Gabbie was staring intently into the camera as she spoke about how much she still missed her best friend. Mel winced at her exaggeration. Gabbie had only moved into Laurel Street six months before Erin had disappeared. She hadn't known her like Mel had.

'No one knows what happened to the missing girl,' the interviewer was saying, 'and many years on, this local community is still feeling the effects.'

Gabbie interrupted her. 'We do know what happened,' she said.

'You have a theory about what happened?' she asked.

'There was a man following us. He worked on the estate. We saw him in the woods that night.'

The programme cut back to the studio. 'There are many theories about what happened back then,' the anchor said. 'But only one thing is certain. Erin Radley hasn't been found in the last twenty-five years. And with each passing year, it gets less likely that she will be.'

Mel stared at the television, open-mouthed. She could hardly believe what Gabbie had said, so clearly pointing the finger at Joe. Wherever Joe was now, she hoped he wasn't watching.

Half an hour later, when Mel was starting up the stairs to go to bed, the doorbell rang. It was past eleven, far too late for anyone to call round.

'I'll get it,' Luke said, from the living room sofa. 'Maybe one of the neighbours needs help with something.'

Mel waited on the stairs, listening to him opening the door.

'Oh,' he said. 'Gabbie?'

'Is Mel in?'

Mel came back down the stairs at the sound of Gabbie's voice. 'Is everything alright?' she asked her friend.

'Yeah,' Gabbie said, slurring her words. 'It's fine. Did you see my interview? Did you think it was OK?'

'Umm... yeah. But Gabbie, I'm not sure it was a good idea to mention Joe.'

'Oh,' Gabbie looked crestfallen. 'I just wanted to raise awareness about the case, you know. I thought you'd want that too. I'm sorry if it upset you.'

'It's alright,' Mel said, her irritation with her friend fading as she apologised.

'I hate today,' Gabbie continued. 'I can never sleep afterwards. Do you want to have a drink with me? I brought wine.' Gabbie raised her arm and Mel saw the bottle of chilled white wine in her hand.

'Gabbie, I'm sorry, I can't,' Mel said. 'It's late, and I'm absolutely shattered.'

Gabbie's face fell. 'I thought it would be like the old days. Sneaking out together at night for a drink on the green.'

'We're not teenagers anymore,' Mel said softly.

'I know, but... god, I could do with a drink.'

Mel put her hand on Gabbie's arm. She was reminding Mel of her mother, how she had always needed a drink to get through. How Mel's role had been to calm her, to soothe her emotions. 'It's OK,' she said. 'I can't do tonight, but let's have a drink together another night.'

'Oh,' Gabbie said. 'Why don't you come round to dinner on Saturday? With me and Stuart? Would that suit you? We'd love to have you round.'

Mel glanced back at Luke, and he nodded. 'That would be perfect,' she said.

FIVE

'Are you sure we needed to dress up?' Luke said uncertainly as they walked across the green to Gabbie's house for dinner on Saturday night. He had reluctantly put on smart chinos and an ironed shirt. Mel had squeezed into a long navy dress that had been loose when she'd bought it years before, but now clung to her figure. She carried Lily, while Luke carried a travel cot for her to nap in while they ate dinner.

'Definitely,' Mel said, reassuringly. 'Gabbie messaged me earlier saying it was a great excuse to get into our best clothes.' Mel had been looking forward to the dinner all day. It was good to have Gabbie so close again. Recently, with their busy lives, they had only managed to meet up once a year in the summer, when Mel was on school holidays.

When they knocked Stuart opened the door with a smile, and pecked Mel on each cheek in turn. He was dressed almost identically to Luke, except his shirt was pale blue, whereas Luke's was green.

Mel felt strange stepping into the house that she and

Gabbie had coveted as teenagers. Back then the owners had been an elderly couple and Mel and Gabbie had never set foot across the threshold, just admired it from afar.

Mel recognised the hallway from Gabbie's Instagram photos, mirrors on each side reflecting a vase of fake orange and white flowers on a mantelpiece over and over again. When Mel slipped off her shoes they sat alone on the pale tiles, looking out of place and messy.

'Let me take your coat,' Stuart said. Mel handed a sleepy Lily to Luke and Stuart whisked her coat away into an understairs cupboard. 'I'll get you a bottle of wine,' he said. 'Or a glass, if you'd prefer.' He laughed, and Mel and Luke exchanged glances.

'A glass will be fine,' Mel said.

'If you say so. Gabbie's told me all about what you were like as teenagers. How much wine you could put away.' It was true that when Mel was a teenager she'd been a big drinker, but since then she'd rarely drunk at all, having seen how alcohol had eaten away at her mother.

'You'd think Stuart was never young himself,' Gabbie said with a smile, as she appeared behind Stuart in a cornflower-blue dress which matched her eyes and clung to her curves. Her blonde hair was neatly blow-dried and her make-up immaculate.

'Come on in,' Stuart said. 'Gabbie's cooking a moussaka.'

'It smells delicious,' Mel said, as she stepped into their house.

'It's not quite ready yet,' Gabbie said. 'It needs a bit more time in the oven. But I've got cheese to go with the wine while we wait.'

'Where should we put Lily's travel cot?' Mel asked, as they went into the living room. It was sparsely furnished, with white sofas facing a TV that took up the whole wall, and a huge blue rug in the middle of the room with a glass coffee table on top.

Every surface was clear of clutter. When Gabbie had been growing up, she'd liked 1960s chintz and china animal ornaments. There was no sign of any of that now.

'Oh, wherever,' Gabbie said airily.

Mel moved the coffee table a little and set up the travel cot. Lily had fallen asleep in Luke's arms, and he managed to place her in the cot without disturbing her. Mel covered her with a blanket.

'There we go,' Mel said. 'Fast asleep for now. That's a change.'

'She's so gorgeous,' Gabbie said, handing Mel a glass of wine. 'You're so lucky.'

'And you,' Mel said, walking into the open-plan kitchen. Stuart was taking Luke to see his home gym at the back of the house. 'I can't believe you ended up living here.' This house had had everything they wanted as children: a swimming pool, a tennis court. They used to sneak out onto the tennis court at night, sitting in the corner of the court drinking cans of beer and crushing them in their fists, so that the local boys were blamed.

'That's the reward you get for marrying an investment banker.'

'What's that when it's at home?'

Gabbie laughed. 'Someone who can't do his own washing.'

Mel smiled. 'How's your job going?' she asked. Gabbie worked in communications for the council.

'Oh, it's fine. I don't love it, but I don't hate it. At least it's local. Stuart has to go to London a few days a week with his job. He's always back late. He works hard.'

'The wine's good,' Mel said, taking a sip.

'Stuart chose it from his wine cellar. I've got lots of cheese to soak it up.' She went over to the big American fridge and rooted around, pulling out packets of cheese and tearing each one open with a knife. She placed them haphazardly on a breadboard, then reached into her cupboard and pulled out a couple of packets of crackers.

'There you go,' she said, pleased with herself.

'Thank you.'

They looked out of the window and Gabbie pointed to the crumbling building close to the house. 'We're thinking of doing up the old pool house,' she said.

The swimming pool had fallen into disrepair when they were children and had been that way ever since. Mel and Erin had sometimes played there, before Gabbie had moved into the road.

'That's great,' said Mel, feeling a twinge of jealousy.

'Let me show you what we're planning,' Gabbie said. 'You can borrow my trainers. We're still the same size, aren't we? Size 7?'

'Yeah,' Mel said as Gabbie went to a small cupboard in the laundry room and pulled out two pairs of trainers.

She opened the patio doors and a cold waft of air came in. She placed the trainers outside on the patio, by the doors.

'Sorry,' she said. 'We need to put them on outside. Stuart doesn't like the kitchen floor getting dirty.' She laughed. 'It's easiest if you sit down with your feet sticking out the door.'

They sat next to each other doing up the trainers. 'Don't we need coats?' Mel asked, shivering in her dress.

'We'll only be outside a couple of minutes,' Gabbie said. She grabbed Mel's arm. 'Come on – I can't go back inside now I've got my shoes on.' Mel frowned. Gabbie sounded like a child.

But she followed Gabbie outside, her breath creating steam circles in the cold night air.

'Here we are,' Gabbie said, pushing open the door of the pool house.

They stepped inside. In the entranceway there was a small changing area, with benches and forgotten pegs on each side.

They went through to the pool itself, sunken into the ground, overgrown with plants. Around it were dusty sunloungers, lost in the undergrowth.

'This could be spectacular,' Mel said.

'I can't wait to do it up,' Gabbie said. 'You'll be able to use it whenever you want, of course.'

'Brilliant,' Mel said, trying to imagine this place transformed, shining and modern, with white tiles and sparkling water. She imagined gliding through the blue pool, the sun shining through a clean glass roof. 'Then I'll be round all the time,' she said.

Gabbie's watch beeped and she looked down. 'The moussaka will be ready,' she said.

They went back into the house, and Gabbie showed her to the dining table. The table had folded cloth napkins to mark each place setting and winter candles and holly sprayed silver in the centre. Stuart poured more wine, while Gabbie dished up the meal.

'So, how are you settling in?' Stuart asked, once they were tucking into their food.

'Oh, really well,' Luke said. 'We love it here.'

'It feels like coming home,' Mel said. 'I've missed the place.'

'Everyone's made us feel so welcome,' Luke said. 'Although we came back at a strange time. The memorial...' he trailed off.

'Yes, well,' Stuart said. 'I go to support Gabbie. The best thing is to just get through it. And try not to drink too much.' He glanced at Gabbie, and Mel thought of her slurred television interview.

Gabbie got up suddenly from the table. 'I forgot to close the curtains,' she said. She glanced at Luke as she went over to the window. 'She's watching us again.'

Mel looked up out of the window and could see that Tamsin was up in her studio at the manor house opposite, painting.

'Stuart thinks we should report her,' Gabbie asked.

'To who?' Mel asked.

'To the police. We should be able to sit in our own house eating a meal without being watched,' Stuart said, flushing.

'Don't report her,' Mel said, feeling sorry for Tamsin. 'She's harmless. She's just lonely,'

Stuart changed the subject. 'So where are you from, Luke?'

'Scotland, can't you tell from the accent?'

'Ah, yes. And are your parents from there originally?'

Mel squeezed Luke's hand under the table. They both knew what Stuart was getting at.

'My mum's British Indian. She was born in London. And my dad's English. I moved to Scotland when I was a kid.'

'I see,' Stuart said, taking a sip of wine. 'Gabbie tells me you're a handyman?' Mel winced. He'd met Luke before, but clearly didn't remember much.

'Yep. Have been for over ten years. First up in Scotland, then in London.'

'Ah, great. I was wondering if I could rope you into some extra work on the estate. We don't have a maintenance man, but there's always lots of things that need doing.'

'What kind of work?'

'Oh, whatever comes up. Fixing things, unblocking drains, maintaining some of the brickwork on the garden walls. Everything and anything. We'd pay you, of course. I manage the fund on behalf of the residents of the street. We all put in some money each year.' He smiled. 'Actually, I think your contribution is overdue.'

'Oh, I'll transfer the money tomorrow,' Mel said, blushing. It had completely slipped her mind.

'I'm happy to take on the jobs,' Luke said. 'I've been looking for more work round here.'

'Good man,' Stuart said, reaching across the table to shake Luke's hand. 'To be honest, I'm not particularly inclined towards manual work.' Stuart looked down at his hands and laughed softly. 'Don't like getting my hands dirty, so to speak.'

Gabbie laughed. 'He really doesn't,' she said. 'He's terrible at fixing things.'

'Alright,' Stuart said. 'Calm down. I don't criticise your cooking, do I?' The moussaka was slightly burnt at the edges and Stuart shoved a bit into his mouth pointedly.

Gabbie looked tearful all of a sudden, and for a moment Mel thought she might get up and leave the table. But she didn't. Instead, she took a huge gulp of wine.

'This dinner's delicious,' Mel said brightly, glancing at Luke.

'It is,' Luke murmured in agreement. 'You'll have to give us the recipe. I'd like to have a go myself. Although I can't say I'm a great cook. I don't think it would turn out like this.' He smiled bashfully.

'Thank you,' Gabbie said. 'At least some people appreciate me.' Her eyes were still watery, and she stood up, glass in hand. 'Right,' she said. 'Dessert soon. Maybe Stuart will like that a bit better than the main course. But in the meantime, does anyone want more wine?'

SIX

The next morning, Mel took Lily for a walk down the street in the pushchair, to gather her thoughts before she started work the next day and Lily started nursery. Luke was off out in his van, dropping some of the things they'd cleared out of the house at the charity shop and putting up notices in the local shops about his handyman services. They'd had a busy week. Mel had prepared for school and cleared out some of her grandmother's things, while Luke had done odd jobs like putting the stair gates up and changing the lock on the front door. It had felt good, working together as a partnership to create a family home. They'd had big plans for decorating the rooms and buying new furniture, but that would have to wait until they had a bit more time.

She felt a mix of excitement and dread about starting school. She'd missed teaching – the class of eager six-year-olds in London always competing for her attention – but she knew it would be difficult to separate from Lily after a year's maternity leave.

'Look,' Mel said to Lily as she walked along the road. 'The first snowdrops. Spring is on its way already.' The delicate white flowers lined the verge of the street, the first ones starting to flower.

'It's so pretty, isn't it?' Mel said.

Lily giggled and Mel's heart contracted. She would miss her when she was at nursery.

A chocolate-brown Labrador appeared beside them and began sniffing round Lily's pushchair. Lily smiled in delight as its nose rubbed against her trouser leg.

Mel reached down and stroked it and looked up to see the owners approaching. She recognised the man's thick dark beard. He was the man who had berated her the day they moved in, told her she wasn't looking where she was going.

'Hello,' Mel said with a tentative smile. 'Your dog's beautiful.'

The woman, clad in a thick green winter coat and a bobble hat, beamed. 'Thank you,' she said. 'He's very friendly. I hope he wasn't bothering you.'

'Oh no, not at all. Lily loves him.'

'She's gorgeous.'

'Thank you. I'm Mel,' she said, reaching out her hand. 'My husband and I have just moved in up the road.'

'Ah, yes,' the man said. 'Of course. I saw you move in.' He didn't mention rapping on her window and Mel decided to let it go.

'Well, I'm Heather and this is Greg. We live towards the end of the road, in Gardener's Cottage.'

'Great to meet you.'

'You too. It's brilliant to have some new life on the street.' The couple started to walk away, and then the woman turned back suddenly. 'You wouldn't happen to be free this morning, would you? In about an hour? I'm having coffee with a few of the ladies from the street. Gabbie should be there. And her mum. Do you fancy joining? You can bring the little one, too.'

'Sure,' Mel said. 'I'd love to.' It would be nice to get to know others on the street a bit better, and it might be useful to make a good impression on Heather, as she'd clearly got off to a bad start with Greg.

An hour later, Mel was sitting in the living room of Gardener's Cottage with a cup of tea and a chocolate digestive in her hand. The dog, Charles, lay at her feet, in front of the roaring fire. Gabbie's mum, Deena, and Heather were entertaining Lily on the floor in the middle of the room.

'It's great to have another young family on the street,' Heather said.

'Yes,' Deena said. 'There's a bit more for kids to do here now. There's another family, the Dawsons, they live in Rose Cottage and have a six-year-old called Freya. A few years ago they built a tree house in the woods for the kids to play in.'

'Lily's a bit young for that,' Mel said.

'There's a baby swing down there, too,' Heather said. 'And a slide. They set up a play area for the local kids.' Mel shivered. She hadn't been to the woods in so many years, but now she was living back here, surely she'd have to. Lily loved nature; it would be a shame to deprive her of the woods on their doorstep.

'That's kind of them. I'll have to take Lily.'

'Otherwise the nearest playground is in Burton and you'd have to drive.'

Mel nodded. Lily adored collecting sticks and watching squirrels. Mel knew she'd love it down there.

'It's so good to have you back,' Deena said. 'Gabbie will be here soon. It's great to see the two of you back together again on Laurel Street.'

'It's good to be here,' Mel said, smiling. It felt like she was back where she belonged.

'You know, I've been a bit worried about Gabbie. She hasn't been herself lately. She's seemed – I don't know – a bit down. Maybe she's told you more about it?'

Mel shook her head, thinking of her friend's erratic behaviour after the memorial. 'She hasn't said anything to me. But I haven't been back long.'

'Maybe it's nothing. A mother always worries. But I suppose you already know that with Lily.'

'I definitely do,' Mel said, thinking how much more anxious she'd become since having a daughter.

'It gets harder as they get older, you know. That's the thing they never tell you. The bigger they are, the harder it gets. Even when they're adults. Well, then it's harder again, I think. Because you're not allowed to help them, even though you can see what's best for them.'

Mel wasn't quite sure what to say. Luckily they were interrupted by the doorbell.

'That will probably be Gabbie now,' Deena said brightly.

Heather went to the door, and in a moment came back with a woman with curly brown hair wearing well-fitted jeans and a red cashmere jumper, with matching red lipstick. 'This is Roz,' she said to Mel.

The women shook hands as Mel introduced herself. Roz's hand was freezing cold from the bitter weather outside.

'I live next door to you,' Roz said. 'In the cottage with the old oak tree.'

'I'm so glad to meet you,' Mel said sincerely. She was pleased to have a neighbour around her age.

'Where are you from?' Roz asked.

'We moved from London,' Mel said. 'But I originally grew up here, in the house we now live in. I lived with my grandmother as a teenager.'

'How lucky for you,' Roz said, looking Mel up and down.

'Well, yes. It's a lovely place to grow up.'

'It is, I'm sure. People work very hard to afford the houses on the street. It's idyllic.'

'Sure,' Mel said. 'I'm a teacher myself.' She didn't want Roz to think she wasn't working.

'Oh, that's interesting. Where do you teach? I'm a governor at the local school.'

Mel shifted uncomfortably. 'Woodside School?' she asked. 'I'm starting there tomorrow. Teaching year two.'

'Oh, well done you. It's a great school to be a part of,' she smiled. 'If you need any inside information, just let me know.'

The doorbell rang again, interrupting them. Mel was closest to the door, so she got up and went into the hallway to answer it.

'Gabbie!' she said as she opened the door.

'Oh – Mel? I didn't expect to see you here.'

'Heather invited me.'

'You could have said no,' Gabbie whispered. 'I'm only here because my mum likes me to come. These things are usually so tedious. They like to talk about petty neighbourhood disputes. Noise and unruly behaviour, that kind of thing.'

'I wouldn't have thought you get much of that round here?'

'Exactly. We don't. Usually it's because someone had Radio 4 on too loud in their garage. Something like that.' Mel stifled a laugh and they went into the living room together.

'Gabbie! How's Stuart?' Deena asked.

'He's fine. Out golfing today.'

'He must be very good at golf,' Deena said. 'He's there so often.'

'He is,' Roz said. Mel raised her eyebrows.

'Roz is captain of the ladies' team at the local club,' Heather explained.

'I like to keep fit in my spare time,' Roz said breezily.

Deena was still crouched with Lily down on the floor. 'Isn't Lily lovely?' she said, looking pointedly at Gabbie.

Gabbie's face darkened. 'She is,' Gabbie said, forcing a smile. 'She's beautiful, Mel.'

'So do you think you and Stuart will...?' Deena let the sentence trail off, but everyone knew what she meant. They all stared at Gabbie.

'Mum, you know I don't want to talk about it.'

'You're not getting any younger.'

'I know that, Mum.'

'Is there any neighbourhood business anyone wants to discuss?' Roz asked, and Mel smiled at her gratefully for changing the subject and rescuing Gabbie from her mum's questions.

Heather nodded. 'Well, I thought it might be useful if we talked Mel through a few street guidelines, as she's new.'

'Guidelines?' Gabbie said. 'What on earth are you talking about?'

'You'd know if you ever paid any attention, Gabbie,' Deena snapped.

'One of the things,' Roz said, 'is that we like to keep everything looking presentable.' She looked at Mel. 'You've got a van on your drive. Are you planning building work?'

'No,' Mel said. 'Well, not right away. My husband's a handyman. It's his van.'

'Oh, I see,' Roz said. 'Well, just so you know, if you do any work on your house, we all like to let each other know when there's going to be any noise.'

'OK,' Mel said, wondering where this was going.

'And the van – perhaps you could park it further onto your driveway? It looks a bit... well, out of keeping with the street.'

Mel's mouth dropped open in surprise. Surely they could park however they liked at their own house. She dug her nails into the palm of her hand to stop herself reacting. She didn't want to fall out with Roz. 'We'll see what we can do,' she said.

'Are you in Laurel Street's WhatsApp group?' Roz asked. 'If

not, I can add you. It's where we keep each other updated on what's happening on the street.'

'No,' Mel said. She wasn't sure she wanted to be added if it was full of petty issues like Luke's van. 'I'm not sure—'

'Luke's already in it,' Gabbie said. 'We use the group to discuss maintenance that needs doing on the street too. Luke's taken on a lot of that work.'

'Ah, OK,' Mel said. 'Maybe you should add me then.'

'Great,' Roz said with a smile.

'I'm glad that's sorted,' Deena said. 'And I can vouch for Mel. She knows the street. She'll fit in perfectly. The person we really need to talk about is Tamsin.'

'Yes,' Gabbie said quickly. 'She's still watching us. She was watching us last night, wasn't she, Mel?'

Mel nodded reluctantly. 'I don't think she means anything by it. Her studio overlooks your house. She likes to keep an eye on things on the street.'

'She's always been a bit strange,' Deena said. 'Ever since Erin went missing. Awful business, of course.' She shivered dramatically. 'But things do have to move on. It's been twenty-five years.'

'She's still grieving,' Mel said. She remembered Deena and Tamsin being close when Deena had first moved into the road. But perhaps it had been a friendship of convenience because their daughters were the same age.

'I used to tell you to stay away from her,' Deena said to Gabbie. 'There was something not right about her after Erin went missing. You know, she's kept her room exactly the same, waiting for her to come back.'

'Things have been so difficult for her,' Mel said. She needed to stick up for her friend.

'Yes, very sad,' Deena said, taking a gulp of her coffee. 'But we must keep an eye on it. For Gabbie's sake. Watching someone like that all the time. Well, it's almost stalking.'

SEVEN

When Mel got back home, Luke had messaged her to say he wouldn't be back for lunch, so she ate with Lily and then decided to go out again. She wanted to make the most of her final day with her daughter before she started work tomorrow.

The sun was shining and it felt like spring was coming early. She walked down to the green and then lifted Lily out of her sling and placed her on the home-made wooden swing that hung from the ancient tree. She held her daughter and moved her gently, but she was too little for the swing and it was too unstable.

Mel remembered a recent Instagram post from Gabbie, a picture of two horses. *My loves*, the caption had read. Mel took a left down the bridle path that ran between Gabbie's house and the neighbouring cottage, and took Lily to the stables that were a few dozen feet from the house. Mel introduced Lily to Gabbie's horses, taking off her mittens and reaching out her daughter's small hand to stroke their noses. Lily squealed in delight.

'I'll teach you to ride when you're older,' Mel said, as she put the mittens back on. Mel had learnt to ride on Erin's horses as a child, and she was determined to give Lily everything she'd had in her childhood and more. Lily would grow up with the love of two parents, in a close-knit family.

Mel looked down the bridle path towards the woods. She thought of the play area that Heather had mentioned. She should go and check it out. They were planning to live here for years, to make their home here. She couldn't avoid the woods forever.

The sun warmed her face as she walked down the path breathing in the fresh air, grateful to be here, back home. Lily's warm body pressed against hers and she clutched her daughter's mittened hand that hung down from the sling. From the path she could see the backs of the cottages with their neat gardens. When she was little, she'd been envious of the people who lived here. She used to walk through the woods to her grandmother's house from the small flat she shared with her mother and her boyfriend. Laurel Street was like another world, where people had whatever they wanted. When she'd first met Erin it had seemed like she'd had everything: a trampoline, a swing set, a paddling pool, a climbing frame.

'We are so lucky to live here,' she whispered into Lily's mop of hair. She thought of her grandmother, who had rescued her from her previous life with her mother and brought her to live on the street when she was eleven, not long after Erin had disappeared. Back then, she had felt like the others looked down on her, particularly Gabbie's family. She had felt like the poor girl from the village, the one with the alcoholic mother, who didn't quite fit in. She'd always felt she had to be careful what she said, to make sure she made a good impression and told people what they wanted to hear. Things had got better when she was a teenager, but she'd never quite lost the feeling.

Before Erin disappeared she had played in the woods all the time, often with Erin, but frequently on her own. Mel tried to conjure the spirit of that brave little girl now as she approached the woods. She took a deep breath as she carried Lily through the trees. Memories flooded back to her. These woods had been so much a part of her childhood. Her mother had walked her through them in all weathers to her grandmother's house. She remembered being late for her grandmother's Sunday lunch once. She must have been about seven or eight, and her mother had hurried her along, twigs cracking under their feet as they ran together, giggling as they raced across the little bridge over the small stream that flowed through the middle of the woods. Her mother's drinking had been more intermittent then.

There had been good moments before her mother had succumbed completely to her addiction, after Erin disappeared. Mel had always held out hope that she'd get better again. But as Mel's teenage years passed, she worked hard to fit into Laurel Street, and she started to feel like she was part of the community.

The air in the woods was still and calm, and Mel breathed in. She put her hand on a nearby tree, feeling the rough bark under her palm. Heather had told her that the play equipment was in the clearing in the middle of the woods, close to the stream. Mel walked on, down the familiar path. The woods were silent except for her own footsteps, and Mel found herself alert to any sounds. Occasionally there was a rustle among the dried, dead leaves as squirrels and mice scampered. A blackbird swooped down from above and landed on a branch of a tree.

'Look, Lily, did you see the bird?'

Mel thought of her mother, spending these moments with her at the same age.

She walked on to the clearing, her body tensing, her breathing shallow. The last time she'd been in the clearing, she'd been with Erin and Gabbie, sharing her chocolate for the midnight feast. She'd dreamt of that evening so often, so many different iterations of the same scene, until she was no longer sure what was a memory.

The clearing was different now, a swing set in the middle of it, with a baby swing. The set was dirty and mud-spattered, but the plastic seat itself was clean, as if someone had made an effort to wipe it.

As Mel put Lily into the seat, tingles started to run up her spine. It was an automatic reaction, that feeling of being watched. When they'd been kids, Joe had always been around whenever Erin was. He was always in the background, doing some work nearby. Erin had romanticised it, called him her 'guardian angel', but Mel hadn't liked the way he followed them, the special interest he took in Erin.

She pushed Lily on the swing from the front, smiling at her and playfully reaching out and grabbing her feet as Lily came towards her. Lily beamed and laughed, her little head shaking with glee.

Mel chatted to Lily like she always did, about anything and everything. She talked about Luke's job and how it was good he was getting work; about their new house and all their plans to decorate; about her grandmother and how she had looked after her on the street.

She was in the middle of an anecdote about her grandmother, when she suddenly froze. She hadn't heard anything, but the feeling of being watched had intensified.

She missed the next push on the swing and Lily cried out in objection. 'Ma-ma, Ma-ma!'

Mel's eyes darted round the clearing, looking at each tree in turn, to see if someone was behind them. The woods were private property, belonging to Tamsin, but the public had a right of way. Someone could easily be walking through. People liked to walk their dogs here.

She breathed in and counted to ten, but her heart kept pounding, her body convinced it was still under threat.

She knew it was just the location. She shouldn't have come back here on her own, with just Lily. She felt hopeless all of a sudden. No matter what she did, her fear would never fade. Mel felt tears form in her eyes. Why was she still letting her fear control her?

'Let's go, Lily,' she said.

'No!'

As she bent over to pull Lily out of the swing, she glanced up and her eyes locked with a set of pale blue eyes staring out at her from a gap between the trees. It was a man in a long green coat, his hood pulled up and tied under his chin, covering most of his face.

Mel felt something hit her in the stomach from below, and she jumped. When she looked down she saw that Lily was still fidgeting, her little feet kicking out violently.

'Don't kick, Lily!' she said. She glanced up again and the man was gone.

Mel looked round in all directions. Something about those blue eyes had seemed so familiar.

Joe, she thought, fear taking over.

But of course it wasn't. How could it be? He had left the area years ago, hounded by the press from his home in a nearby village.

'Hello?' she called out, hoping the man would speak to her, tell her he was a neighbour, a dog walker, anyone.

But the man didn't respond. She couldn't see him, but she was sure he was still there. Fear clawed at Mel's chest as she looked all around. Why had she called out? He could be dangerous. Just watching like that. Wasn't that what stalkers did? It wasn't only Joe she needed to be afraid of. There were countless men just like him, seeking out women on their own to hurt.

'Come on!' she said to Lily, trying to pull her out of the swing. But Lily struggled, refusing to remove her legs from the holes, as she kicked and screamed.

To her left she saw the back of the man's coat moving

behind the trees, a set of keys jangling as they swung from a chain attached to his pocket.

'Lily, please!' Mel could hear the panic in her voice and she pulled her out with more force than she intended and Lily screamed louder.

Mel knew she had to calm down and get them both out of the woods. It was a ten-minute walk to the path. Another ten minutes to the house. What would she do if he tried to follow them? He could easily overpower her.

'It's OK, Lily,' she said, looking at her red-faced child as she tried to strap her back into the sling. Above the noise of the screams, she heard a twig snap behind her. She spun round, Lily nearly falling from her arms.

Struggling with the buckle on the sling, it finally locked into place. Mel started to walk to the edge of the clearing, back through the woods. She tried to walk purposefully but quickly, all the time her heart beating uncontrollably and Lily screaming in the sling in front of her. She wouldn't hear someone behind her, so she kept looking round, watching out for him, expecting him to reach out and grab them at any moment.

But he didn't. And then they were back on the path and on their way home.

EIGHT

When Mel arrived at the nursery for the drop-off on Monday morning, she was a bundle of nerves, worrying about meeting her colleagues on her first day at her new school and concerned about leaving Lily at nursery. Luckily today was a training day, so she wouldn't be teaching, but would need to make a good impression.

She rang the doorbell at the nursery and stroked Lily's thick mop of dark hair. Mel had done the settling-in sessions with Lily the previous week, and she wanted to be the one to drop her off on her first day. Luckily she had managed to find a nursery that opened early, at 7.30, so she could be in school for 7.45.

The door opened and a smiling woman said hello and then turned to Lily and beamed. 'Hi, Lily!'

'Look, it's Jodie,' Mel said, smiling down at her daughter. Mel tried to hand Lily over to Jodie, but Lily struggled and burst into sobs, her little hands clinging to Mel's neck. Mel felt a pain in her chest. How was she going to leave her?

'Don't worry,' Jodie reassured her. 'They're all like this at first. Do you have time to come in with her and sit for a bit?'

Mel shook her head. 'No,' she said. 'I have to get to work. I'm a teacher at the school. It's my first day.' She thought of Luke. 'Her dad could do it,' she said. 'I'll ring him.' Luke had offered to drop Lily off this morning, but Mel had insisted that she do it herself.

'Oh, don't worry about that,' Jodie said, expertly removing a screaming Lily from Mel's arms. 'We're used to these situations. You get to work.' Mel looked at her writhing, inconsolable daughter, overcome by guilt. She desperately wanted to stay with her, but she really couldn't be late.

'Honestly, no worries,' Jodie said, turning Lily around and bouncing her up and down on her hip. 'As soon as you're gone, she'll calm down. It's always the way.'

'I'll be back later,' Mel reassured Lily, wiping away her tears with her fingers. 'I promise.'

Mel rushed back to her car in the car park, but when she sat behind the wheel, she could still hear Lily's echoing cries and she burst into tears.

She was ten minutes late when she arrived at the school. Before she'd left the nursery she'd needed a few minutes in the car to take some deep breaths and wipe off the mascara that had run down her cheeks with one of Lily's baby wipes. She turned up flushed and breathless, and greeted the others with a smile.

'We're very strict with the children on punctuality,' Mr Gresham, the head teacher, said pointedly. He wasn't the same head as Mel had had when she'd been at the school herself, but he might as well have been. Mel had always been late then, too, her mother never quite capable of leaving early enough to get her to school on time, as much as she tried.

'Of course,' Mel said. 'I had to drop my child off at nursery this morning and it took longer than I expected.'

'OK, you must allow more time, in that case.'

'Yes, it won't happen again.'

'OK, sure. Well, we don't have a naughty table for teachers.' He laughed at his own joke and a couple of the other teachers snickered, but most looked down at their shoes. 'Right,' he said, 'Mrs Singh is our new year two teacher. Say hello, everyone.' The others nodded and smiled at her.

By the time Mel left at the end of the day, she was exhausted. She'd been taken through all the policies and procedures at the school and listened to presentations on the changes to the English and Maths teaching plans. The kids would be in with her tomorrow, and she couldn't wait. Some of the teachers at this school had made such a difference to her when she was little, giving her sandwiches when her mother had forgotten to make her lunch, or waiting with her when her mother was late to collect her. She wanted to be there for the children in her class in the same way.

When she collected Lily from the nursery, she was playing happily with some blocks in the corner of the playroom.

'Look, Mummy's here,' Jodie said as she saw Mel. Lily turned round and beamed, then started crawling straight towards her.

'Hello, Lily,' Mel said, sweeping her child into her arms. Lily smiled happily, but Mel felt like crying again. All day Lily had been in her thoughts, all day she'd been worried that she was still screaming her head off at nursery, that she wouldn't forgive Mel for leaving her. But clearly she had been fine.

'See you tomorrow, Lily,' Jodie said as she waved her off.

It was dark by the time they got back. Laurel Street was pitch-black except for the lights in Tamsin's studio. Everyone else was at work in offices somewhere. Mel suddenly felt the isolation of the countryside, the distance between them and the nearest town.

She saw a small light at the edge of the road and noticed a man in dark clothes crouched over by the side of Gabbie's garage. For a moment she shivered. But then the man stood up and waved at her approaching car. It was just Luke.

'What are you doing?' she asked as she pulled over and wound the window down.

'Oh, Stuart's got a damp problem in his garage. I said I'd take a look.'

'Lily had a good first day at nursery,' Mel said.

'Ah, good,' Luke said. 'Well, I'd better get back to it. I've got a few bits and pieces to do for Stuart, but I'll be home in about an hour.'

When Mel got home she pulled up onto her drive and went to the wooden door of her cottage. She was about to put her key in the lock when she noticed something odd. There was a nail in the door, right in the centre, below the small picture window. It looked like the kind of nail that could be used to hang a wreath at Christmas, but she was almost certain that it hadn't been there before. There was a tiny sliver of paper attached to it, and Mel realised that it had been used to attach a note.

Mel glanced around and saw a piece of folded white paper had blown between the pots of dead flowers. She lifted it out and unfolded it, wondering briefly if a package had been delivered for them.

In neat handwriting across the middle of the page, it said simply:

You don't belong here.

NINE

On Saturday, Mel felt exhausted from her first week at work, and Luke let her have a lie-in while he looked after Lily, driving her out to buy some new clothes in the shops in the nearest town. The first week of school had flown by, and Mel had spent each evening planning her lessons for the next day. She hadn't had time to do anything but work and look after Lily, but the note that had been pinned to her front door had played on her mind.

You don't belong here.

It felt so personal, as if someone knew Mel's biggest insecurity. As a child she had always felt like she hadn't belonged on Laurel Street, that she was the poor relation from the village. As a teenager she'd worked so hard to fit in, and had finally felt like Laurel Street was her home.

Now someone was trying to tell her she had been right when she was a child: she didn't belong in Laurel Street.

She'd told herself not to let it get to her, that it was probably just a petty neighbour. She thought of Roz and her comment about Luke's van. She'd never asked him to move it. Maybe that's what the note was about.

Mel rolled over in bed and tried to get back to sleep and make the most of her lie-in, but she couldn't settle. She dragged herself out of bed, got dressed, then went to Lily's room to sort through the cupboards and remove some of her grandmother's things. She bagged up clothes for the charity shop and then looked at the boxes at the bottom of the cupboard. Opening one up, she discovered it contained her grandparents' old letters and photos, and for a while she got lost in them. There was a photo of her grandparents young and newly married, standing in front of the cottage, and so many of her mother: her mother as a child on the swing on the green; her mother smiling as she opened Christmas presents; her mother with her first bike, a red ribbon tied round the handlebars. Her mother had had everything here: her own horse, a swing set and a tree house in the back garden that her father had built. But when she'd been seventeen she'd thrown it all away and left home to live with Mel's drug-dealing father in the village on the other side of the woods. Mel's parents had split up when she was two, and she didn't remember her dad.

Her mother and her grandmother had never fully reconciled, but her grandmother had still left her mother half her house in her will.

Mel felt a pang of longing. Her mother had never quite managed to be the mother she wanted, but sometimes she had tried. It was hard to understand someone who could be so loving one minute and so completely disinterested the next. She remembered her mother comforting her when she'd been picked on at school by another girl in her class, then marching into the school and demanding the teacher sort it out. And she remembered her mother having several lunchtime glasses of wine to get her through the day, and then slumping down on the sofa and sending Mel out to the woods to play with Erin, telling her not to come back until dinner.

Her mother had been just about holding it together before Erin's disappearance, but afterwards she became completely subsumed by alcohol, unable to perform the most basic tasks for Mel. She was always drunk when she collected her from school, and in the end Mel had insisted on walking back on her own. Then her mother got another unsuitable boyfriend, and Mel had hardly felt welcome in her own home anymore. Luckily her grandmother had taken her in, and Mel had suddenly had the life she'd always wanted, living in a happy, warm and secure home.

In the cupboard, there was a pack of letters from her mother to Mel's grandmother, held together with an elastic band. The writing was faded but still legible. Most of the letters begged for money, and asked for help with Mel. She could tell by how desperate the letters got that her grandmother must have always refused to help. She understood why. Her mother, despite her good intentions, would have only ended up spending the money on drink.

After Mel had moved away from her grandmother's house, she used to get similar emails from her mother asking for money. Now that they had both inherited Mel's grandmother's house, Mel gave her rent every month to cover her half of the house.

Mel put away the letters and thought of the email that her mother had sent just the other day. She'd wanted to sell the house and divide the proceeds. She said she'd split up with her boyfriend in Spain and had nowhere to go. Mel had told her no, that she and Luke were living there now. Then her mother had suggested that she move in with them. Mel knew it would never happen. Her mother had been in Spain for the last fifteen years. She hated Laurel Street and had always said she'd never come back.

Luke returned to the house with Lily and came up to see Mel.

'How's it going?' he asked.

'I'm trying to sort out Lily's room, but I haven't made as much progress as I'd have liked. I got caught up looking at old photos.'

'Are those your mother?'

'Yeah. You know she suggested coming to stay with us?'

'Is it because she wants to see Lily? My father wants to see her too.'

'No, I don't think it's that. She's just trying to get money out of me. I didn't think you were in contact with your father.'

'I wasn't. But this year I sent him a Christmas card, with a picture of Lily. I wanted him to know he had a granddaughter. But now, of course, he wants to see her.'

'How do you feel about that?' Mel asked, thinking of their lonely Christmas, just the three of them, how Lily would miss out on having grandparents.

'I don't know. He was never there for me in my childhood. I'm not sure how great a granddad he'd be if he couldn't even be a dad.'

Mel put her arms round Luke as they watched Lily crawl on the floor. 'We've got our own family now,' she said. 'Our number one priority is Lily. You should introduce him if you think it would be good for her.' She thought idly of her own father. She hadn't considered telling him about Lily. She didn't even have his contact details. 'It might be nice for Lily to have one grandfather,' she said.

'I'll think about it,' Luke said. 'I've got to go out again now. I ran into Gabbie on the way over. They have a blocked drain-pipe that needs fixing.'

'OK, then. I'll see you later. Will you be back for lunch?'

'Doubt it. I need to go and price up a couple of jobs in the village this afternoon. I'll make myself a sandwich, have it in the van.'

'OK, then, see you later.' Mel was pleased that Luke was building up his business so quickly. His services always seemed to be in demand. There was always work on the estate, and Gabbie and Stuart seemed to have a whole list of things at their house that needed fixing. And the notices Luke had left round the village were starting to pay off, too.

By five o'clock it was dark and Mel decided to light the fire. She remembered her grandmother having it lit in her childhood, how warm and cosy it had made the room, even in the coldest winter. It took a couple of firelighters to get the old wood going, but soon it was roaring. She kept Lily close to her, away from the fire, building up her tower of blocks with her and knocking it down again and again, as she laughed.

Then she gave Lily some milk and a portion of cucumber sticks in the kitchen, but she slumped down in her highchair, her head flopping to the side as she yawned. Her eyes started to close. Mel knew that sleep was inevitable, so she took her to her cot and laid her down for a nap. It would mean her sleep would be disrupted at night, but there wasn't any alternative other than to let her nap when she was like this.

Mel kissed her cheek then went back down to the living room and got out her marking to do. As she marked the tenth sheet of sums, exhaustion hit her and she put the papers down and stretched out on the sofa. She watched the fire crackle, spreading warmth into the room, and felt lucky to be there, in such a cosy house, living with a family of her own. She thought for a moment of the note saying *You don't belong here* and felt a twisting in her stomach. Even after all these years there was someone who thought she shouldn't be here, that she wasn't good enough.

You couldn't be liked by everyone, that's what her grandmother had always said. Mel just had to let herself settle in and enjoy her new life. She thought of the family she and Luke would have here. Two children or three? There was so much freedom here, so much nature to explore. But she'd always keep a close eye on Lily. She wouldn't let her wander off, or go out on her own in the freezing weather. She wouldn't let what happened to Erin happen to her. For a moment she thought of the man in the woods last week, but then she let the thought go. When she'd run into Gabbie's mum, she'd asked her who he might be and she'd thought it was the neighbour who lived at the end of the road. Mel was sure it must have been him. Being back in the woods had just made her panic, thinking of Joe. But there was no one here to be afraid of anymore.

Mel started to relax as the room got warmer, and she drifted into a peaceful sleep.

She woke suddenly to footsteps outside. The fire had nearly burnt out and she felt a rush of guilt at falling asleep with it lit. What if she'd burnt down the house with Lily inside? She waited for the sound of Luke's key in the lock, but there was nothing. Instead the footsteps continued, round to the other side of the house. Mel stilled her breathing. The living room curtains were open but she couldn't see anything out of the windows. It was pitch-black outside. Whoever was out there would be able to see in, even if Mel couldn't see out. She heard a scraping from the patio, like the sound of flowerpots moving, and then the footsteps retreated again. They didn't go back round to the front of the house onto the gravel, but they stopped completely, as if someone was still out there, lying in wait for her.

TEN

Mel didn't move, fear binding her to the sofa. For a few minutes the house was silent, and she was starting to think she'd imagined the footsteps when they started up again and she jumped. She stayed completely still as she heard the person walk back round to the front of the house and their footsteps crunch down the gravel driveway and away.

She was relieved when she heard Luke's key in the lock half an hour later.

'You're home,' she said, wrapping him in a hug.

'That was a nice greeting,' he said, his cheeks dimpling.

'Yeah, well. Something odd happened earlier. I thought I heard someone outside.'

'Oh? Well, people do come and go along this street. Maybe someone walking a dog.'

'It was right by the house. I heard footsteps. But it could have been a dog walker,' Mel conceded. 'If the dog was sniffing round the house, they might have come to pull him away.' She felt relieved. 'That makes sense,' she said. 'Maybe it was that.'

Luke squeezed her tightly. 'Don't worry,' he said. 'This isn't London. You don't need to be so worried about security. If someone's near the house, there's probably an innocent explanation.'

'Of course,' Mel said. 'There aren't many break-ins round here. It's safe. The right place to bring up Lily.'

'It really is,' Luke said. He pulled some chocolates and a bottle of wine out of his bag. 'I picked these up at the supermarket in town.'

'What are they for?'

'No reason, just something to enjoy together. We've both been so busy lately.'

Later, after they'd eaten their dinner, they sat on the sofa drinking the rest of the wine and eating the chocolates. At 10 p.m. Luke yawned and said he was heading up for an early night. Mel sat in front of the television watching the latest reality series with a small glass of wine, when she heard a tapping at the window and froze.

Not again. Luke had reassured her about the person outside earlier, but now she felt vulnerable again, under threat. Her heart raced. She wondered if she should go upstairs and fetch Luke, but she hesitated. The tapping got louder.

'Mel?' A voice called through the window. 'Mel?'

'Gabbie?' Mel got up and went over to the window and drew the curtains back. Gabbie was leaning towards the glass. She stepped back and Mel opened the window. 'Why didn't you ring the bell?' she asked.

'I didn't want to wake Lily. Don't you remember how I used to throw stones at your window when we were kids? And then we'd sneak out in the middle of the night.'

'Yeah,' Mel said. Her grandmother had never had any idea what they got up to. Mel waited for Gabbie to say why she was here.

'I'm bored,' Gabbie said. 'Do you want to go for a walk?'

'What, now? It's so late.'

'We could go and sit on the green like we used to.' She pulled a bottle of wine out of her bag and grinned lopsidedly. 'I brought this with me.'

'I'm tired, Gabbie.'

'Please... I... I need to tell you something.' Mel looked at Gabbie's bloodshot eyes and realised she'd been crying.

Mel felt a wave of sympathy wash over her. 'Let's go then,' she said. 'I'll see you outside in a second.' She wrote a quick note for Luke in case he woke up, then put on her coat and boots and left the house.

They walked down the dark road together, towards the swing.

'Was it you who was walking round my house earlier?' Mel said.

Gabbie looked at her, confused. 'No, why?'

'Oh, I thought I heard someone, that's all.'

'It wasn't me. But sometimes I do walk on my own at night, down to the green,' Gabbie said. 'I just need to get away.'

'Get away from what?'

'Oh, nothing. Just the monotony of it all, I suppose. It feels like every day is the same. Get up. Go to work at my tedious job at the council. Cook dinner, which most of the time I eat on my own. Wait around for Stuart to come home from whatever late-night work function he's got on, make the briefest chit-chat, go to bed.'

'It's hard sometimes,' Mel said, thinking of Luke and Lily. She was so lucky to have them, but Luke hadn't been around much since they'd moved. She'd hoped that he'd be spending his spare time doing up their cottage, but instead most of his time was taken up doing maintenance work for Laurel Street and for Stuart and Gabbie.

'I guess it's just normal adult life, but I'm just so... bored...'

'I get it,' Mel said. She remembered living here as a

teenager, when she'd felt that longing for the outside world. 'Do you remember when we both planned to run away to London?'

'Yeah,' Gabbie said. 'And I lived in London for years. The whole time I longed to be back here. I was so pleased when we could afford the house. And now I'm here, I long for London. It's stupid, really.'

'It's not stupid,' Mel said calmly. 'I'm sure it's normal. The grass always seems greener.'

'Maybe. I thought Stuart and I would have a family by now, but every time I mention kids he shuts me down.'

'Oh, Gabbie,' Mel said, touching her friend's arm lightly.

They were approaching the swing on the green next to Tamsin's house, and Gabbie sat down on it heavily, unscrewed the wine and took a big swig. She passed it to Mel and started to swing, the branch above her creaking, although she was as light as a feather.

'I feel so trapped already. I'm only thirty-five, but I feel... old... like I'm running out of time. I'm not happy with Stuart and I don't know why.'

'I'm so sorry,' Mel said.

'I have everything I ever wanted in that house. We're even going to do up the pool. We'll have our own swimming pool. Can you believe that? But I'm still not happy.'

'Maybe you could spend more time with Stuart?' Mel said. It sounded like they hardly saw each other.

'Even when we're together we have nothing to say to each other,' Gabbie said, taking a swig from the bottle of wine.

She glanced up towards Tamsin's house and they both saw the light was on in her studio. Gabbie pointed up at the house. '*She's* always watching me. Judging me. I don't even have privacy in my own home. It's like she can see through me, see my marriage disintegrating.'

'I'm sure she doesn't think that.'

'I don't know, Mel. She creeps me out. From her windows

she can see directly into my house. She's always painting, always peering in. And what's she painting? Is it me? My life?'

'She paints the landscape,' Mel said. 'I think it's always been an escape for her, after what happened to Erin.'

Gabbie nodded sadly. 'That was so awful for her.' She stared into the distance. 'Do you ever feel guilty about it?' she asked.

'About what?' Mel said, her heart rate quickening. She took the wine bottle from Gabbie and tipped it back.

'About leaving her that day. We both left her. And Joe was out there. We knew that.'

Mel sighed. 'Of course I feel guilty, but I try not to think about it. I can't think about it.'

Although Gabbie and Mel had been close when they were teenagers, they had never spoken much about Erin. She sat like a shadow between them, part of all the things that remained unspoken. Neither of them had gone to the woods after she disappeared. They roamed everywhere else, the fields, the gardens, drinking on the tennis courts. But they never went back to the woods together and they never spoke about it.

Gabbie nodded. 'It's weird being back. I wanted to come back, for Stuart to buy the house. But now I think I'm too close to Tamsin, too close to the past. I didn't realise she'd be watching me all the time.' Gabbie glanced up at Tamsin's house. 'Can you see?' she said. 'She's watching us now.' Gabbie took the bottle back. 'She's judging me, I'm sure.'

'Let's go somewhere else then,' Mel said. 'Get out of her sight.' Although she was sure Tamsin wasn't judging them. It seemed to Mel that she was just lonely.

'I know!' Gabbie said suddenly. 'Let's go down to the stables. We can ride my horses.'

'I haven't ridden for a while,' Mel said. She used to ride twice a week when she lived in Laurel Street, but she hadn't kept it up in London.

'It's not like you ever forget. Remember when we used to fly down the bridle path?'

Mel had always used to ride with Erin when she was young, on the two horses the family had owned. Once she'd disappeared, Gabbie's family had bought the horses from Tamsin, to help Gabbie deal with the loss of her friend. And Mel had started riding every weekend with Gabbie instead. It had seemed like such a natural transition, but now Mel thought about how Tamsin must have seen it. Her and Gabbie continuing without Erin.

'But we've been drinking,' Mel objected. 'It's not a good idea.'

'It doesn't matter,' Gabbie said. 'Come on, live a little. We'll be fine.'

And then she was off, wine bottle in one hand, running down the dark path to the stables. Mel ran after her, trying to watch her step in the dark. A part of her felt worried but another part of her felt exhilarated. She felt alive again. Not a mother, not a teacher, not someone always making sensible decisions. But a real person.

When they got to the stables, Mel felt bad as Gabbie woke the horses up.

'Are you sure this is a good idea?' Mel asked.

'I've done it before. At night. Honestly, you must experience it. Riding in the moonlight is really something else.'

Gabbie gave the horses some pony nuts, then put on the bridles and reins and led them out of the stables. She jumped on bareback, and Mel did the same. Mel patted her horse and stroked its side. She loved the feel of it underneath her, its strong, athletic body.

'Good boy,' she whispered softly, as Gabbie led them down the bridle path that ran through the fields and then alongside the woods. The track was straight and wide, and Gabbie picked up speed, galloping off. Mel followed, the cold air on her face, the wind in her hair. She felt alive.

They rode for two miles, and then stopped beside a dark field, next to the outbuildings of a farm. Gabbie dismounted and sat down heavily on the dirt.

Mel sat beside her. Miles away at the bottom of the hill, lights of a nearby village twinkled. Only a few people were up at this hour. It felt like the world belonged to them.

'I'm thinking of leaving Stuart,' Gabbie said quietly.

'What?' Mel said, moving closer to her friend and putting her arm around her. 'You can't leave Laurel Street. I've only just moved in.'

'I know I can't. I've set up my life exactly how I want it. The perfect house. An attractive, well-off husband. A good local job where I don't have to work long hours. And good maternity pay.' Gabbie half-smiled. 'Can you believe I checked that? Before I signed up, I rejected a better-paid job because of the commute and the maternity package. I thought it wouldn't work if we had children.'

'That just sounds sensible,' Mel said.

'I suppose so. But Stuart still has his well-paid job. He hasn't changed anything because we might have children.'

Mel remembered Gabbie saying that he avoided the subject of children entirely. 'It will be OK,' she said softly.

'I'm thirty-five, Mel. If I want kids, I know I should stay with Stuart. And he's given me the life I've always wanted. But...'

'But?' Mel probed.

'I'm not sure if this life *is* what I want anymore. You know, every night once Stuart gets home, I go out for a walk. Even if it's raining. I just walk up and down the street, headphones in, music blaring. It's the only time I feel close to being free. And yet, I don't leave the street. I just walk up and down. Feeling trapped.'

Mel didn't know what to say. 'You know you can talk to me any time?'

'Of course,' Gabbie said. 'Thanks. I'm so glad you're back.'

'You don't have to stay here if you don't want to,' Mel said gently. 'If you're unhappy.'

'But I don't know why I'm unhappy. This is the life I planned. And I can't leave now. If I want kids I have to stick this out.'

Mel squeezed Gabbie's hand as tears rolled down her friend's face.

'But... honestly...' Gabbie continued. 'The best thing to do is to keep going. I'm sure my mood will improve. I just have to stay.'

'Forever?' Mel asked softly. She hated seeing her friend like this. When they'd been teenagers, Gabbie had wrapped the boys round her little finger. They used to fight over her.

Gabbie laughed bitterly. 'I guess until the kids grow up.'

'That's a long time,' Mel said.

'Yeah,' Gabbie said, staring out over the fields. 'I'll be imprisoned in this paradise for years.'

ELEVEN

On Sunday, Mel went over to the manor house. Everything Gabbie had said the night before had made her think of Tamsin, how difficult it must have been since Erin went missing, how everyone else's lives had continued, but hers had stopped.

Mel sat upstairs in Tamsin's studio and watched her play with Lily. She was sitting on the floor with her, painting lines on a huge piece of white paper. Lily was laughing hysterically.

'You're so good with her,' Mel said.

'Well, I had practice with Erin. And it's good to have a little one around again.' Tamsin stared out of the window wistfully. 'If Erin's still out there, maybe she has a kid, too.'

'Maybe,' Mel said.

'I often imagine the life she might be leading now. Even if she was kidnapped and adopted by another family, she'd be an adult now with her own life. There's still time for her to come back.'

Mel nodded, blinking back tears. Sometimes she thought

the same, that Erin could be out there somewhere. But Tamsin's hope made her feel so desperately sad.

'I could be a grandmother,' Tamsin said.

'You'd make a brilliant granny.'

Tamsin smiled and changed the subject. 'So, how's the teaching going? I bet you have lots of cute little children in your class.'

'Yeah, year two, so six- and seven-year-olds. They're growing up fast. Actually I have someone from the street in my class. Freya.'

'Oh, that's right. Her parents live at the end of the road.'

'Great, I haven't met them yet. Their nanny picks them up.'

'Don't worry, they're lovely. I should introduce you to them. I was thinking about throwing a party.'

'A party?' Mel said, surprised.

After Erin disappeared, the regular neighbourhood parties that Tamsin and her husband had thrown in their huge house had stopped entirely. The last party had been the New Year's Eve party twenty-five years ago, when the girls had snuck out to have a midnight feast in the woods and Erin had gone missing.

'Yeah, I think it's about time. I don't know everyone here so well anymore. If I throw a party, we can all get to know each other a bit better. And it's a chance to welcome you back to the neighbourhood, too.'

'That sounds brilliant. I can help you organise it,' Mel said. Now everyone was back at work, including her and Luke, she didn't run into the neighbours so often.

'I've noticed you and Gabbie are close again,' Tamsin said.

'Yeah, it's good to be reunited.' Mel flushed. Sometimes she felt guilty about her friendship with Gabbie when she talked to Tamsin, even now. If things were different, she would have been catching up with Erin as well.

'I saw you having dinner at her house last weekend. Do you think she's happy?'

Mel frowned. 'I'm not sure,' she said tactfully, not wanting to reveal Gabbie's problems.

'She has everything she ever wanted in that house,' Tamsin said. 'But when I speak to her there's no light behind her eyes. I've been worried about her, and trying to look out for her. But there's not much I can do to help. Maybe you can. She needs a friend.'

'I'll try my best,' Mel said, thinking about how Tamsin had the best intentions watching Gabbie, but Gabbie only found it intrusive.

'Oh look,' Tamsin said, pointing out the window. 'Luke's over there now.' She lifted Lily up to see. 'Look – there's your daddy.'

Down below them Luke and Gabbie were talking in the kitchen.

'Luke will be fixing something for her,' Mel said, feeling the need to explain.

'How's his business going?'

'Oh, fine,' Mel said. 'Quite well, actually. He has a lot of work. A lot of it from Gabbie and Stuart.' She laughed, but she wasn't sure why. She looked back down into Gabbie's house. Luke and Gabbie were standing in the kitchen now, by her expensive coffee machine. She was showing him how to work it, standing beside him while he put in one of the pods. She put her hand over his while he pushed it down, and he turned to her and smiled, his face close to hers. She took a step back, laughing at something he said.

'He's taking a break,' Tamsin said. 'He's been working hard all morning.'

Mel kept watching, feeling uncomfortable with the intrusion, but unable to look away. Luke had his coffee now and was standing by the machine as Gabbie made hers. She said something and touched his shoulder lightly. He laughed, throwing his head back. Mel swallowed. She'd forgotten the way Gabbie had with men, the mildly flirtatious way she always spoke to them. She knew it was harmless. Gabbie hardly knew she was doing it. It was just the way she was.

Mel made herself step away from the window and changed the subject. 'So, what food shall we have at the party?' she asked.

Mel stayed at Tamsin's for a couple of hours before heading back to have lunch with Luke. She'd tried not to keep watching him at Gabbie's house, tried not to check up on him, but she'd been aware that he'd been inside for over an hour, and she wasn't sure how much of that time he'd been actually working, rather than chatting to Gabbie. She supposed that as long as Gabbie was paying him it didn't matter. Luke had always said how important it was to maintain good relationships with clients if he wanted repeat business. Maybe Gabbie was confiding in him about her marriage. The thought had made Mel uncomfortable. She supposed she could ask Luke what they'd talked about. But she didn't want to sound like a paranoid wife.

She pushed Lily's pushchair past the swing on the green and thought of her ride with Gabbie on the horses last night. It had made Mel feel alive, although she'd been hungover this morning. As she passed Gabbie's house, she looked down the path where the stables were. There was a man standing on the footpath beside the field, a short distance away, staring down towards the woods.

She froze, fear surging through her body. She recognised his long green coat. It was the man from the woods. His hood was down now and she could see his messy grey hair framing his face.

Mel swallowed. *Joe.*

This time she was certain. Something about the way he

stood, his weight more on one leg than the other, slightly hunched over. His hair had greyed but it was definitely him.

Mel felt weak, the security of her world crumbling around her. What was he doing here? Why had he come back?

He turned and caught sight of her, and began to walk purposefully towards her.

She started to turn the pushchair, but it wouldn't move. Panicking, she tried to force it, before she realised that the brake was on. As she released the brake with her foot, he was already upon her.

'Mel,' he said, his voice calm and steady, but instantly recognisable, even after all these years.

Fear swelled in her stomach. *It was him. He was back.*

She moved the pushchair quickly, but he was beside her.

'Is that your daughter?' he asked, staring into the pushchair. 'Is that Lily?'

He knew Lily's name.

Mel's chest contracted as she increased her pace, breaking into a run and bouncing the pushchair over the speed bumps in the road, Lily squealing. She didn't dare look behind her, focusing on the path ahead. She raced past the other cottages and finally reached her home, panting and out of breath. Then she turned, expecting to see him right behind her, to feel his breath on her neck. But he wasn't there.

TWELVE

There was no one behind her. No sign of Joe. Relief flooded through her as she reached for her key, fumbling in her pocket, expecting him to appear any moment.

She heard footsteps on the gravel behind her and dropped her key, scrabbling on the ground to pick it up.

'Hi, Mel.' The voice stopped her in her tracks. It was Roz.

She wasn't sure if she was relieved or upset to see her. She was the last person Mel wanted to see, but at least she was another person.

'I have to get inside,' Mel said.

'Is everything alright? I need to speak to you.'

The key turned in the lock and Mel pushed the door open, then pulled the pushchair inside.

'Everything's fine,' Mel said. She wanted to get out of sight of the road. She couldn't talk to Roz on the doorstep. 'Why don't you come in?' she asked. There was safety in numbers.

Roz looked surprised. 'OK, then. We can talk inside. It won't take long.'

Roz followed Mel through to the kitchen, Mel carrying Lily.

Mel closed all the curtains as she walked through the living room.

'Do you want a drink?' Mel asked. 'Cup of tea?'

'No, thank you, I'm fine. I just wanted to talk to you.'

'What about?' Mel was dreading the sound of Joe coming up to the house, footsteps on the gravel drive. Had that been him the other day? It must have been.

'Just general neighbourly concerns,' Roz said.

'Concerns?'

'I don't think you understand how it works round here. The little rules that mean everyone gets along well.'

'Rules?' Mel raised her eyebrows, hugging Lily.

'Yes, just keeping the place looking presentable. Keeping our gardens tidy, for example, grass cut.'

'I'm sorry – we haven't had time to do the garden yet. We've both been busy with work. And clearing out the inside of the house.'

'Hmm...' Roz said. 'Yeah, I've seen the boxes piled outside your garage. You will dispose of them, won't you?'

Mel nodded, perplexed.

'Good, well, the main thing I wanted to discuss was the boundary.'

'The boundary?'

'Yes, a couple of your trees are growing over the fence. Their branches hang onto my side. I want you to cut them back.'

'I can ask Luke to do that,' Mel said. She wouldn't be rushing. She didn't want to do any favours for this woman.

'The boundary line is very clear. It's the centre point of the end of the wall that separates our gardens. I noticed that when you put your bins out the other day, they encroached a bit onto my side. You need to keep them completely within your boundary in the future.'

'Sure,' Mel said, in no mood to argue, while she was still thinking of Joe outside.

'And make sure you take them back in once they've been emptied. The other day I got home from work at nine and yours were still out.'

'OK,' Mel said, although what she really wanted to do was tell Roz to get lost. 'Was that everything?'

Roz nodded. 'I think so.'

'Well, thanks for dropping round. I'll show you out.'

Once Roz had left, Mel went upstairs and looked out of the window. There was no sign of Joe on the road or in the fields behind the house. She looked over towards the woods and wondered if he was there, hiding like he always did. She picked up the phone and rang Gabbie.

'How are you feeling today?' Gabbie asked, as soon as she answered. 'I've got a dreadful hangover. It was a fun night, though, wasn't it?'

Mel had almost forgotten about the previous night. She'd had a headache when she'd woken up in the morning but it had cleared now. But then she hadn't had anywhere near as much to drink as Gabbie.

'I'm OK. Listen, I—'

Gabbie interrupted. 'I'm sorry I rambled on and on about Stuart. I didn't mean to. I was just in a dreadful mood. Really, our marriage isn't as bad as I made it sound. You won't tell anyone, will you?'

'No, of course not. Listen, Gabbie. I think I just saw Joe.'

'Joe?' Gabbie took a sharp intake of breath. 'Where?'

'Here, on the street. I saw him the other day, too.'

'What? He's come here?' Gabbie sounded alarmed.

'Yeah. He seemed to want to speak to me. He asked me about Lily.' Mel's hand trembled as she remembered him saying her daughter's name. Her voice shook. He must have heard Mel saying Lily's name when they'd been in the woods. How could she have been so stupid to have said it in front of him?

'Don't let him anywhere near Lily,' Gabbie said.

'Of course I won't. I don't think he knows where I live. Although he must know I live on the street, otherwise I wouldn't be walking in the area.' Mel's stomach knotted.

'What do you think he wants?'

'Maybe it's to do with your interview on the news,' Mel said. Gabbie had made it clear that she blamed Joe for Erin's disappearance. And she'd mentioned Mel by name.

'I only said what people already know. I was trying to get publicity,' Gabbie said defensively. 'I'm sure it's not that.'

'But maybe you blaming him again made him angry. He's kept a low profile, stayed out of the press.'

'You think he's come here to get back at me?'

'He might have come back to punish both of us. For telling the police we saw him that night. Now he'll know that we're the reason he was arrested, the reason people hounded him out of town.'

'He did it, Mel! That was the reason he was arrested.'

Mel's mouth went dry as she thought of what Joe might have done to her friend. She went upstairs and peered out of the bedroom window. 'He's probably still hanging around,' she whispered as she scanned the fields below.

'Oh my god. Really?'

'Yes.' Mel's heart pounded. 'Go upstairs,' she told Gabbie. 'Look out of your window. I saw him near your house.'

She heard Gabbie's footsteps on the stairs. 'Can you see him anywhere?' Mel asked. 'Is he still around?'

'No...' Gabbie said slowly. 'He's not in the fields. Hang on, I'm going to look out of the front bedroom... No, he's not over this side either.'

'Right,' Mel said. 'Good.' But was it good? If he wasn't by

Gabbie's house, then he could be somewhere else. Somewhere closer. Or hiding.

'Are you sure it was him?' Gabbie said desperately. 'Couldn't it have been someone else? A delivery man? A neighbour?'

'I don't think so,' Mel said, suddenly having doubts. She hadn't seen his face close up. 'There was something about him. The way he walked. His posture. I just... recognised it. And then he came close. It was definitely him.'

'What can we do?'

Mel shivered. 'I don't know.' How could she hide from him? Did he know where she lived? He'd seen her with Lily. 'What about Lily?' she asked. 'Would he hurt her?'

'Oh my god, Lily,' Gabbie said. 'He likes young girls. Think of all the times he took Erin to the storage hut for their little chats.'

'I know.' Erin had always said they just talked, but she'd never let the other girls come in with her. 'And he never got charged for that.'

'There can't have been enough evidence,' Gabbie said. 'Not without Erin there to tell them.'

'God, I can't believe he's back,' Mel said. She wasn't sure if she could make a home here for her family with Joe hanging around. She didn't feel safe.

'Should we go to the police?' Gabbie asked.

Mel laughed. 'And tell them what? That he was standing in a field, far away? That he tried to talk to me? He hasn't done anything wrong. There's no way we can stop him.'

'I guess you're right. We must look out for each other. If you see him again, just phone me.'

'I will do.' Mel swallowed. There was nothing else she could do to stop him. She felt like a sitting duck, just waiting for Joe to pounce.

THIRTEEN

By the second week of the school term, Lily had settled in well at nursery and Mel was getting used to the routine of dropping her off and picking her up. On Wednesday, Jodie handed Lily over with a smile and Mel bundled her into the car, taking off her coat to put her into the car seat and secure the straps snugly. Luckily Lily was in a good mood today, all giggly and smiley, as Mel couldn't stop thinking about the awful day she'd had at the school. A parent had complained to the school about her teaching 'style', and she was the one who had been hauled into the head teacher's office, as if she were the naughty child. Unfortunately the parent knew the head teacher from the golf club, and he seemed to take her side over Mel.

When Mel had come out of the head teacher's office, she'd seen Roz waiting in the corridor to speak to the head. Mel had blushed, wondering if she'd heard every word through the thin walls. Roz had been polite and friendly, but she'd left feeling embarrassed.

Luckily she was going over to Gabbie's house straight from

the nursery, so she'd have the chance to offload about her day. Gabbie had had the afternoon off to go to the dentist.

As Mel drove down Laurel Street, she felt her body tense. Since she'd seen Joe, she'd been constantly looking out for him. Whenever she drove down the street, she scanned the footpaths and fields. Whenever she went out for a walk with Lily and Luke, she was always on guard. She was starting to wonder if it had really been him, or just her imagination. It had been twenty-five years since she'd seen him.

When she knocked on Gabbie's door, Gabbie welcomed her inside her spotless house.

'Be careful, the floor's wet,' she said, as they went to the kitchen. 'I just mopped it. Do you want a coffee? Or a glass of wine?'

'A coffee, please.' She chose one from the machine and they sat on the sofa in the living room. Mel told Gabbie what had happened at school with the parent and the head teacher.

'I wouldn't worry,' Gabbie said. 'People really get worked up over nothing round here. They don't have enough to think about.'

The topic of conversation quickly changed to Gabbie and how much she missed London. 'You know we shouldn't talk about this here,' she said suddenly.

'What? Why?'

'Oh, I don't know. Sometimes I worry that Stuart will install a camera to watch me when I'm at home. They're really tiny these days, you know?'

'Did he say he was going to?'

'Not exactly. He just made a joke about keeping an eye on me, how he always knew what was going on. Let's go and talk in the pool house.'

'Are you sure? It's so cold out there.'

'Come on, Mel,' Gabbie said. 'Please.' She went to the

utility room and passed Mel some boots to wear. Mel wrapped Lily back up in her coat.

They went down to the pool house and Gabbie pushed the door open. She'd cleaned up the benches either side of the hallway and put in a couple of pot plants. Mel held Lily on her lap, not wanting her to crawl on the dirty floor.

'What's going on?' Mel asked, thinking about what Gabbie had said about a camera. She thought of the other day when she'd watched Gabbie chatting to Luke in the kitchen from Tamsin's house. She hadn't been worried about cameras then. 'Why would Stuart want to watch you?'

'I don't know.' Gabbie put her hands to her head. 'He just... well, he likes everything a certain way. Nothing out of place. I hate the idea of him watching all the time. When I'm on my own I sometimes relax the rules a bit.'

'The rules?'

'Nothing unusual. Just keeping the house clean and tidy. Stuart's a perfectionist, that's all. But everyone has their quirks, don't they? Stuart likes everything put away properly. I don't know why I'm even complaining.' She blushed. 'I'm the one who can be messy. It's me with the problem, not him. It's better to be clean and tidy, isn't it?'

'I don't know,' Mel said. 'You want your house to feel like home.' She looked at her friend. The way she was talking made it sound like she was still a child. She remembered Gabbie drunkenly saying she was thinking of leaving Stuart.

'Is everything else OK?' she asked, putting a hand on Gabbie's arm.

The colour rose in Gabbie's face. 'I shouldn't have told you I was thinking of leaving him the other day. I was drunk. I really want to make things work with me and Stuart.'

'It's OK,' Mel said. 'You needed to talk things through.'

Gabbie sighed. 'It's me, not him. I'm too hard on him. You shouldn't judge people on what they say in anger, should you?'

'What do you mean?' Mel asked, concerned. 'What does he say in anger?'

'Oh, nothing. Just little things, you know. Picking at me. My looks. My career. Anything, really. When we fight, I say horrible things to him too. It's the way it is. All couples fight, don't they?'

'I guess so,' Mel said. 'All couples must disagree sometimes.' She squeezed her friend's hand. 'You don't have to stay with him if you don't want to. If he's nasty to you.' Lily started to fidget in Mel's arms and she knew she had to get back.

'He's fine,' Gabbie said. 'Really he is. I'm lucky to have him.' Gabbie seemed downcast.

Mel wanted to ask her more, but she needed to go home and give Lily something to eat and get her ready for bed. 'I'm so sorry, I have to go. It's Lily's bedtime.'

'Oh, it's OK, I've gone on. And it's so cold. I should be getting back inside anyway.'

'You know you can talk to me any time,' Mel said, as she carried Lily back to the house. 'About anything.'

'Yeah, I do. You're my oldest friend.'

'I mean it,' Mel said, as they took off their boots in the patio doorway. 'If you need to talk about Stuart, or your relationship, anything at all, just give me a ring and I can pop round.'

Gabbie took the boots from Mel and turned into the house. Suddenly she froze. Mel glanced up, her heart pounding, Gabbie's fear contagious. She half-expected to see Joe looking at them from the kitchen. But it was only Stuart. He had changed out of his work clothes and into a gym kit and trainers.

'Hi,' Gabbie said. 'I didn't expect you back.'

'No, well, I didn't expect to see you here either.'

'I had the dentist. I told you this morning.'

'Oh, I see.' Stuart glanced at Mel. 'I'm going for a run,' he said. 'I haven't had any exercise all day.'

'OK. Well, what do you want for dinner? It's nice to have you back early. We can eat together.'

'For dinner?' Stuart looked confused. 'Umm... well, I don't know. Whatever you think's best.'

'Curry?'

'If you like.' He turned and left, and a few seconds later they heard the front door shut behind him.

Mel and Gabbie stood in silence for a moment.

'I'm sorry he didn't say hello to you, Mel,' Gabbie said. 'He's been so busy lately, so stressed with work.'

'It's OK,' Mel said. Gabbie shouldn't have to apologise for her husband. 'I have to go and get Lily to bed. She's exhausted after nursery. But remember, you can call me any time.'

Mel put her shoes on and then hugged Gabbie goodbye, squeezing her tightly.

FOURTEEN

When Lily woke on Saturday morning at 6 a.m., Mel rolled over and groaned, wishing she was still asleep.

'Ma-ma! Ma-ma!' The cries got louder, and Mel eased her feet out from under the warm duvet and placed them on the cold wooden floor.

'Don't worry,' Luke said. 'I'll go.'

'Are you sure?'

'Of course. You did the night shift.'

Mel didn't need telling twice. She rolled over and went back to sleep.

When she got up a couple of hours later, Lily and Luke were playing on the living room carpet, Luke helping Lily to place wooden pieces in a puzzle.

'Shall we go out?' Luke said, jumping up as soon as he saw her.

'Sure. Where were you thinking? We have the party later,

remember? I said I'd help Tamsin out before, so we can't go out for the whole day.'

'Oh no, I was just thinking of the morning. I have to be at Stuart and Gabbie's around lunchtime. Something else needs fixing. Honestly, those two keep me in business.' He grinned and ran his hand through his thick, dark hair.

'It's good you've found work so easily.'

'Yeah, it's a real relief. I hate not having enough to do.'

'They are paying you properly, aren't they?'

'Yeah, well,' Luke said, blushing. 'Mates' rates.'

'Don't sell yourself short,' Mel said, squeezing his arm. 'Maybe once things are on a bit more of an even keel you can cut down the weekend work? It's nice to spend time as a family.'

'Sure,' Luke said. 'I'm still trying to make a good impression at the moment. So I can't really say no to work. Besides, I've got this morning to spend with my two favourite people. Stuart was telling me about a walk through the woods. Lily would love it. There's even a little stream down there. And a swing.'

'I know,' Mel said hesitantly, remembering how she'd thought she'd seen Joe there last time. She hadn't mentioned that to Luke – he would only think she was paranoid.

'Come on, Mel. It would be good to get out and get some fresh air. And the woods will be paradise for Lily. You know how much she loves collecting sticks. And there might even be squirrels.'

Mel smiled. Lily had always been fascinated by squirrels, and had watched them obsessively in their nearest park in London.

'OK, then,' she said. If she was going to live here, she should live here fully. There was no need to be afraid. No matter whether Joe was hanging around or not, she would be with Luke. And he'd never let anyone hurt them.

. . .

They walked through the field to the woods, Lily strapped to Luke in the sling. On the way down Luke made up a song to sing with Lily, pretending to be a pirate searching for treasure in the woods. Mel laughed at his booming voice, but she kept looking round, constantly alert, searching for Joe.

They entered the woods and Lily giggled as Luke handed her a dirty stick. She swung it round her head, nearly hitting Mel in the face, and Luke laughed. He turned over a log to show her the squirming woodlice underneath and held Lily close to them so she could see.

When they got to the stream, Luke took Lily out of the sling and held her up as he pointed out the round pebbles on the riverbed and the reeds growing on the edges. They looked for frogs together, unsuccessfully.

'Don't go too close,' Mel said. 'It's deeper than it looks. Come this way and I'll take you to the bridge.'

Luke followed Mel and she showed them the little wooden bridge where it was safe to cross. It hadn't rained recently and the stream looked peaceful and smooth-flowing.

Mel remembered dropping sticks from the bridge with Erin and seeing whose came out the other side first. Now Luke was doing the same thing with Lily, holding her up so she could drop her stick and then taking her to the other side of the bridge so she could watch it appear again.

The sound of a twig breaking somewhere in the woods made Mel jump.

'What's wrong?' Luke asked.

'I don't know,' she said. 'Just on edge.' She thought about mentioning Joe, but decided against it. She didn't want to ruin their trip to the woods.

'This is where Erin went missing, isn't it?' he said. 'I can understand why it makes you feel odd being here.'

She nodded. 'It's the last place I saw her.'

Luke squeezed her hand. 'I wanted us all to come here,' he

said. 'As a family. We're so lucky, with all this nature on our doorstep. I want us to enjoy it. What happened here was so sad, but Lily has her whole life ahead of her. We need to enjoy the area we're living in.'

Mel knew Luke was right. She'd thought she could come back here and forget the past, forget what had happened to Erin. But for her the past felt alive, memories good and bad lurking behind every tree in the woods and down every foot-path. It wasn't as easy to start again as she had thought it would be.

FIFTEEN

Late afternoon, Mel went over to Tamsin's to help her prepare for the party. They were setting things up so that the huge art studio was centre stage, so people could admire the views over Laurel Street and beyond. Mel helped Tamsin to tidy it up and clear the space. They moved the finished canvases to the spare room, leaning them against the wall carefully, and piling others on the bed. They folded up the easels and put them in the study, along with Tamsin's multiple works-in-progress, and her paints.

'Gosh, I haven't seen the room like this in years. It looks so empty without my paintings. I wish I'd got round to hanging some of them on the walls.'

'You should do,' Mel said. 'I can help you another time. After the party.'

They dusted the room, getting into the nooks and crannies of the ornate fireplaces at either end.

'Should we light the fires, do you think?' Tamsin asked.

'Yeah, good idea. It will seem more homely. And it's freezing outside. People will appreciate a nice warm fire.'

'OK, I'll get them going now.'

Once that was done, they moved drinks trolleys of spirits into each corner of the room, ready to serve the guests. The fridge was overflowing with wine and beer and party food, and Mel started getting the cheeses out, so she could stuff even more white wine in the fridge. She put the bottles of red out on the kitchen counter.

'You've bought enough food and drink for an army,' she said.

'Oh, people round here can really drink.'

Mel thought of Gabbie. 'I think I've witnessed that.'

'Oh yeah, last week when you were swigging wine on the green like teenagers.' Tamsin chuckled. Mel was surprised she was so open about the fact that she'd been watching them. She remembered Gabbie asking her not to tell anyone what she'd said about Stuart and her marriage, and Mel changed the subject. 'Let's put some crisps and nibbles out in the studio too,' she said. 'So people can help themselves.'

They went back through to the studio carrying bowls of crisps and nuts and placed them around the room on small tables.

'Are many people coming?' Mel asked Tamsin.

'I think everyone on the street is,' Tamsin said with a smile.

Then she turned her head, looking down on Gabbie's house with a frown.

Mel could see that Gabbie was already in her party dress, standing by a mirror in her bedroom, putting on her make-up. Stuart came up behind her, put his arms round her and she seemed to flinch.

'They're not happy,' Tamsin said sadly.

'We shouldn't watch,' Mel said quickly. But then Gabbie turned around towards Stuart and said something. Whatever it was made him angry and he stepped closer to her. For a moment Mel held her breath. Then Gabbie started gesticulating, raising her hands in the air and pointing her finger at him.

Stuart was shaking his head, then pacing the room. He got closer to her again, right up in her face.

She barged past him into the other room, but he followed.

Mel's heart beat faster. They were out of sight now, and she couldn't see what was going on. 'Do you think we should check they're OK?' she asked Tamsin.

'They're fine,' Tamsin said. 'They often fight like this.' Mel felt tense and uncomfortable. She didn't think she should witness something like that, without then doing something about it. And what else had Tamsin seen?

'You must see everything,' she said.

'Too much, probably. I worry a lot.'

Mel thought of Joe. Surely Tamsin would have seen him too. 'Have you seen any strange men hanging around?' she asked.

'No,' Tamsin said. 'Why?'

'I saw someone odd the other day, that's all. On the path to the woods.'

'When?'

'Last weekend, walking back from your house.'

Tamsin shook her head. 'After you left, I went to the other room to do some washing. I wasn't watching. But I haven't seen anyone I don't know around Laurel Street in recent weeks. It might have been one of the neighbours you haven't met yet. You'll probably meet them tonight.'

Mel couldn't bring herself to tell Tamsin that it had been Joe. She didn't want to upset her, to bring back what had happened to Erin. 'Probably,' she said.

'If I see anyone odd, I'll let you know,' Tamsin said.

Gabbie came back into the bedroom now, and slumped down on the bed. Mel felt relieved. At least she was physically OK. But she could tell from Gabbie's hunched shoulders that she was crying.

'Roz has a lot to answer for,' Tamsin said, watching.

'Roz?' Mel asked.

'She's been having an affair with Stuart. They go running together sometimes. And a few times a week when he gets home from work, he goes over to her house first for about an hour before he returns to his wife.'

'What?' Mel said, horrified.

'Yeah, it's been going on for at least a couple of months. I'm not sure if Gabbie knows.'

Mel thought of Gabbie, so distressed by the state of her marriage, thinking of staying with Stuart, having kids with him. 'Why haven't you told her?'

Tamsin looked surprised. 'We're not that close. And it's none of my business.'

'Oh god,' Mel said. If Tamsin hadn't told Gabbie, then she should. She was Gabbie's friend. But how could she tell her? The party was starting in less than an hour. She didn't want to make things worse. And if she told her at the party, she'd ruin it for her. Maybe she could tell her tomorrow. Take her out for lunch away from Laurel Street. Give her some time apart from the neighbours so she could calm down and take stock.

Yes, that's what she'd do. In the meantime, she wouldn't mention it; let Gabbie enjoy the party before her world crashed down around her.

'She'll be OK,' Tamsin said. 'People recover from affairs all the time. There are worse things that can happen.' Of course there were. Tamsin knew that better than anyone. How could anything else ever compare to what had happened to her?

'Yeah,' Mel said dully. 'I must go back and get ready soon. And prepare our overnight things.' Mel and Lily were going to stay over at Tamsin's tonight. Tamsin had kindly organised for Jodie from Lily's nursery to come round and look after a few children of the guests during the party. Tamsin had set up a playroom in one of the rooms downstairs, away from the adults. Mel thought back to the New Year's Eve when Erin had snuck out of the window in the basement and met her and Gabbie in the woods for their midnight feast. They had been left to their own devices that evening.

'I'll take you downstairs, show you where you'll be sleeping,' Tamsin said. 'I'm afraid it will be on the floor if you want to be close to Lily. The kids are bringing sleeping bags. Have you got one for you?'

Mel nodded. 'How long's Jodie staying for?' she asked as they went down two flights of stairs to the first floor.

'I've booked her until midnight. The kids should all be asleep long before then.'

'Right,' Mel said. 'And I'll be close by after that, in the room next door. I'll listen out for the kids.'

'The older ones should be no trouble. Their parents will collect them in the morning. Let me show you where you'll be sleeping.'

Tamsin pushed open the door to the first floor corridor, and the cold air hit Mel. Tamsin frowned. 'I don't usually use these rooms, so they get a bit cold. I'll turn the heating up.'

Mel went down the familiar hallway. Before Erin disappeared, Erin and Tamsin used to have bedrooms on this floor. Mel could remember visiting, playing with Erin in her room, running up and down the corridors and stairs of the big house. They'd had such good times together. The house had been like a second home to Mel when she was little. Mel felt her stomach knot. It hurt to think of it.

Erin's room had been the first door on the left, and Mel pushed it open without thinking. The room smelt slightly stale and mouldy, but other than that it was the same as when Erin had lived here. Mel's heart quickened and tears welled up in her eyes. It was like stepping straight back into the past. Tamsin hadn't changed a thing. Erin's My Little Pony duvet covered the bed, which at ten she had insisted she'd grown out of. There was a line of soft toys along the pillow, books still on her bookshelf, hair ties and hairbands and a small brush on her bedside table.

'Wow,' Mel said, swallowing her emotion.

'Don't go in there,' Tamsin said, pulling Mel away and shutting the door firmly. 'I don't want it disturbed. In case she comes back.' Tamsin's voice shook and she couldn't look Mel in the eyes.

Mel squeezed her hands together to calm herself. She knew in her heart Erin wasn't coming back, but she couldn't say that to Tamsin. And if she did return, she wouldn't appreciate a ten-year-old's room. But she could see how Tamsin couldn't let go. To clear out the room would be to extinguish all hope, to admit that Erin was gone forever. And no one was ready to do that. Even Mel still held onto a sliver of hope that Erin would one day return to Laurel Street, with the same ready smile and some reasonable explanation of why she'd been gone.

SIXTEEN

After Mel had gone home and changed, she came back to Tamsin's with Luke and they dropped Lily off downstairs with Jodie before coming up to the party. As Mel pushed open the huge wooden door to the top floor, the noise hit them, chatter and laughter echoing over classical music.

Mel walked over to Tamsin and kissed her on the cheek. 'Thanks so much for organising this. Everyone's here.'

'Mel! Luke!' Gabbie rushed over, glass of wine in hand. 'Isn't this party just so brilliant? I'm so glad you coming back has given Tamsin the excuse. This is the perfect house for a party, isn't it?'

'Yes, it's perfect,' Mel said, thinking of what Tamsin had told her earlier about Stuart and Roz. Gabbie seemed so fragile. Mel wasn't sure if she would be able to take it when she found out.

The buzzer rang at that moment and Tamsin started to go back to the kitchen to the entryphone.

'Gosh, you're going to be back and forth all night,' Gabbie said. 'Maybe you should just prop the door open.'

'Maybe. But I want to know who's coming into my home.'

'I wouldn't worry,' Stuart piped up, appearing from behind them and topping up Gabbie's wine. 'It's only locals round here. It's not like anyone's going to wander by and see there's a party going on and come in from the street.'

Tamsin smiled. 'You're right, of course. And the kids are safe with Jodie. I'll prop the front door open.'

Mel thought about Joe hanging around and felt a shiver of worry. But Tamsin was right. Lily would be safe with Jodie.

'And it makes it easier for me to go out for a smoke, too,' Stuart continued. 'If I need one. I gave up years ago, but I can't resist when I have a drink.'

'Oh, me too,' said Luke. 'I'm a social smoker at parties.'

'Come on,' Gabbie said, taking Mel's hand and grinning at Luke. 'Let me introduce you to everyone.'

Mel went through a dizzying series of introductions to the neighbours she hadn't met and reconnected with some of the ones she already knew. She fought back the desire to say something to Roz, but stuck to a curt, 'We've met,' leaving it at that. Luke peeled away to talk to Stuart and Roz introduced Mel to the parents of the child who was in her class.

'Thanks for putting the swing and climbing frame in the woods,' Mel said. 'Lily and I went down the other day.'

'Well,' the woman said, smiling, 'we thought it was about time the woods lost their association with that...' she looked around, lowering her voice 'tragedy... I felt we needed to make the woods more child-friendly again. A place for the next generation to enjoy.'

Mel nodded, glancing round to check Tamsin couldn't hear them. She saw her sitting on a sofa in a corner of the room, deep in conversation with Gabbie.

'Well, it was a good idea,' she said. 'You know, I'm your daughter's teacher at the school.'

'Oh, yes,' the man said. 'The new teacher. Well, I hope you're settling in OK.'

'I'm enjoying it,' she said. 'I love the kids in my class. Freya's such a lovely girl.'

'She is,' the mother said, her voice a shade colder than before. 'And she always likes her teachers. She talked about last year's teacher all the time.'

Last year's teacher. Right. Not Mel. Maybe this woman was friends with the mother who'd made the complaint about her. It was a small world round here.

'Well, she's a very good teacher,' said Mel. She looked round for a way to exit the conversation, but she couldn't see Luke anywhere. 'I'm going to get a drink,' she said. 'Can I get you one?'

'No, thanks,' the couple said in unison, pointing to their full glasses.

Mel went down to check on Lily before she got a drink, but she was fine with Jodie, already fast asleep in her travel cot. Back upstairs at the party, she helped herself to a glass of white wine. The liquid slipped easily down her throat, and she felt herself start to relax. She went to the window that looked out over Gabbie's house and the fields beyond. She could see, in Gabbie's living room, a red light moving back and forth across the empty room. Mel stared at it curiously, and then realised it must be the robot vacuum that Gabbie swore by.

Mel looked at the disused building next to the house. The pool house. Everything was in a state of disrepair now, crumbling. Mel hoped that Stuart would do it up as planned, return the swimming pool to its former glory.

'There you are!' Gabbie came up behind her and tapped her on the arm. 'Is everything alright?'

'Yeah, I was just... looking.'

'Were you thinking about Joe?'

Mel looked at her friend in surprise. 'What makes you say that?'

'Something weird happened the other day. I thought I saw

him too.' Gabbie shivered. 'Down by the stables at night. It was almost like he was waiting for me.'

'Did you speak to him?' Mel felt hot and she swept her hand through her hair, agitated.

'No, I turned round and headed back to the house, pretended I had to go back and get something.' Gabbie wrapped her arms around herself anxiously, her wine glass tilting precariously in her hand.

'And what did he do?'

'Nothing, but it really creeped me out.' Gabbie's voice got higher, and her knuckles turned white around the stem of her wine glass.

Mel sipped her drink. Gabbie's eyes wandered and then settled. She seemed distracted by something over in a corner of the room. Mel followed her gaze and saw Stuart laughing loudly with Roz, her hand on his arm. Gabbie downed her glass of wine.

'What does he think he's doing?'

'Gabbie...' Mel said, seeing the flash of anger in her friend's eyes.

'He's flirting with her. In front of everyone. How can he do that to me?'

'I'm sure he doesn't mean to,' Mel said, instinctively trying to defuse the situation. How could she get her friend out of this? 'Why don't we go outside? Talk there?'

'What? Why? I can't just stand here and watch this.' Gabbie strode over to Stuart and Roz, Mel following behind her.

'What are you doing?' she said to Stuart. 'With her?' Her voice was at a higher pitch than normal. She swayed in her heels and Mel took her elbow to steady her.

'Come on, Gabbie,' she said. 'Let's go.'

'Yeah,' Stuart sneered. 'Why don't you just go? You're

drunk. Making a fool of yourself. Your friend thinks it's best that you leave.' Stuart slurred his words.

'You're flirting with her,' Gabbie said, her voice wobbly.

Roz put her hand on Stuart's waist in a possessive gesture, and Gabbie looked at her, horrified. 'Why are you touching him?' she screamed.

'He's not your property,' Roz said.

'He's my *husband*.'

'I wasn't flirting,' Stuart insisted, pulling away from them both. 'But so what if I was? It's not like you never flirt. I've seen you.'

'I don't,' Gabbie said, tears in her eyes. 'Just because you're not interested in me anymore doesn't mean I'd turn to someone else. I'm not like you!'

Stuart snarled. 'Why do you think I'm not interested? When I married you, you were sparkling and full of life. You had so much going for you. Now you've become so dull. You just want to live in the countryside and start a family.'

'That's unfair, Stuart. We made the decision to move together. Now I hardly see you.'

'Let's just go, Gabbie,' Mel said. She was aware of the hush in the rest of the room, the neighbours listening to the conversation.

'No,' Gabbie said. 'I'm not going. I'm not leaving them together. Things aren't right at the moment. I need to know why. What's going on, Stuart?'

'Nothing,' Stuart said, flushing, as he glanced at Roz.

'Oh, just put her out of her misery,' Roz said. She put her hand on his arm and stared directly at Gabbie. 'Just tell her you're sleeping with me.'

Gabbie looked blankly from Roz to Stuart and back again. Then she seemed to become suddenly aware of her surroundings, noticing she had an audience for the first time. Her eyes darted from face to face and she burst into tears.

'I'm going home,' she said, putting her head down and stumbling towards the door, knocking a full glass of red wine onto the rug as she went.

'I'll come with you,' Mel said.

But Gabbie pushed her away. 'No – I need to be on my own.'

SEVENTEEN

For a moment everyone stared at the spot Gabbie had just left. Then the chatter in the room resumed and it was like nothing had happened. Roz and Stuart backed into a corner, speaking to each other in hushed whispers. Mel went to the kitchen, grabbed some kitchen roll and started dabbing the red wine out of Tamsin's antique rug.

'Is everything OK?' Tamsin asked. 'I mean, I heard what happened...'

'Gabbie's left,' Mel said. 'And your rug...'

'Oh, don't worry about that, it's ancient.' But Tamsin took the kitchen roll from her and began mopping it herself.

'I need to go after Gabbie,' Mel said. 'Check she's OK.'

'Of course, see you later.'

Mel went down the stairs and out into the cold night air. The chill caught her arms instantly, wrapping itself around her, under her skin and into her bones. Her coat was upstairs.

She ran quickly across the street to Gabbie's house and rang the doorbell, her breath visible in front of her. She waited, running her arms over her bare skin to warm up.

No answer. She rang the bell again. 'Gabbie!' she shouted. 'Gabbie! Are you OK? It's just me, Mel.'

Mel thought anxiously of how drunk Gabbie had been, how unsteady on her feet. Could she have had an accident? But Tamsin's house was next to hers. There was no way anything could have happened to her on the way back home. Maybe she'd had a fall inside the house. Mel rang the bell again.

She remembered what Gabbie had said about going for walks late at night. Could she have done that again? Mel thought uncomfortably of their late-night ride on the horses. She wouldn't have gone down to the stables, would she?

Mel shivered violently. It was so cold, and Gabbie hadn't had a coat either. She walked to the path that led down to the stables and peered into the dark. She couldn't see her. Gabbie was probably fine, she reassured herself. She was probably inside her home, sleeping off the alcohol. Mel would speak to her tomorrow. She looked at her watch. It was 11.50 p.m. She needed to take over from Jodie watching Lily from midnight.

She sighed and was about to walk back, when she heard a high-pitched female voice, talking rapidly, the words unclear. The sound was coming from the abandoned pool house.

Mel crept towards it, suddenly afraid. She thought of how she'd seen Joe hanging around recently. She needed to see what was going on.

She got to the pool house and peered through the half-open door. She could see two people in the little hallway, sitting on the bench together.

Gabbie. And Luke.

Mel held her breath as she watched the two of them, huddled together. Luke was smoking a cigarette and he offered it to Gabbie, their fingers touching as she accepted it gratefully.

Mel could only catch some of the words Gabbie was saying. *Stuart. Roz.* Gabbie was explaining what had happened in a monologue. Luke was nodding understandingly. Mel was about to go in, say hello, suggest they go into the warm, but something stopped her. After all, Gabbie had told her not to follow her. But she'd wanted to talk to Luke. Mel watched as Gabbie laughed at something Luke said and then reached out to touch his arm. Mel remembered what Stuart had said about Gabbie flirting, remembered Luke stopping for ages at Gabbie's house when he went to fix something, remembered watching them have coffee together from Tamsin's house.

Mel and Gabbie had always had the same taste in men, negotiating over the boys in school. But when it had come down to it, it had always been Gabbie who had ended up dating the boy they were both interested in. Mel had been invisible. Her friend had been confident and self-assured, with shiny blonde hair and the perfect figure. Mel had always been in her shadow.

And now Gabbie was here with Luke. Her husband.

Gabbie still had her hand on Luke's arm. He didn't move away, letting her hand stay there. And suddenly Mel knew where this was going. Luke was no different to the others. He wasn't the perfect, loyal husband she had thought he was. He would choose Gabbie, too.

Mel watched as Gabbie put her hand round the back of his neck and lifted her face up, so her lips met his, and kissed him.

EIGHTEEN

Mel saw Luke lean into the kiss for a few seconds, before he pulled away. The betrayal surged through Mel's body, and her hands clenched into fists.

She was about to barge into the room and ask Gabbie what on earth she was doing, when her phone vibrated in her pocket and she pulled it out.

Jodie.

The time was in the corner of the screen. It was a few minutes past midnight and she was late to take over with Lily.

Moving away from the pool house, she whispered into the phone. 'Hello? Jodie? I'll be there in a minute.'

Lily's screams echoed in the background and Mel paused, alarmed. 'Jodie? What's wrong with Lily?'

'She's got a bit of a fever. I've given her Calpol, but I can't calm her down. She's crying out for you,' Jodie said.

'I'm coming straight away,' Mel said, running from the pool house back to Tamsin's house and up the stairs to Jodie and Lily.

'She's calmed down a bit now,' Jodie said as she handed her over. Lily's body was shaking with sobs, but she was no longer screaming.

'Do you think I need to call a doctor out?'

'No, not yet. Just keep an eye on her overnight. Her temperature's already starting to come down.'

Once Jodie had gone, Mel rocked Lily back and forth in her arms until she closed her eyes and drifted off. The other children were all asleep in sleeping bags on the floor. Her mind was spinning, replaying the kiss between Gabbie and Luke again and again. She thought of the life she'd built with Luke, the future they'd planned together. Gabbie had clearly instigated the kiss and Luke hadn't looked like he was into it, but he hadn't pulled away instantly either. How could he put everything they had at risk?

Mel lay Lily down in her cot and looked at her sleeping daughter. She desperately wanted to leave Tamsin's and go back to the pool house to check Luke and Gabbie weren't still together, to check that Luke hadn't given in to Gabbie's advances. But she was torn. She couldn't leave Lily, or the other kids she was responsible for.

She went to the room across the corridor where she would be sleeping. Her sleeping bag was laid out neatly, a glass of water beside it, which Tamsin must have left for her. Mel paced up and down, her fury rising. She felt like a trapped animal, thinking of Luke and Gabbie out there together, with her stuck here, unable to get to them.

Mel went to the window, but she was at the other side of the house, looking the wrong way, with no view of the pool house. *Luke had pulled away*, she reminded herself. He would have left Gabbie by now, gone home to their cottage and his bed.

She could ring him, check where he was. Her finger

hovered over his number and then she pressed call. She listened to it ring a couple of times and then hung up. She couldn't face him now; she didn't want him to witness her anger. She needed to calm down first, get her thoughts in order.

A message popped up on WhatsApp from Luke.

> Everything alright?

> Lily's been unwell but OK now. Did you get back to the cottage OK?

> Yes, safe at home. See you tomorrow.

Mel frowned at the screen. The problem was, she didn't know whether to believe him. This was all Gabbie's fault. How could she do this to her? Mel's rage rose inside her and her pulse quickened as heat flushed her face. She picked up her phone to ring Gabbie, but then stopped herself, taking deep breaths to try and calm down. Gabbie would be too drunk to make any coherent sense. She picked up the water glass from the floor and threw it at the wall with all her might, watching it smash into pieces.

Half an hour later she had cleared up the glass as well as she could and was lying on Tamsin's cold wooden floor in her sleeping bag, her mind still spinning.

She tried to close her eyes and sleep, but it was impossible. Images of Luke and Gabbie kept flashing through her mind. She was so furious with Gabbie for behaving the way she'd always done, just like when they were teenagers. And furious with Luke for betraying her.

Sleep eventually came in dribs and drabs, and she tossed and turned, trying to get comfortable. Lily woke up in the night a couple of times, and Mel thought about Luke as she cradled her in her arms. She needed him to be a father to her. She hadn't known her own father growing up, and she was determined that things would be different for Lily. Luke had promised her that she would always have two involved parents, something that neither of them had ever had themselves.

When morning finally came, the other parents came to collect their children and Mel concentrated hard on being polite, even though she hadn't slept properly and felt exhausted.

Luckily Lily seemed much better this morning. She was her smiley, happy self and her temperature was gone. Mel took her upstairs and started to clear up from the party while Tamsin played with Lily. Mel put half-eaten food into bin bags, wine glasses into the dishwasher, and lined up the empty bottles for recycling.

'Thanks for your help,' Tamsin said, 'but I can do the rest.'

Mel insisted on giving the place a quick hoover before she left, and taking the bottles down to the recycling bin. On the walk back with Lily, she lingered by Gabbie's house, looking over to the pool house where she'd seen Luke and Gabbie the previous night. How was she going to face him? She felt like she was on the edge of a precipice, like her whole world might be turned on its head.

When she put her key in her front door she still didn't know what she was going to say to Luke. The key was stiffer than usual in the lock, and when she looked more closely at the keyhole she could see it was scratched, as if someone had been trying to pick the lock. Her body tensed, thinking of Joe. She was sure the lock hadn't been scratched before. It must have happened last night.

As she pushed the door open, she called out 'Hello?' There was no answer. Lily fidgeted in her pushchair and Mel took her out and carried her through to the living room and then to the kitchen.

'Luke?' she called up the stairs.

Still no answer. She went upstairs with Lily and looked for him in each room.

But he wasn't in. He had gone.

Mel wasn't sure what to do. She had been going over possible scenarios with Luke in her head all night. She'd imagined confronting him about the kiss and him apologising. She'd imagined not saying anything and seeing how he behaved, watching him for signs of guilt. She'd imagined asking him if he'd seen Gabbie last night and him denying it. She'd rehearsed countless possible conversations with him in her head. But the one thing she hadn't thought of was him not being here at all.

Mel swallowed, fear gripping her heart like a vice. Had he even come home at all last night? Had he got back from the party? What if he was still with Gabbie?

Mel hugged Lily closer, and then got her some milk. She tried to calm down. Luke couldn't be at Gabbie's house. Stuart would be there too. Could they have run away together? No; she was being silly. She reminded herself that she'd seen him pull away from the kiss. She had to trust him. Frowning, she checked her phone to see if he'd contacted her since she last checked. There were no new messages.

She looked out of the window and noticed for the first time that his van wasn't on the drive. He'd gone off somewhere. Mel felt her chest tighten. Had he left her? Or was he just running an errand? She picked up her phone and tried to ring him, but he didn't answer. Her head throbbed as she tried not to think about what might have happened.

She had to get out of the house and clear her head. She couldn't stand sitting here on her own. With Lily back in her pushchair, she left the house.

Halfway down the street, she saw Stuart in his running kit.

He was the last person she wanted to see and she tried to avoid meeting his eyes.

'Morning,' he said, gruffly. She didn't know how he could even speak to her after last night.

'Morning,' she said back.

'Gabbie's gone, you know,' he said, offhand, stopping beside her.

'What?'

'She's left me. Can you believe it? She didn't even tell me she was going, she just left a note.' Stuart's face was flushed. 'She was gone when I got back this morning.'

'What? Really?' Mel tried to hide the panic in her voice. Gabbie missing. Luke uncontactable. They must be together.

'Yep. She left me a note last night. She's gone. Maybe it's for the best. We need a break from each other.'

'Right,' Mel said, thinking of Luke. What had happened after that kiss? Why hadn't she gone back to check on him and Gabbie? She should have left Lily with Tamsin and gone to see what they were doing.

Stuart continued up the street towards Roz's house, and Mel stood still for a moment, shell-shocked, before she walked on towards Tamsin's and Gabbie's houses, in a daze. As she walked by Gabbie's house, she saw Luke's van parked outside. It hadn't been there half an hour ago when she'd left Tamsin's after clearing up. He must have driven out somewhere and then come back to Stuart's house.

She breathed deeply. At least she knew where he was now. And Gabbie and Stuart weren't in. She needed to talk to him.

She carried Lily round the side of the house and saw Luke fiddling with a drain near the pool house. Just being next to the pool house brought back memories of the night before. Mel was surprised by the tears that pricked her eyes, the rush of emotion that overcame her.

'Luke?' she said, tentatively.

He turned. 'Oh, hi, Mel, how are you doing? I thought you'd still be at Tamsin's.'

'I've been back a while. I didn't know where you were.'

He pulled his hand out of the drain and stood up slowly, stretching out his stiff back. 'I should have left a note, then. Sorry.' He flushed. 'I just thought I'd get up and get on with work. Stuart had a few things that he needed sorting. I drove to the hardware store this morning to get some materials, and here I am.'

'Back at the pool house,' Mel said.

Luke's brow creased. 'Stuart needs the drain clearing. It's blocked down the bottom there. He wanted it done this morning.'

'You were here last night, too.'

'Last night?'

'With Gabbie. I saw you.'

'She was really upset, Mel. She needed someone to talk to. Stuart's been cheating on her.'

'And you were her shoulder to cry on?'

'No one else was around.'

Mel winced. She had offered to go with Gabbie, offered to help. But Gabbie hadn't wanted her. She'd wanted Luke.

'What happened between you?' she asked, giving him a chance to come clean, to admit to the kiss.

'We talked,' Luke said. 'And then I encouraged her to go to bed. It was freezing cold last night.'

Mel could feel heat rising in her body, her temper fraying. 'You did more than talk,' she said. 'I saw you, Luke. You kissed her.'

'It wasn't like that,' he said quickly. 'She was upset, really emotional, and drunk, and she kind of leant in. It took me by surprise.'

Mel remembered how it had looked. How Gabbie had taken the initiative, but Luke had been slow to pull back.

'You didn't pull away,' Mel said.

'I did! I was just so shocked.' Luke stepped towards her. 'Look, Mel. I'm really sorry. What can I do to make it up to you?'

'It's not that simple. You kissed my friend. Was it the first time, or has it happened before? Is there something I should know?'

'No!' Luke said. 'Nothing like that... it's never happened before. I don't have any interest in Gabbie. It was a mistake.' He rubbed his dirty hands on his workman's trousers. 'I'm so sorry, Mel. It should never have happened. I love you and Lily. You're the only people who are important to me.'

Luke and Mel ate lunch in silence, chewing their sandwiches slowly and fussing over Lily whenever she made the tiniest noise or wanted food. They didn't know what to say to each other, and Mel didn't want to start another argument.

'Did you know the lock to the house was damaged?' she asked.

'What? No, I hadn't noticed.'

'When I came back it was all scratched. Did someone try to get in?'

'I didn't hear anyone, but then I was out like a light.'

'I see.' Mel wondered if Gabbie had followed him last night, if she'd tried to get into the house after him, intending to seduce him. Or if he hadn't heard anything because he hadn't been there at all, he'd been off somewhere with Gabbie.

Mel finished her sandwich and put her plate in the dishwasher, then continued to help Lily with her food.

Their meal was interrupted by the doorbell and Luke jumped up to answer it.

'Mel!' Luke shouted from the hallway, his voice full of alarm. 'Come here!'

Mel put down Lily's sandwich and rushed through the living room towards the door.

'It's Angela,' Luke called. 'She says she's come to live with us.'

'What?' Mel felt her pulse quicken. This was the last thing she needed. She got to the doorway, saw the familiar figure standing there.

'Mum?' she said.

NINETEEN

Mel's mother was dressed in a leather jacket and floral leggings, and her short black hair was streaked with grey. Mel could see her age in her face: the frown lines on her forehead, the puckered lips from a lifetime of smoking. There was a battered motorcycle parked behind her, which must be hers.

'Mel!' she said. 'I am *so* glad to see you.' Her mother wrapped her arms around Mel and squeezed her so tightly she could hardly breathe.

Mel let her arms hang limply by her sides, not returning the hug. Her mother shouldn't be here. She was supposed to be in Spain. In the last fifteen years Mel could count on one hand the number of times she'd visited. Mel had built her own life entirely by herself. She didn't want to let her mother waltz back in and ruin it.

She could smell her mother's perfume. She'd put far too much of it on. But there wasn't the familiar smell of stale alcohol underneath. Instead the perfume covered a damp smell and a whiff of stale smoke.

'What do you want, Mum?' she asked.

'I split up with Jonathan and left Spain for good,' she said. 'I came here to see you and Lily. I'm sober. I have been for six months.'

'Six months?' Mel didn't believe her. She'd lost count of the times her mother had turned a corner, stopped drinking, before meeting a new boyfriend or going out for a drink with an old friend and sliding back into alcohol dependency. It had been an endless cycle throughout her childhood. Once her mother slipped back, she returned to the life she had before. The house was always messy; sometimes she forgot to wash; she would drink in the morning, the day, the evening. Mel could remember the dizzying drives to school, when her mother was all over the road. She could remember waking her up in the morning and trying to force her to drink water; she could remember helping her tidy the house for social services.

But she wasn't always bad; sometimes she cared. She'd kiss Mel goodnight and say she loved her, but the next day tell her she was a bad child, that she couldn't cope with her, that Mel had turned her to drink.

'Yes, six months,' her mother said. 'I did it for Lily. I didn't want her to have a drunk for a grandmother. Are you proud of me?'

Mel sighed. 'Of course, Mum.' Wasn't she going to ask Mel how she was? Or about her life? Didn't she care? 'Why are you back here?' she asked.

'I wanted to see you, reconnect. And have a relationship with Lily. I know I wasn't a good mother, but I want to put things right as a grandmother.'

'It's not that simple,' Mel said. She didn't want to be put through her mother's drama again, and she certainly didn't want it to affect Lily.

'But I've changed, I'm a different person. Honestly, Mel, you have to believe me. I've given up the drink for you. Because I want to be part of your life, your family's life. I want to live here with you.'

Mel took a step back, feeling ambushed and confused. Her mother owned half the house – she couldn't say no. But she hadn't expected her back; Angela had never had any interest in Laurel Street, had always wanted to get away from her own mother.

'Oh,' she said. 'Why didn't you call me before you turned up?'

'You wouldn't have believed I was sober. I had to see you face to face. I came round last night but you weren't here.'

'I was at a party at Tamsin's.'

'Yeah, I saw the party. When you weren't at home I went over to see if you were there, but I saw Tamsin and she told me to get lost, that you didn't want to see me.'

Tamsin hadn't mentioned it. Was her mother telling the truth, or was this another one of her lies? It was true Tamsin had never liked her. Mel thought of the scratched lock. They'd changed the locks since they moved in. Her mother would have had the previous key. 'Did you try and get in last night?' she asked.

'Yes,' she said. She looked crestfallen. 'You weren't here and I couldn't find you, so I tried to use my key, but you've changed the locks. How could you?'

'It was just for security,' Mel said. 'The locks haven't been changed for years. Lots of people would have had a key. And I didn't think you'd come back and try to get in.'

'It's half my house,' her mum said. 'Now can I come in?'

'Are you sure you don't have anywhere else to go?' Mel felt cruel as she said it, but she was just trying to protect herself.

'No, I own half this house. I want to live here.'

Mel stepped back reluctantly, not sure what she could do. 'OK, then.' Her mother picked up her dirty blue holdall off the ground beside her and lifted it over her shoulder, straining under its weight.

She stepped forward and touched Mel's shoulder and Mel

felt an unexpected surge of longing. Despite all her defences, a part of her wanted a close relationship with her mother. No matter how old she got, she still couldn't help hoping that one day her mother would transform into the caring, nurturing woman she'd always wanted. She was sober now. Maybe there was hope.

Her mother followed her into the house. 'My goodness,' she said. 'You've cleared it out quickly.'

'We had to,' Mel said. 'We needed space for us and Lily.'

'Where have you put all Mum's stuff?'

Mel felt an odd possessiveness when her mother called her grandmother 'Mum'. They'd never been close.

'Most of it's gone to the charity shop. Some's in the garage.'

'You could have let me go through it. My own mother's things. This house was a part of my childhood. Her things meant something to me.'

'I'm sorry,' Mel said, putting her hands to her temples.

'I was going to clear it out myself. I wanted to spend time with her belongings, remembering her, before I let them go. And there were a few things I wanted to keep. Vases, wedding china, things like that.'

'Those are in the garage,' Mel said. 'You can have them if you like.'

'OK. Well, they *are* mine. I'm her daughter. It's not for you to give them to me.'

'I'm sorry you didn't get to go through everything,' Mel said, feeling guilty. 'I assumed you weren't interested.' She stopped herself from saying that she'd thought her mother would have been too drunk to care.

'Of course I was interested. She was my mother. My only connection to my past, my childhood. Surely you can understand that?'

But Mel couldn't. The woman standing in front of her was her only connection to her past, and they'd cut ties long ago.

'Everything OK?' Luke said, interrupting them.

Mel hesitated. She knew Luke wasn't going to like what she was about to tell him.

'Mum's moving in,' she said, knowing she didn't have the power to stop it happening.

'Right. Mel – can I talk to you for a minute in the living room?'

She nodded. 'You can wait in the hall, Mum,' she said. Her mother put down her holdall. The damp smell was stronger now she was inside the house.

Luke led Mel into the living room, shutting the door behind him. 'She can't stay here,' he said to Mel. 'She's no good for you. She makes you unhappy.'

Mel's head was pounding. She didn't want this anymore than Luke did. 'She doesn't have anywhere to go. The rent money we're paying her for her half of the house isn't enough to get her own place. She wants to stop that arrangement and live here instead. This house is as much hers as it is mine.'

Luke paced up and down. 'You know this is a bad idea. We've started our own lives here. Away from our toxic parents. It was the only thing we could do. To protect ourselves. If you let her in, you're throwing that all away.'

Her mother pushed open the door suddenly and their conversation stopped.

'Can I use your washing machine?' she asked.

'I'll show you where it is,' Mel said, as Luke stared at her, incredulous.

He followed them to the washing machine. Inside the house, Angela's damp smell was even more pungent. 'Why don't you have a shower in the downstairs bathroom?' Mel said.

'Sure,' Angela said. 'I'd love a shower, thanks.'

'There should be some shampoo and shower gel in there. I'll get you a towel. I can put your stuff in the wash if you like?'

'No, I can do it,' Angela said. 'You don't need to go through my dirty things. I'll put a wash on after my shower.'

When Angela was in the shower, Luke turned back to Mel. 'You know this is an awful idea, don't you?'

Mel shook her head. 'We don't have any choice,' she said. 'She says she wants to be a good grandmother to Lily, and Lily needs that. We're going to have to give her a chance.'

Luke put his hand on her shoulder, the pressure a little firmer than normal. 'It's up to you,' he said. 'But I think we're making a huge mistake. Your mother could ruin everything.'

TWENTY

The next day, while Mel was at school, Luke helped her mother to clear out the cupboards in the guest room to make space for her things. Her room was across the corridor from theirs, and suddenly the cottage felt smaller, with Angela always around.

Over the next few days, Mel's mother made a big effort, tidying and cleaning while Luke and Mel were at work, and going to the supermarket on her motorbike to do the shopping. But Mel felt uneasy around her, and couldn't relax when she returned home with Lily after work. It didn't help that Mel was particularly busy, preparing for the parents' evening on Wednesday night, and she didn't have much time to speak to her mother.

The parents' evening was exhausting and the school hall was freezing cold. Afterwards, Mel was grateful to get home to the warm. Luke made her a cup of tea before leaving on an urgent work call. Mel had hardly seen him lately. The weather had turned colder and people were calling him out to deal with frozen pipes and damaged central heating.

On Thursday it started to snow, first a dusty kind of fairy-tale snow, with snowflakes that caught in the wind. Then later it got thicker and settled. When she got home after picking Lily up, Mel turned on the patio light and took her daughter out in her wellies, gloves and thick coat. Lily was just starting to take her first few tentative steps and they made footprints in the snow, Mel holding Lily up as she walked, Lily looking down in wonder at her own tiny prints.

Her mother came outside, and Mel felt a moment of irritation at her interrupting a special moment between herself and Lily. But then her mother joined in too, laughing as she made her own footprints, and helping Lily track them. Mel felt caught in a strange whirl of emotions – of love, of longing and of loss. She wanted so much for her mother to be a proper mother to her, a grandmother to Lily, but still she couldn't bring herself to trust her. Her mother would pick Lily up when she cried, but Mel always took her back immediately, unable to quite cope with their level of intimacy. She wasn't ready for that yet.

That evening there were severe weather warnings for the next day, and in the morning the local schools were closed due to dangerous conditions. Mel was glad to have a full day with Lily. Since she'd started working again and Lily had gone to nursery, life seemed to be rushing by at record speed and she appreciated the chance for a slower day, to savour Lily growing up before her eyes.

'I don't have to go in today,' she told Luke on Friday morning. 'Maybe we can take Lily for a walk in the snow together.'

Luke turned to her, his expression unreadable. He'd been back late the night before from a call-out and he hadn't got into bed until 2 a.m. She'd sat up half the night worried because of the conditions outside. 'I've got a full day of work,' he said. 'Did you see the message on the street WhatsApp group? Stuart wants me to clear the snow from the road so that everyone who needs to can get out.'

'That will take ages. Is he paying you for it?'

Luke shifted uncomfortably. 'It wasn't clear.'

'No one's going anywhere in this weather,' Mel said. 'I'm sure it can wait until tomorrow. Why don't you come out with us?'

Luke shook his head. 'The old woman at the end of the road has a carer coming. She needs to get in.'

'I doubt the carer will make it anyway,' Mel said. 'All the country roads are bound to be treacherous.' She began to worry about the woman. 'I'll drop round later to see if she needs anything.'

'Good idea,' Luke said. 'Just in case.'

'Is everything alright between us?' she asked tentatively, stroking his arm. She thought of the kiss he'd shared with Gabbie, how often he was out of the house. He'd said the kiss meant nothing, but she wasn't sure she believed him. Ever since it had happened she'd had a hollow feeling in the pit of her stomach that she couldn't quite shift, the sense that her marriage had taken a different direction and she couldn't control it.

'Yeah,' he said. 'Fine. Although I wish your mother wasn't here. She makes me feel uncomfortable.'

'What about Gabbie?' Mel probed.

'What about her? I haven't heard from her. I guess she's sorting her life out now she's left Stuart.'

'OK,' Mel said, not quite satisfied with the answer.

An hour later she was walking down the snowy street with Lily snug against her in the sling, her mother beside her. Lily was facing forward and Mel was pointing out the snow-covered scenery: huge fir trees, with the branches sagging under the heavy snow, the snowed-in cars, the little footprints of tiny birds who had hopped along the road before them.

'Dog, dog, dog!' Lily started shouting suddenly. 'Dog' was one of her first words. She had always been fascinated by them and would point them out when they walked through the park in London. Just ahead of them, Roz's golden retriever had appeared, sniffing around in the bushes. Roz was the last person Mel wanted to see, but soon she rounded the corner, hand in hand with Stuart, both snug and warm in hats and gloves. He leant over to kiss her, and they made a picture-perfect image, underneath the snowy trees.

'Good morning,' Stuart said to her.

'Morning,' she replied, relieved when they'd passed by, their blissful smiles annoying her no end. She thought of Gabbie, and was angry on her behalf, despite the fact that she'd made a move on Luke. It seemed so unfair that Stuart and Roz could be so happy, when they cared so little about the damage left in their wake. It was less than a week since the party, and it seemed early to be flaunting their relationship so blatantly.

'Who was that?' her mother asked, once they were out of earshot.

'That's Stuart, Gabbie's husband. And the woman was Roz.'

'Oh,' her mother said. 'So... Gabbie's split up with her husband?'

'Yes, the night of the party. She found out he was cheating on her with Roz.'

'That must have hurt.'

Mel nodded. 'Yeah, she's left him.' Mel hadn't heard from her since the party. She wondered if Luke had. He'd been so secretive recently.

'Do her parents still live on the street?'

'Yeah, in the same house as always, just up here.'

'They never liked me much,' Angela said. 'Thought I wasn't good enough for you to mix with their daughter.'

Mel bit her tongue. There had been a reason for that. Her mother had always been drunk.

'Here's their house,' Mel said. The lights were off and Mel remembered Gabbie's parents saying at the party that they were leaving the next day to go on holiday to the Canary Islands.

It occurred to Mel that when Gabbie left Stuart, it would have been sensible for her to go and stay with her parents. But she clearly hadn't done that as all the lights were off in the house, and there was no sign of life. She must have gone to stay with a friend.

'I was surprised you wanted to come back and live in Laurel Street,' her mother said.

'I was happy here. With Granny.'

'Lucky you. She was kinder to you than she ever was to me. But then she felt I let her down, getting pregnant so young. And with your father, too. She hated him.'

'She always said you chose the wrong man. That you chose excitement over stability.'

'What have you chosen with Luke?' Angela asked. 'Stability?'

Mel tensed. 'No, well, yes, kind of. I mean, I know he'll be loyal to me, I know he won't leave.' She thought of him with Gabbie and wondered if she was so sure of that anymore.

'Well, that's good,' Angela said. 'And I'm glad you were happy here. It was hard to leave you with your gran, but it was the best thing for you. I couldn't look after you anymore.'

'I know,' Mel said, remembering.

'I never wanted to hurt you, Mel. But after everything that happened with Erin, I couldn't cope anymore.'

'We don't have to talk about this,' Mel said. It was only going to upset them both.

'Maybe not. But I just wanted to clear the air, say I'm sorry. I was neglectful back then. I didn't mean to be, but I was. I neglected myself as much as you. I made some serious mistakes.'

'So did I,' Mel said.

'You were only a child. I should have been a better mother. I shouldn't have let you play in the woods alone late at night. There were so many things I shouldn't have done.'

'Don't worry, Mum,' Mel said, although her mother's behaviour had haunted her well into adulthood. She felt a glimmer of hope, almost like she might be able to trust this version of her mother. 'Maybe we can start again.'

Angela nodded. 'Yeah,' she said. 'I'd appreciate that.'

Mel reached out and took her mother's hand in hers. It was the first time she'd ever apologised to her about the past. Family was so precious. Maybe her mother deserved a second chance.

TWENTY-ONE

That afternoon, Mel went round to see Tamsin with Lily. On the way over, they passed Luke, still shovelling the snow, his cheeks rosy from the cold.

'How's it going?' she asked him.

'Nearly there,' he said, looking at the rest of the snow-covered road ahead of him. Mel wondered whether Stuart was abusing her husband's good nature, getting a kick out of working him hard for no reason.

'Stuart's paying me an hourly rate,' Luke said, reading her mind.

'The lady at the end of the road is fine,' Mel said. 'I checked.' She'd gone over with Lily at lunchtime and had fixed her a sandwich and sat for a while to chat, while Lily crawled on the floor and pulled herself up to standing using the coffee table. The woman had said that her carer had already cancelled her visit and she'd be fine for one day on her own.

'OK,' Luke said. 'But we'll all want the road clear for the weekend.'

'I suppose so,' Mel said, trying not to feel resentful about missing out on family time with Luke.

When they got to Tamsin's house, Tamsin led them inside and smiled down at Lily. 'Are you enjoying the snow?' she asked. Lily nodded enthusiastically.

'Erin used to love the snow,' Tamsin said wistfully to Mel. 'You two built a huge snowman on the green one year. Do you remember?'

'Yes,' Mel said, remembering Joe helping them as Tamsin watched from the window. That was long before any of them had realised what he was like.

'How are you both? Do you want a cup of tea?' Tamsin asked Mel.

'Yes, please,' Mel said, gratefully. She had come out partly to get away from her mother, who she had known wouldn't want to go to Tamsin's house. She remembered what she'd said about Tamsin turning her away from the party.

'Did you know that my mother's come to live with us?' Mel asked, peering into Tamsin's studio as Tamsin put the kettle on. The studio had been completely returned to normal. Tamsin's easels and canvases were laid out across one side of the room and she'd somehow restored the clutter of her artistic life.

'I saw you walking with her earlier today,' Tamsin said. 'I wondered how you were getting on.'

'She says she's sober now and she seems like a different person.'

'I wouldn't trust her,' Tamsin said. 'When you came to your grandmother, you were a wounded child. Your mother hadn't cared for you properly. You needed so much love and affection from your gran and me and the others before you truly blossomed.'

'I know,' Mel said. 'But she's changed. She wants a relationship with Lily.' Mel looked at her daughter crawling across the floor.

'Well, be careful. I should have told you that she tried to come into the party at the weekend. I turned her away. I didn't think you'd want to see her.'

'Yeah, she said.'

'I hope you don't think I overstepped?' Tamsin asked. Mel didn't know what to say. A part of her did think she'd over-stepped, that she could have at least told Mel her mother was there. Then she could have made the decision whether or not to see her herself.

'It's OK,' Mel said. 'All resolved now.'

Lily crawled into Tamsin's studio and Mel and Tamsin followed. Mel went to the window, and looked out at Gabbie's house. The lights were on and she could see Stuart in the kitchen.

On the easel by the window she could see a sketch Tamsin had begun. It was of Gabbie, her mouth stretched into a scream, her hands washing up a broken glass. Stuart was a distant figure in the corner of the canvas, his arms folded.

'What's this?' Mel asked.

'Oh, it's just something I started working on, after I found out Gabbie had left. I was sad about what Stuart put her through. And when I started drawing Gabbie it was her distress that came through, the raw pain. She's been unhappy for a long time. I wish I'd seen it more clearly before.'

'She's best away from Stuart,' Mel said.

'Have you heard from her? Has she told you where she is?'

'No,' Mel said. 'I tried to ring her but I couldn't get through.' The day after the party she'd called her to confront her about kissing Luke, but the phone had gone straight to voicemail. She'd assumed Gabbie hadn't picked up because she felt ashamed.

'I haven't heard from her either. I've tried to text and call just to check she's alright, but I've had no response at all.'

'Oh,' Mel said. 'Maybe she's embarrassed, doesn't want to speak to anyone.'

'Maybe. You know, my mind's spinning being up here on my own. I'm concerned about her.'

Mel frowned, worry easing its way through her bones. She wondered if anyone had heard from her since the party. She thought of Gabbie's parents' dark house. She hadn't gone to stay with them. 'Do you think we should call her parents? They're on holiday.'

'I wouldn't want to disturb them. I'm probably just being paranoid. After what happened to Erin, you know...'

'Yeah, I understand.'

'I worry so much, being on my own.' Tamsin stared out of the window. 'You know, in the days after Gabbie left, Stuart always had the curtains closed. His behaviour is really odd.'

'I suppose now she's left him, he thinks he can do what he likes.'

'I worry that he might have hurt her, so he can move Roz in.'

'I don't think that's what's happened,' Mel said firmly. 'Gabbie's left him. He said she left a note. She'll be staying with a friend somewhere. I'll try and ring her again now.'

Mel found Gabbie's number on her phone and pressed call. It went straight to voicemail. Then she tried to WhatsApp her. She saw the little tick that meant the message had left her phone. She stared at it, waiting for it to become two ticks, but it didn't.

'I can't get through to her,' she said to Tamsin. 'I'll try again later.' But a knot of apprehension was tightening in her gut. She couldn't shake the feeling that something was really wrong.

TWENTY-TWO

Mel took Lily back home in the pushchair, lost in thought. It was concerning that neither she nor Tamsin could get hold of Gabbie, but then Gabbie had never been close to Tamsin, and she could easily have been ignoring her. And she was hardly going to want to speak to Mel after she'd drunkenly kissed her husband.

Luke was no longer outside shovelling snow, and when she passed Gabbie's house she saw him through the window, sitting with a cup of tea at Stuart's table, chatting to Stuart and Roz. He didn't seem to hold anything against Roz, the way Mel did.

When Mel got home, her mother had tidied the house and was upstairs in her room, reading a book. 'How are you doing, Mum?' Mel asked from the doorway.

'I'm fine. I was thinking I might paint this room, if you don't mind? I'd like to brighten it up.'

Mel hesitated. She and Luke had spoken about paint colours for the house, but they hadn't got far with the plans for decorating. She'd imagined them carefully designing each room and then going round flea markets and choosing the perfect pictures for each wall. But neither of them had had time. Luke was doing more work on Gabbie and Stuart's house than their own, and the combination of her job and looking after Lily took up most of Mel's time.

'Sure,' she said to her mother. 'That's a lovely idea.' She wanted to ask her mother to run the colour choice past them first, but it seemed unfair. Her mother owned half the house, and was just as entitled to paint it as they were.

'Thanks. I appreciate it. Everything alright between you and Luke?'

'Yeah, it's fine,' Mel said, brushing away the question.

'He never seems to be around much,' Angela probed.

'Yeah, well, he's been busy working.' Mel smiled tightly. 'Earning money for the family.'

'That's good. Well, as long as you're happy.'

Mel left the room quickly as a rush of emotion welled up inside her. Was she happy? Since they'd moved, she'd been so busy organising everything that she hadn't given it much thought. But she'd seen so little of Luke lately, and it was starting to worry her.

When Luke came back that afternoon, he said hello to her briefly, and then went straight upstairs to have a shower. 'I need to warm up a bit,' he said, 'and wash the dirt off me.'

'Do you want me to make you a sandwich?'

'Yes, please. Thanks, love.' He disappeared upstairs, whistling.

Mel got out the bread for the sandwich and saw he'd left his phone on the side. Her hands reached for it, wanting to check it, but she stopped herself. She thought of Gabbie, the kiss between them, how Luke was out of the house so often. Could he be meeting up with her? Cheating on Mel?

She was sure he wasn't. He was unfailingly loyal. But Mel felt a sudden urge to check. Just in case. She needed to put her mind at rest. Stop it spinning.

She could hear the water running in the shower upstairs

and she reached for his phone again, and typed in the passcode. Her birthday. For a second she thought it wouldn't work, that he'd probably have changed it if he was hiding something. But the phone unlocked immediately. Mel wondered if she should stop now, put the phone down, stop invading his privacy. But she just had to check. She'd check once now, and then never do it again.

She went into his WhatsApp messages first, and saw tons of messages between him and Stuart about the work he was doing on their house and around Laurel Street. There was nothing interesting there. Then there were a few messages between him and Roz, which also seemed to be connected to the work for Stuart. Then several messages from various groups, one to do with Lily's nursery, which she was on as well, one group of his friends from the gym back in London, one with friends from university. She scrolled further until she saw Gabbie's name.

'What are you doing?' Luke's voice was directly behind her. As she turned to face him, she could smell the fresh, clean scent of his shower gel. He snatched the phone from her. 'Why do you have my phone?'

'I – I was just looking.' She wondered if she should tell the truth, or at least part of it. 'I've been worried about Gabbie. I thought you might have heard from her.'

'Why didn't you just ask me?' Luke said. 'I would have told you I haven't.'

'I'm sorry,' Mel said quickly. 'I should have asked. Sorry, I haven't made your sandwich yet. I'm just starting now.'

'You have to trust me, Mel,' Luke said, his voice rising.

'I know, I do.'

He looked down at his phone, scrolled through his messages himself, as if to check what she'd seen. 'I love you,' he said. 'But if this marriage is going to work, you can't behave like this.'

TWENTY-THREE

Saturday 28th January

Mel got up early on Saturday morning and made breakfast for her and Lily. She hadn't slept well, tossing and turning all night, thinking about Laurel Street, how different her life was here to how she had imagined it. She'd thought she'd just slip into the idyllic life she'd seen on Gabbie's Instagram, but the truth was, that had all been a farce.

In the month they'd lived here everything she'd depended on had started to fall apart. She didn't know if she could trust her husband anymore, Gabbie had left and Joe, the man who had given her nightmares ever since Erin disappeared, was back in the street. Not to mention her mother being back, although if anything, she was turning into a helpful presence and Mel was glad to be rebuilding her relationship with her.

Mel checked the fridge to see what food they had in, but it was empty except for a children's shepherd's pie. She sighed loudly. She'd have to go to the supermarket later. Since she'd started working at the school, she always felt like she was chasing her tail, never having time for the most basic household chores. Luckily her mother had been keeping on top of the cleaning.

'I can go to the shop if you need me to,' Angela said, appearing behind her and making her jump.

'Really?' Mel smiled. 'That would be brilliant. I was going to do an online order but I ran out of time so it's not coming for a few more days, and now we're out of everything except pasta.'

'Yeah, of course,' Angela said. 'I can take the bike. I won't be able to get much, but enough to get us through until the food order comes.'

'Thanks, Mum, that would be great.'

'Are you sure everything's OK between you and Luke?' her mother asked.

'Yes, of course. Why?' Mel's heart raced. What did she mean?

'You just seem a bit distant from each other, that's all. Disconnected.'

'It's hard with a small child,' Mel said, although both of them knew that wasn't the real reason. Luke was always working. He didn't seem to want to be at home anymore. For a moment Mel wondered if he might be trying to avoid her mother.

'I know,' her mother said. 'He's kind to you, though, isn't he?'

'Yes,' Mel said, although recently they'd hardly spoken. 'He always puts me first.'

'Well, that's good. I've been through my fair share of men, and sometimes it's hard to find one like that. I mean, some of them start off like that, but then they change...' She let the words hang in the air.

'Me and Luke are fine,' Mel said. 'We hardly ever argue.' He'd promised her that today, they'd spend some time together, just the three of them, and she just hoped he wouldn't get caught up in some urgent work for Stuart or one of his other clients.

An hour later, Luke had kept his promise and he and Mel were walking down the street with Lily. They were planning to walk through the woods to the village and have lunch together there.

'Come on, Lily,' Mel said, holding her daughter's hand tightly, helping her to keep her balance as she concentrated hard on putting one foot in front of the other. One day after school, Mel had been to the nearest town and bought her new trainers that flashed when she trod down, and Lily was fascinated by them, stomping on their kitchen floor again and again to see them light up.

Laurel Street was the ideal place for her to practise walking, and they went along at a snail's pace. The road was flat and there were hardly ever any cars or people about. Once they got onto the footpath, where the ground was uneven, they would put Lily in the sling.

As they went past Gabbie's parents' house, Mel spotted their car on the drive.

'They must be back from holiday,' she said to Luke.

'I guess so.'

Mel paused outside the house, holding Lily's hand. She thought of the conversation she'd had with Tamsin yesterday about Stuart. Did Gabbie's parents even know she'd left him?

Holding Lily's hand while she took her faltering steps gave Mel an excuse to peer in through the windows of the house. She could see Gabbie's mother loading clothes into the washing machine.

'Do you think we should knock?'

'Why?' Luke asked.

'Just to see how they are. To see if they've heard from Gabbie.'

'She wouldn't have called them on their holiday,' Luke said firmly.

'I suppose not,' Mel said. 'Maybe I'll pop round later.'

But she didn't need to go round later because at that moment Gabbie's mum looked up and met Mel's eyes. She got up quickly and hurried towards the front door.

'Mel?' Deena called from the doorway.

'Hi,' Mel said, with a tentative smile, picking Lily up and walking over.

'Oh, Lily's adorable, isn't she?' Gabbie's mum brushed her hand over Lily's hair absent-mindedly. 'They're so lovely at this age.'

Mel nodded. 'I'm very lucky.'

'Have you seen Gabbie today?' Deena asked. 'She hasn't been answering my calls this morning.'

'I haven't seen her since the party.' Gabbie's parents had left the party early to get some sleep before their flight the next day. Hadn't Gabbie let them know she'd left Stuart and moved out of the street?

'Really?' Deena looked confused.

'Yeah,' Mel said. 'I haven't seen her this week.' She shifted awkwardly from one foot to the other and glanced at Luke. She was going to have to break the news to Deena. 'Can I come in?'

'I'll take Lily for a walk,' Luke said quickly, eager to avoid any confrontation.

'Yeah, come in,' Deena said. 'Is everything alright between you and Gabbie?'

Mel flushed, thinking of the kiss Gabbie had shared with Luke.

'I think so,' she said.

A frown creased Deena's brow. 'What's going on, Mel?' she asked.

Mel sighed. There was no nice way of putting this. 'Gabbie's left Stuart,' she said.

'Left him?'

'Yes, after the party. She'd had enough, I think.'

Deena put her hands on the edge of the kitchen work surface, squeezing until her knuckles went white. 'What's she playing at? She's done this before, you know. Just upped and left for a few days, not told anyone where she was going.'

'Has she?' Relief shot through Mel. She'd been starting to wonder if Tamsin was right, and something had happened to Gabbie.

'Yeah, she didn't answer my calls for days. And then one day she suddenly reappeared, acting like nothing had happened, said she'd been staying with a friend in London.'

'Oh,' Mel said.

'She worried us so much, but it was nothing. She gave some spurious reason for leaving – she'd had some kind of argument with Stuart. But all married couples argue, don't they?'

'I guess so,' Mel said, thinking of Luke. She tried her best to avoid the sort of echoing arguments that she'd overheard when she was a child, but they still argued sometimes.

'I should go and see Stuart, see what's going on. Why on earth would she leave him? I thought they were planning kids.'

Mel swallowed. 'He was having an affair.'

'What?' A shadow fell across Deena's face.

'He'd been cheating on Gabbie. He admitted it at the party.'

Deena's face was ashen. 'How could he do that to her? He wouldn't have time. He's always working or at the golf club.'

'It was with Roz,' Mel said gently. She knew Deena liked Roz.

'Roz?' Deena looked like she was going to keel over. 'No, it can't be. You must have got the wrong end of the stick.'

Mel put her hand on Deena's arm to steady her. 'It's true,' she said. 'She said so herself.'

'I can't believe the audacity of that woman.' Deena's hands clenched into fists by her sides. 'She should be ashamed of herself. God help me when I next see her. I feel like killing her.'

'I know. It was such a shock to find out.'

'Gabbie must have been beside herself,' Deena said. 'The poor thing. And just when she and Stuart had finally settled into their house.' She looked at Mel, bewildered. 'But why didn't she make Stuart leave instead of leaving herself? They own the house together.'

'I think she just wanted to get away. They told her at the party in front of everyone.'

'That evening? She was drunk even when we left. I hope she hasn't done anything stupid. I'll try and ring her again.' Gabbie's mum fetched her phone from where it was charging next to the fridge and called Gabbie. 'No answer,' she said. 'It's going straight to voicemail. She must have it switched off.'

'She must have,' Mel agreed. 'Look, I'm sure she's alright. Maybe staying with a friend, like last time. But she hasn't been answering my calls either.'

Deena put her head in her hands. 'Oh god, I can't believe this is happening. And with Gabbie so fragile, too. This could send her over the edge.'

Mel swallowed. 'Gabbie's a strong woman,' she said, although she wasn't sure it was true.

'I need to speak to Stuart,' Deena said, grabbing her coat and heading to the door. 'Find out exactly what happened.'

'I'll come with you,' Mel said, following behind as Deena slipped on her shoes and sped off down the street.

When they got to Gabbie's house, Deena marched up to the door and pressed her finger on the bell. When no one came immediately, she pressed it again.

'Hello?' Stuart opened the door. Roz appeared in the hallway behind him for a second and then scurried off.

Mel could see Deena trying to control her fury. 'What's she doing here?' she spat.

'None of your business,' Stuart said.

'It is my business. This house is my daughter's home.' Deena tried to barge past him but he held his hand up to stop her.

'You can't come in,' he said.

'But we need to. Gabbie's missing. I can't get hold of her.'

'She's not missing. She's just left me.'

'If that was the case then she would have contacted me.'

'Not necessarily. She didn't contact you last time she left, did she?'

'No,' Deena said. 'But this is different.'

'Have you heard from her at all since?' Mel asked Stuart.

'No,' he said.

Mel swallowed. 'She hasn't arranged to come back to collect her things?'

'She left me a note when she left. And she took a bag with her.'

Mel looked at Deena and saw tears in her eyes. 'Please could we just come in and have a look? She might have left some clue as to where she's gone.'

Stuart was angered now, his face reddening. 'I've told you, you can't come in. It's my house. You need to leave. Now.'

Deena started to sob as he shut the door on them, her breath catching in her throat. Mel put her arm round her.

'I can't believe he would speak to me like that. He was always so nice to me before.'

'Showing his true colours,' Mel said, darkly. 'You never know what goes on behind closed doors.'

'Where do you think she is?'

'I – I don't know. She'll be with a friend, surely?' Mel felt her stomach contract. She'd been in this position before, with Erin. She'd been so certain she'd run away.

Deena turned to Gabbie's four-by-four on the drive. 'She hasn't come back for her car.'

'She wouldn't really need it if she was with a friend in London, would she?'

They peered into her car, but there was nothing inside.

'Do you think she's been at work this week?' Deena said, as they walked down the driveway.

'I can phone them on Monday and check,' Mel said. 'But I would have thought so. Unless she's taken holiday.'

'She's only taken one bag. It doesn't seem enough.'

They walked past the garage and saw the side door was ajar. 'Let's check in here,' Mel said.

She went through the door and flicked on the light. Inside there were rows of bin bags, each one tied neatly with a twist tie. Mel opened the first one and peered inside. It was full of Gabbie's clothes. She looked up at Deena and then looked round the garage at all the other bags. 'He's already cleared out all her things,' she said.

'Maybe she said she'd come and get them?'

'No, he said he hadn't heard from her at all.' Mel thought of how Tamsin had told her that the curtains had been shut at Stuart's house in the days after the party.

'Deena,' she said softly. 'I don't think we should wait until Monday to phone Gabbie's work. I think we should call the police right now.'

TWENTY-FOUR

When Mel hung up the phone after speaking to the police, she felt a sense of relief. Her voice had shaken as she had told them about her missing friend, memories of the interviews she'd had with the police after Erin's disappearance still fresh in her mind, even after so many years. She'd been terrified of the police back them, the way they'd towered over her, the way they'd questioned her again and again about what had happened in the woods with Erin.

This time it had been easier as she'd explained that Gabbie had gone missing after the party, and that evening had been the last time she or Deena had seen her, and how no one had been able to get hold of her since. They'd asked her about the note she'd left Stuart and what she'd taken with her, but Mel couldn't tell them anything about that. They'd asked about her state of mind, and Mel had explained that she'd been drunk and unhappy. Then they'd spoken to Deena to get further information.

It was nearly lunchtime by the time Mel got back to her house and saw Luke and Lily.

'How was Deena?' he asked.

'Worried about Gabbie,' Mel said. 'We all are.' Since she'd spoken to Tamsin the day before, Mel had tried every possible means of getting hold of Gabbie – WhatsApp, Instagram, text, her Facebook page that she rarely used, a Twitter account she'd probably forgotten she'd even set up, LinkedIn, Snapchat, TikTok. Her Instagram account was unusually quiet. The last thing she'd posted was a picture of the sun setting behind the cottages of Laurel Street a few days before the party.

'Maybe she wanted to disappear,' Luke said.

'What do you mean?'

'I mean, maybe she was embarrassed about her marriage breaking up. Or maybe she just needed time away from it all, to think. When I saw her that evening, she talked about wanting to be alone.'

'Maybe,' Mel said, unconvinced. 'But we found loads of her stuff bagged up in Stuart's garage. We called the police.'

'The police?' Luke's eyebrows shot up.

'She's a missing person. No one knows where she is.' Mel clenched her hands together, thinking of her friend. Now Mel was sure something had happened to her. She wished she'd paid more attention before, wished she'd realised earlier how strange Gabbie's exit from Laurel Street had been. But she'd been so distracted by her mother coming back, and her job, that she hadn't given it enough thought.

Wherever Gabbie was, Mel was convinced her phone was no longer working. It always went straight to voicemail as if it was switched off or had run out of battery, and her WhatsApp said she'd last seen her messages a week ago, the day of the party.

Mel checked Gabbie's Facebook page now. No updates for over a week, although that wasn't unusual. She hardly used it these days. Scrolling through the local Facebook groups, Mel saw that the police had put out a missing person appeal for Gabbie on social media and it was being shared widely. There were already several comments on the post on the Facebook page for the village, people expressing their concerns for Gabbie and their hopes that she'd be found safely.

The Laurel Street WhatsApp group was eerily quiet. Either people hadn't seen the appeal or they had seen it and didn't know what to say. After all, Stuart and Roz were in the group.

Mel was aware of an uncomfortable feeling of guilt rising up inside her. Should she have contacted the police before? She had initially taken what Stuart said about Gabbie leaving at face value.

At least now her disappearance was getting the attention it needed. She googled Gabbie's name and the appeal was the top result. But there were no newspaper articles yet. Maybe it was too early. She thought of her friend Ashley in London, who was working for one of the broadsheets. Maybe she should speak to her, get the newspapers interested in Gabbie and raise her profile.

'Come and eat something,' Luke said. 'You haven't looked up from your phone since you got back. I've made sandwiches.'

Mel reluctantly put her phone down and got up. 'Thanks,' she said, pecking him on the cheek. She remembered they'd said they'd walk down to the village for lunch. 'I'm sorry we didn't end up going out to eat,' she said.

Luke shrugged. 'No problem.'

Ten minutes later, as they were finishing their lunch, Mel heard the sound of a car on the road and went to the window. 'They've come,' she said to Luke breathlessly. 'The police are here.'

There was only one police car this time, not like when Erin went missing, when there'd been lots. But Mel felt the same hole in the pit of her stomach, the same vicelike fear. Mel thought of Tamsin on her own, in her huge house. She'd be able to see everything that was happening from there. It would bring everything back for her. 'I need to go and see Tamsin,' she said.

'Right now?' Luke asked, getting up from the kitchen table. 'You haven't been home long.'

'I think she might need me,' she said.

Luke rested his hands on her shoulders, with a sigh. 'OK, then,' he said. 'I'll take Lily to the play area in the woods.'

'Thanks.'

'And try not to worry too much about Gabbie. I'm sure she's fine. She'll be back in contact soon, like nothing's happened.'

'I hope so,' Mel replied.

When Mel arrived at Tamsin's home on the top floor of her mansion, her friend was dressed in paint-splattered clothes, and her hair was unbrushed and messy. As she waited for the kettle to boil to make tea, she paced up and down.

'I hate this,' she said. 'Seeing the police on the street again.'

'I know,' Mel said, reaching out and touching her arm. 'It brings it all back. Let's take the tea and sit down.'

Tamsin led Mel into the studio, and Mel saw the picture on the easel by the window overlooking Gabbie's house. It was the painting of Gabbie, her mouth open in a scream, her eyes wide. It was nearly finished now, and Tamsin was halfway through painting a dark, dark night in the background.

'I haven't been able to stop thinking about her,' Tamsin said softly, 'imagining something awful's happened to her.'

'It's a good likeness,' Mel said, looking at the picture.

'Thanks. Painting's the only way I know how to cope.'

They both stared at the painting for a moment longer. Tamsin had really captured the fear in Gabbie's eyes.

'Come and sit down,' Tamsin said. She moved piles of sketches off the chaise longue by the window.

'Thanks,' Mel said, as they looked down into Gabbie's house. They could see two policewomen sitting with Stuart at the kitchen table. He was bent over, his head in his hands. Was he playing the part of the grieving husband, or had he told them the truth about his affair with Roz?

'I'm so glad they're taking this seriously,' Tamsin said, pushing her messy hair back from her face.

'Are you alright?' Mel asked, looking into Tamsin's bloodshot eyes.

'Yes. It just seems like the start of everything. When the police came round about Erin that first morning, I truly believed that she was just missing, that she'd walk back through the door any minute.'

'I remember too. It was just so awful.' Mel took her friend's hand and squeezed it.

'I'm worried about Gabbie,' Tamsin said.

'I know,' Mel said. 'But the police are really on top of it. They've already put an appeal out on social media. Lots of people are interacting and commenting. And people are keeping an eye out for her. I'm sure it won't be long before someone finds her.'

Tamsin frowned. 'Everything's escalating now. People being encouraged to look for her. Lots of publicity. But what if she's hiding? What if she doesn't want to be found?'

Mel froze. 'What would she be hiding from?'

'Stuart. If he was hurting her, then she might be hiding.'

'You mean hitting her? I never saw any hint of that.'

'There aren't always signs to see. People hide it well.'

'I think she would have told me,' Mel insisted. 'Or I would have guessed. There would have been signs.'

'Most people are ashamed when they're hit.' Tamsin put her hand over Mel's. 'They try to hide it from others, pretend everything's alright, they think it's a sign of weakness. I tried to hide it when my ex hit me.' Tamsin's face had flushed with embarrassment. The hand holding her mug was trembling.

'Your ex hit you? Do you mean Erin's stepfather?' The memories came back. Erin had always been complaining about her family, particularly her stepfather. Mel had been too jealous of Erin's big house and the huge number of toys she had to pay much attention.

'Yeah.' Tamsin looked down at the floor. 'I adored him, but he really undermined my confidence. So much so that I thought I deserved it when he hit me.'

'No one ever deserves that.' Mel moved closer to her friend and took the shaking mug from her hand, then put her arm round her.

'No, but I took too long to chuck him out. I should have got rid of him long before. But I just wanted to give Erin a happy family, even if it was a pretend one.'

'I understand,' Mel said. She knew how much energy it took to keep up appearances, to pretend everything was fine.

'I don't think Erin knew. I worked so hard to keep it from her.'

Mel nodded, although when she thought back, she was sure Erin had known what was going on. And Mel had seen bruises on Erin's arms, too. At first Erin said they were from falling over, but later she'd said someone was hurting her. After she'd disappeared, Mel had assumed the bruises were something to do with Joe, but they could have been from her stepfather.

'What happened to your ex?' Mel asked.

'Oh, I don't know. I asked him to move out soon after Erin disappeared. After that, I never heard from him again.'

Tamsin looked at Mel. 'Erin was fine, wasn't she? She was a happy little girl. She never knew what was going on.'

Mel squeezed Tamsin's hands. 'She was really happy,' Mel said. 'Always smiling.'

But they both knew there was more to it than that. Erin had had her red rucksack with her that night. She'd wanted to run away. Tamsin had always maintained that it had just been a childish impulse, but Mel remembered how often Erin had talked about running away from her unhappy home life, how desperate she'd been to escape.

TWENTY-FIVE

Tamsin and Mel sat in silence watching the police talk to Stuart. A second police car arrived, and a meticulous search of the house began, the two additional police officers going through each room in turn. Mel watched them take computers and iPads from the upstairs bedroom. Then they moved on to the bathroom, out of sight.

'They must suspect him,' said Tamsin. 'Otherwise they wouldn't be searching like this. There are so many cases of husbands murdering their wives. Moving their mistresses in.' Tamsin let the words hang in the silence.

Mel's stomach turned as she fought a wave of nausea.

'I'm sure it's not that,' Mel said, remembering the bags of clothes Stuart had put in the garage. Could he have done something to Gabbie? It didn't bear thinking about.

'You never know people as well as you think you do.'

'I tried her phone again earlier,' Mel said. 'No answer.'

As they watched Gabbie's house, one of the police officers moved outside and began searching the garage. He opened up each bin bag in turn and rifled through the contents.

'Do you think they'll find something useful?' Mel asked.

'I really don't know. At least they're doing a thorough search,' Tamsin said. 'They did the same with Erin.'

'Do you think they'll search the woods next?' Mel could remember how quickly they had searched the woods when Erin had gone missing. It had been within hours of Tamsin reporting she wasn't in her bed the next morning. The street had been overrun with police, and on that first day, everyone had believed she was just lost in the woods. Mel remembered thinking differently, knowing that Erin had packed her little red rucksack so that she could run away. She'd been certain she had run away like she'd said she would. At that point no one on the street had considered that she might be dead.

'I would have thought they will,' Tamsin said. 'She left on foot. She didn't take her car.'

'Someone could have collected her or given her a lift. Or she could have taken a taxi.'

'Perhaps,' Tamsin said, as they watched a police officer open the pool house door with a key. 'Or,' she said, 'she could still be around here, around Laurel Street.'

Mel heard Tamsin's unspoken words. A week had passed since anyone had heard from Gabbie. If Gabbie was still around Laurel Street, she could already be dead.

Mel left Tamsin's house half an hour later, feeling guilty about leaving Lily for so long. Now she was at nursery all week, Mel only had the weekends with her, and she knew she had to cherish that time.

'Hello!' She forced a smile when she went through the door of her home. She lifted Lily up into her arms and hugged her tightly, suddenly feeling overwhelmingly grateful that Lily was hers to hold. She was so lucky.

'Everything OK at Tamsin's?' Luke asked.

'Yeah, the police seem to be making progress on the search. They're going through all the outbuildings.'

'That's good. But I'm sure Gabbie will turn out to be fine,' he said reassuringly. 'It's very clear what happened. She ran away, left Stuart. She even left a note.'

'But what if Stuart's not telling the truth? What if he did something to her?'

'Stuart wouldn't do something like that,' Luke said.

'How do you know? Look what he was doing with Roz, right under Gabbie's nose.'

'Having an affair doesn't make someone a murderer, Mel.'

A loud rap on the door interrupted them. When Mel went to open it, Deena, Gabbie's mother, burst through.

'I feel so helpless just sitting at home waiting,' she said. 'Like I should be doing something, going out looking for her. But I don't know where to start.'

'Come and sit down,' Mel said, leading her through to the kitchen. She could see Luke frowning at her out of the corner of her eye, but she ignored him. 'You can stop here for a bit, and we'll work out a plan.'

'I've called all my family in case she's gone to stay with them. And I've called all her friends I can think of. But I hardly have any of their numbers. Just people she used to go to school with, like you. I hadn't realised how separate our lives had become. I don't know any of the friends she's made since she was an adult. Or any of her work colleagues. So I've drawn a blank.'

Mel sighed. 'I haven't met any of her other friends either. We'd almost lost touch over the years.'

'What else can we do? I've been sharing the appeal over and over again on my Facebook page. And checking all the comments to see if anyone's seen her. And I've messaged all her friends on Facebook to say she's gone missing. No one's seen her.'

'I don't know,' Mel said. 'I've tried all her social media too.'

'The police have called all the local taxi firms and none of them picked up a fare from around here that night. They're also following up any friends' names anyone mentions, so if you can think of any, you must let them know.'

'I will do.'

'Good. We can't let them get all their information from Stuart. We can't trust him, not after what he did with Roz.'

'The police are doing all they can,' Mel said to Deena, resting her hand on her arm.

'They are,' she said. 'They're checking her phone records and bank transactions as we speak. Hopefully that will reveal something. They'll be able to tell exactly where her phone is. And if she's used her bank cards since she left.'

'It sounds like they're putting everything into it,' Mel said, keeping her voice steady to hide her worry. 'I'm sure they'll find her soon.'

Luke's phone beeped across the other side of the kitchen and he reached down to check it.

'Who's that?' Mel said, wondering if it was Stuart, complaining about what was going on, the intrusion into his life by the police. Most of Luke's messages were from Stuart since he'd started working for him.

'Oh, no one,' Luke said. 'It's not important right now.'

'What? Is it Gabbie?' Mel couldn't stop the words coming out, the image of Luke and Gabbie in the pool house suddenly flashing into her mind.

'Why would Gabbie be contacting Luke?' Deena asked, and Mel flushed.

'It's not Gabbie,' Luke said. 'If you must know, it's my father. He really wants to meet Lily. He's been asking more often lately.'

'What have you said?' Mel asked. She knew Luke found his

estrangement from his father upsetting, that a part of him longed to reconnect with him.

'Well, I've been telling him no, that I can't trust him after he abandoned me. But, I don't know. I'm thinking about it. I've seen how well your mother gets on with Lily, and I'm wondering if I should give him a second chance.'

Mel nodded. 'It's up to you,' she said. 'If you want him back in your life, then I'm happy to accept him. But tread carefully – he treated you badly as a kid.'

Luke sighed. 'I'm not sure I can forget that.'

'I'd better go,' Deena said suddenly, her face pale, as she stared at her phone. She stood up. 'Michael's just messaged me. The police have found Gabbie's phone.'

TWENTY-SIX

'What?' Luke said. 'They've found her phone? Where?' He was almost as pale as Deena.

'It doesn't say,' Deena said, leaning heavily on the kitchen counter. 'I feel...' Deena sank to the ground in a faint and Mel took a quick step over to catch her before she hit the floor. She grabbed the tea towel that was hanging on the oven door and placed it under her head as she waited for her to come round.

Lily crawled over, and Luke quickly moved her away.

Mel got a cold flannel and wiped it over Deena's forehead.

'It's OK,' Mel said as Deena's eyes flicked open.

Deena immediately started to try and stand up. 'No,' Mel said firmly. 'Stay where you are. You're not ready yet.'

'Where am I? Has something happened to Gabbie?'

'Just lie still for a minute,' Mel said. 'I'll get you a glass of water.'

Deena sat up, leaning against the kitchen cupboards, and sipped the water.

'Gabbie's missing, isn't she?'

'Yes. And you just told us the police have found her mobile phone.'

Deena looked panicked, her eyes darting from side to side. 'Yes. What does that mean? They've found her mobile phone without her? Why wouldn't she have it with her? Something must have happened to her.'

'Where did they find it?' Luke asked again.

Mel picked up Deena's phone. The message from Gabbie's dad was still on the screen. 'It doesn't say,' she told them. 'It just says the police want to talk to Deena because the phone has been found.'

Deena started to shake violently. 'It must be bad news. It can only be bad news. She's never without that phone. What if she's done something silly?'

'You won't know any more until you speak to the police,' Mel said gently. 'Do you want me to walk you over to your house?'

Deena nodded, and Mel helped her to her feet. She grabbed Mel's arm as she walked shakily towards the door. She'd only just got back from holiday and already she seemed so fragile, ten years older.

Mel supported Deena to her house and through her front door.

'Do you want me to leave?' she asked her, glancing at the policeman and Gabbie's dad, sitting in the living room.

'No,' she pleaded. 'Please stay with me.'

'OK,' Mel said, following her into the room.

She introduced herself to the police officer.

'Ah, Mel,' he said. 'Nice to meet you. You reported your friend missing with Deena. We're keen to interview you again and get a few more details. We'll probably do that tomorrow.' He turned to Deena. 'Are you happy for us to give you an update on the case while Mel is here?'

She nodded and Deena sat beside her husband on the sofa, while Mel took the spare armchair.

'OK,' the police officer said. 'So, based on the information you've given us, we are quite concerned about Gabbie. We've managed to get in contact with her manager at work, who says she wasn't in the office last week at all. Her absence was unexplained, as she hadn't booked holiday or contacted them, but when they tried to ring her, she didn't answer.'

'Why didn't they report that to the police?' Deena asked, and Mel felt a shiver of guilt that she hadn't reported Gabbie missing to the police earlier either.

'They said her behaviour had been getting more and more erratic lately. Sometimes she turned up still drunk from the night before, or very late. So they didn't see it as out of character. But at least they've confirmed she wasn't at work. We've also run financial checks, and she hasn't used any of her cards since she went missing. But that doesn't necessarily mean anything. She could have had cash saved, or else be being supported by a friend, or even a boyfriend. But it means we don't have any idea of her whereabouts from banking data.'

'She would have contacted us,' Deena whispered. 'She would have known we'd be worried.'

'Perhaps. But people aren't always logical when they're stressed and leaving their partners. And it seems like she didn't have access to her phone. When we ran checks on her mobile, we could see that no calls had been made or received since last Saturday. Various people had tried to phone her, but no one got through. In fact, the phone hadn't even been switched on since the evening of the party. The last location we had for the phone was in the area around Laurel Street. So it looked like she hadn't left. Which worried us. We were going to start a search of the local area. But then today, in our search of Gabbie's house and outbuildings, we found her phone.'

'Where was it?' Mel whispered. She thought of Luke and Gabbie in the pool house. It couldn't have been found there, could it?

'It was under the marital bed,' the police officer said. 'She never took it with her.'

'OK,' Deena said, tears running down her cheeks. 'That's good. It wasn't in the middle of nowhere. It was in her house.'

'Yes. Now we don't know if she dropped it there by mistake or left it there deliberately, but it does explain why no calls have been made and why everyone has found it so hard to get in touch with her.'

'So it's good news?' Deena said hopefully. 'She might just not remember our numbers. I changed mine recently. I used to make her memorise my number when she was a teenager, but not anymore. She probably doesn't know it.'

'It's more information for the investigation,' the officer said levelly, 'but it does mean we have no idea where to start our search. Banking and mobile phone data usually give us a clue where someone's gone, but this time we have nothing.'

'So will you search around here? In the woods?' Deena asked.

'No, that wouldn't be a productive use of resources. Gabbie's been away for a whole week. Her phone may be here, but she could be anywhere.'

TWENTY-SEVEN

Sunday 29th January

Mel was up early the next morning. She'd hardly slept all night, her mind racing, thinking of Deena and what she was going through. And of Tamsin, all alone in her huge house, watching another nightmare unfold. Lily woke at five, and Mel went into her room and rocked her back to sleep. She was glad to feel the warmth of her daughter in her arms, grateful to feel her chest rising and falling against her own. She knew how cruel life could be, how quickly someone you loved could be taken away. Afterwards, she couldn't get back to sleep, so she got up and did some marking.

Her phone beeped at 7 a.m., when she was making herself breakfast.

It was Deena.

> Sorry to message so early. Police say there has been a sighting down in Brighton. They think it could be her!

Mel's heart leapt. She replied immediately.

> She always loved Brighton. Fingers crossed it is her!

Deena replied.

> I'll be furious if she's caused all this worry over nothing.

Mel took a sip of her coffee. She was hoping against hope that this *was* all worry over nothing.

Deena messaged again.

> What if it's not her? I can't believe the police aren't going to search the woods!

Mel warmed her hands on her mug, thinking about Gabbie, how she'd liked to take late-night walks on her own when she was drunk. She'd told the police that, but they hadn't taken it seriously enough. Gabbie could have just walked off on her own, tripped over and broken her ankle, been lying injured somewhere, unable to get up. Mel shivered. It wasn't worth thinking about. If that was the case, she'd be dead by now.

But her car was still on the drive. If she had walked off somewhere then there might be a trace of what had happened to her. She might have dropped something on her way, or left some kind of mark of where she had been.

Another message flashed through from Deena.

> I feel like they've given up on her already.

Mel replied.

> They haven't. I'm sure they're doing lots of things we don't know about. But we could search the woods ourselves. With the other residents of Laurel Street.

Good idea.

I'll put something on the WhatsApp group.

Mel crafted a message to the others on the street.

You will all have seen the police presence on our street yesterday, and I am sure you will have heard by now that Gabbie is missing. She hasn't been seen since Tamsin's party last Saturday night. If you have seen or heard anything, please contact the police. Today, Sunday, we would like to arrange a local search of the woods, to see if there is anything there that will help with the police investigation. I suggest we start at 9 a.m., meeting on Laurel Street at the top of the path that leads down to the woods. Please let us know if you are able to join us, and we can split into groups to search.

As soon as Mel had sent the message the replies started coming in. Everyone was keen to help. The only people who didn't reply were Stuart and Roz. Mel sighed. Stuart could at least pretend to care that his wife was missing.

At 9 a.m., nearly every resident on the street had turned up for the search, several with dogs, many clutching flasks of coffee. Stuart and Roz remained at home.

Mel led everyone down to the woods and then split them into groups of two or three people, allocating each a different area. The method wasn't perfect, but it would mean they would cover most of the woods in a couple of hours.

Luke paired up with a retired man who lived on his own, and Mel went with her mother, with Mel carrying Lily in her sling. Mel and her mother walked along the edge of the woods until they reached the section they had agreed to search and made their way slowly in, looking all around them.

'This is awful,' Angela said, after a while. 'To be searching these woods again. It brings it all back to me.'

'I know,' Mel said. 'But we need to focus. I know we'll find something this time.'

The memories flooded back as she walked through the woods. After Erin disappeared, the police had searched the entire area and found no trace of her. When they were teenagers, lots of local children at their school would dare each other to come down to the woods, saying it was haunted. She and Gabbie had never come.

Her mother put her hand on her arm. 'I always avoided the woods after Erin died. I never wanted to walk through them. It was the shortest route to my mother's house, and by then I'd sold my car. But I couldn't bear to walk through.'

Mel sighed. 'Are you saying that's why you didn't visit me often at Granny's?'

'No... well, maybe a bit. I didn't like walking through, remembering.'

Her mother had visited her about once a month after she'd moved to her grandmother's, even though she'd lived so close. When she did visit, she smiled, and slurred and stumbled. She hadn't been a mother to her at all.

'Let's forget about all that now,' Mel said. 'We need to focus on what's happened to Gabbie.' She was trying so hard to remain in the present, like the therapist she'd had when she was a teenager had recommended, but it always felt like the past was chasing her.

'I blame myself for what happened to Erin. I shouldn't have let you play in the woods.'

'We all blame ourselves,' Mel said. She didn't want to have this conversation with her mother.

'I wish I'd looked after you properly, hadn't been drunk all the time. Half the time I just wanted you out of my way so I could be on my own with the bottle.'

'It's OK, Mum,' Mel said. Although it really wasn't. She just didn't want to talk about it. 'You're back now.'

'I don't know what I was thinking back then. Even after that flasher was spotted in these woods, I still let you play here.'

Mel remembered the rumours about the flasher. They had never seen him, but they had always expected him to appear from behind a tree at any moment. The danger of it had made them giggle. They had no idea of the things that could happen to them. They thought there was safety in numbers; that as long as the three of them stuck together, they'd be OK. Now, everyone thought the flasher had been Joe. He'd always been there, waiting for them.

'We all make mistakes, Mum. I know that.'

'I've made so many. I don't know how you can forgive me.'

Mel scanned the ground, looking for any signs of Gabbie. It seemed futile, the woods seemed endless, every tree and stick looked the same. She didn't even know what she was expecting to find. An item of clothing? It was far too late for footprints or anything like that. She thought of Gabbie on the night of Tamsin's party, in her thin dress. It had been freezing then. What if something had happened to her out in the countryside?

Her eyes scanned the path ahead and she suddenly froze. She could see him. *Joe.* He was watching them coming towards him, a half-smile on his face.

'What's wrong?' Angela asked.

'Look,' Mel said, her heart pounding. 'Straight ahead. Do you recognise him?' A part of her wanted her mother to say no, to tell her that she was ridiculous to think it was Joe.

'I think so,' her mother said softly. 'It's Joe, isn't it?'

Joe was turning away now, disappearing into the depths of

the woods. Mel felt the need to run in the other direction, to get away from him, but she stopped herself. Her heart was pounding, her body flushed with a sudden rush of heat. She turned to look at her mother, her mind spinning. 'I think I need to call the police.'

'What? Why?'

Mel tried to stay calm. 'It's too much of a coincidence that Gabbie's gone missing after he arrived back.' She pulled her phone out of her pocket. 'I haven't got reception.' She sighed. 'Have you got any?'

Her mother shook her head. 'I left my phone back at the house.'

'I'll have to call them when we finish the search.'

'We can go back home if you like, so you can calm down,' Angela said, stroking Mel's arm. 'You look a bit pale.'

'No, I don't need to calm down,' Mel said, irritated. 'And Joe can't make us stop the search. That might be exactly what he wants. To scare us off, put us off the search.'

'I think you're jumping to conclusions. You're stressed.'

Mel shook her head. 'I think Joe's been following me...' She took a deep breath. 'And Gabbie, too. She said she saw him, before her disappearance.' Mel had forgotten Gabbie's words at the party, but now they came back to her in a rush. Gabbie had thought he was watching her too.

'He's harmless,' her mother said. 'And why would he be following you both?'

'Mum... you know why... Me and Gabbie told the police we saw him the night Erin disappeared. We told them about him following us. We kicked off that whole chain of events where the press hounded him, called him a murderer.'

Her mother looked uncomfortable. 'That was a long time ago.'

Mel sighed. There was no point disagreeing with her

mother. 'Let's just focus on the search. For Gabbie's sake. We can't give up. I'll call the police when I'm back.' She patted Lily's head and smiled tightly. 'Lily's overheating. I think I'll let her out of the sling so she can cool down.'

Lily giggled. 'Ma-ma, Ma-ma!' she said.

Mel carefully put her down on her unsteady feet and Angela quickly took her hand and helped guide her.

Lily bent down and picked up an old pine cone and showed it to them.

'Wow, Lily,' Mel said, trying to steady her voice, to remain calm after seeing Joe. What if he had something to do with Gabbie's disappearance? What if he didn't want them searching the woods?

Lily took a few more steps and picked up a stick, handing it to Mel's mother. 'Thank you,' she said. As Lily walked further into the woods, Mel realised they were near the abandoned storage hut, where Joe used to keep his tools when they were children, and where he used to take Erin for their 'little chats'. Mel looked up at it, and then stopped in her tracks. There was a book on the windowsill inside the hut, next to a thermos flask.

Mel's breath quickened as she stepped closer and peered in. The book was a recent paperback thriller, a bestseller from a few months ago.

'Someone's been in here recently,' she said. She wondered if Luke was using the hut as part of his work for Stuart, but he wouldn't have brought the book here. He hardly read at all, and when he did it was always the autobiographies of sports players.

'I don't think we can get in,' her mother said. 'It will probably be locked.'

'I just want to see,' Mel said. She couldn't leave now. Not without checking out the hut.

She went to the building. The door wasn't locked and she pushed it open easily. The hut consisted of two rooms, but she could only see into the first. There was a duvet in the corner and an old stained pillow that Mel recognised from clearing out her grandmother's house. They'd put the bedding in the garage to take to the dump. Someone had taken it and brought it here.

Mel looked at her mother. 'Someone's been living here,' she said.

TWENTY-EIGHT

Mel stared at the duvet and pillow on the floor. She hadn't noticed them go missing from the garage because she'd assumed Luke had taken them to the dump. But someone had taken them and brought them here. Mel shivered. Could it have been Gabbie? Would she have slept here? It seemed so unlikely that she'd have chosen to do that when she was so close to her own home, but what if Stuart had upset her? What if she'd been afraid of him?

Then she thought of Joe, and how much time he used to spend in the storage hut. Now he was back, hanging around the street.

'The police need to search this hut,' she said to her mother. 'Someone's slept here. Do you think it could have been Gabbie? Or Joe?'

Her mother blushed furiously. 'It's not Joe,' she said. 'Or Gabbie.'

'How can you be sure?'

Her mother sighed and looked down at her feet. 'Because it was me. I slept here the night of the party. I'd come to see you, but when I got to the cottage you'd changed the locks and I didn't have anywhere to sleep. I remembered the storage hut and I thought I could take shelter there. So, I took some bedding you'd left in the garage and came down here.'

'Oh, Mum,' Mel said, feeling a stab of guilt. 'It was freezing that night. I wish you'd tried to find me.'

'Tamsin had already made it clear I wasn't wanted at the party. Don't worry, I was fine sleeping here. It was only one night. And I'm glad I stayed and reconnected with you. I'm happy to be back.'

They searched for another hour before walking back to Laurel Street. Most of the others had finished searching now, or had stopped for a break. Between them they'd found a couple of old gloves and a child's woolly hat, which they'd handed over to the police.

As she walked back down Laurel Street, Mel saw two police officers coming out of Deena's cottage. She asked if she could speak to them about a suspicious person, and soon they were sitting across from her in her living room and she was explaining Joe's connection to Erin's disappearance.

'He'd been following me and Gabbie,' she said, breathlessly. 'Before she disappeared.' Mel's stomach was twisting itself into knots. The police always made her nervous.

'Following you how?'

'Well, I've seen him around. In the woods, on the footpath. Just watching me.'

'Does he live round here?'

'I don't know,' she said. 'I suppose he could do.' She thought of the storage hut in the woods, how her mother had slept there.

Out of the corner of her eye she saw Lily crawling over to the TV stand and pulling herself up, then reaching out to grab a collection of wires that could bring the TV down on top of her.

Mel jumped up to stop her, carrying her back to the sofa and putting her on her knee.

'And has Joe done anything to upset or alarm you?' the female officer asked.

'Well, just following us, I mean that's suspicious in itself, isn't it? That's what he was doing to Erin before she disappeared.' Mel looked up at them, and could see the doubt in their faces. She had to convince them to take it seriously. 'The thing is, a few weeks ago, Gabbie gave an interview on the news about Erin's disappearance. And she made it clear that we thought it was Joe who had taken her. Then after that, Joe appeared on Laurel Street... I just think it's related. He wouldn't have liked Gabbie connecting him to Erin's disappearance. He would have been angry. What if he hurt Gabbie?'

'OK, that's useful information. We'll follow up on that,' the male officer said calmly, making a note. 'We also wanted to ask you some more questions about the night of the party. Particularly how Gabbie was that night, and what happened before she left.'

They asked again about Gabbie's behaviour at the party. Mel remembered how erratic she had been, how drunk. She told the police officers everything she could think of, including how on edge she'd been about her marriage to Stuart. She explained how Gabbie had seemed afraid of Stuart, how she'd thought he might have set up cameras in their house. The police said they had searched the house thoroughly but there hadn't been any cameras. As they were speaking, Lily started to cry. No amount of jigging up and down on Mel's knee seemed to calm her. She must be hungry.

'Don't worry, we'll be done soon,' the officer said. 'I just want to ask you about the end of the party. We've been told that before Gabbie left, she had an argument with Stuart. Can you tell us a bit more about that?'

Lily cried harder, and Luke came into the room and picked

her up. Mel explained that Lily was hungry and he took her to the kitchen to make her a snack.

Mel turned back to the police officers. 'Yes, she had an argument with Stuart and Roz. They told her about their affair. She stormed out. I tried to follow her, but she didn't want me to.'

'And that was the last contact you had with her?'

'Yes, that was the last time. At the party.' She said it automatically, before realising her mistake. She'd seen Gabbie with Luke, after the party. Mel opened her mouth to correct herself and then closed it again. She could hear Luke humming to himself as he made Lily a snack in the kitchen. She hesitated, unsure what to say.

'Lastly,' the officer said, not noticing her hesitation, 'can you think of anyone who might have a reason to want to hurt Gabbie? Other than her husband or Joe.'

Mel swallowed. For a moment the image of Gabbie kissing Luke flashed through her mind. She thought of how unconcerned Luke had been that Gabbie was missing and how secretive he'd been lately. But Luke wouldn't have wanted to hurt her. She was sure of that.

'No,' Mel replied. 'No one else.'

TWENTY-NINE

Mel let the police out of her house and then stood at the door for a moment, gathering her thoughts. She felt a hand on her shoulder and jumped. 'Everything alright?' Luke asked, embracing her from behind. 'What did the police want?'

'I asked to speak to them,' she said, her voice shaking with emotion. She found herself crying, tears running down her face.

'Hey,' Luke said, wiping them away. 'What's wrong?'

'It's just Joe. He was the maintenance man who used to work on the estate when Erin disappeared. Everyone thought he killed Erin. But he was never charged. There wasn't enough evidence. And now he's back. He's been watching me. He was watching Gabbie, too, before she disappeared. I think he had something to do with it.'

'What?' Luke said, guiding Mel towards a chair in the kitchen, next to Lily's highchair. 'Sit down. So you think he's been following you?'

'I've seen him a few times. He watches me. And once he tried to talk to me – he knew Lily's name. I don't know why he's back or what he wants from me. He moved away after Erin's disappearance. Anyway, I've told the police everything now. It's in their hands.' But that didn't make Mel feel any better.

'What exactly happened?' Luke asked, with a worried frown. 'When Erin disappeared. How was Joe involved?' Luke had asked her this question before, early in their relationship, and Mel had told him, but she hadn't gone into too much detail, preferring to look forward, not back. She'd just wanted to get on with her life.

But now things were different. Joe was back. And now Gabbie had disappeared too.

'Joe worked on the estate,' Mel said. 'He used to do a lot of the odd jobs, a bit like you. But he was a full-time employee. He lived off-site in the village of Burton, about three miles away, but he was always around. Sometimes he even slept in his storage hut. He was a bit odd, a bit of a loner, but people mainly thought he was harmless.'

'But he wasn't?'

'He behaved strangely with Erin. In the six months before she disappeared, they were together a lot. She sometimes said he was her best friend, the only person she could talk to. They'd spend hours together in his storage hut. She said he was the only one who listened to her, who really understood her. And he taught her things, too, survival skills, how to catch rabbits, how to light a fire. Me and Gabbie said we wanted to learn too, but she wouldn't let us. Their friendship was always about the two of them. I didn't understand back then how inappropriate it was. A thirty-year-old man and a ten-year-old girl. Of course they couldn't be friends.' Mel shivered, thinking of Erin in the storage hut with Joe, the door shut, her telling her friends not to come in.

'Maybe he was just looking out for her?' Luke said.

'No, I don't think so. He followed us all in the woods. We played there together a lot. Erin and Gabbie weren't supposed to, they always told their parents they were playing on the green, and no one ever seemed to care enough to check. Often when we were in the woods, we'd look around and he was just there, watching us. It creeped us out a bit, but not too much. I suppose we were used to him being around. And you've got to understand, it was different back then. Even though he was a bit odd, he was well-liked in the community. People spoke highly of him – they appreciated all the work he did on the estate. He could get away with things. That winter, there were rumours of a flasher in those woods. A few older girls had seen him. We never saw him, but we were always alert, looking out for him.'

'And was he ever caught? The flasher? Couldn't he have hurt Erin?'

'Maybe. But after Erin disappeared, everyone decided the flasher must have been Joe.'

'But you never knew for sure?'

'No, not for certain. But the whole of the street was convinced.'

'And the police?'

'The police thought Joe had killed Erin. But there wasn't enough evidence. And no body.' Mel felt tears prick her eyes as she thought of her friend.

'But what actually happened that night? Did you see anything?'

'We were all in the woods. Me, Gabbie and Erin. It was New Year's Eve and the adults were distracted with their party. We wanted a party too. We were going to have a midnight feast in the woods. I met the others in the clearing and we laid the food out. Erin had brought a little red rucksack with her. She said she was going to run away after the party, but we didn't believe her.'

'Was Joe there?'

'Yeah. He was always hanging around. But he didn't disturb us during the midnight feast.'

'And what happened?'

'Nothing at first. We ate the food, laughed, messed about. We were going to pack up and go home. Gabbie and I started putting everything into plastic bags. We got distracted, dividing up all the remaining food. When we looked up, she was gone.'

'She disappeared, just like that?'

Mel nodded, repeating what she'd told the police all those years ago. 'We thought maybe she'd followed through and tried to run away. We looked for her, calling out, but couldn't see her. We ran through the woods, up to the river and back. We didn't see her anywhere. For a long time after she went missing, I believed she'd run away. But everyone on the street thought Joe had hurt her. And now I think that's what happened too. He was the only other person we saw in the woods that evening.'

After Mel had spoken to Luke, she went down the street to see if there was any more news on the search. She ran into Deena and Michael. 'Some of the neighbours have gone back out to the woods,' Deena told her. 'They're continuing the search. But they haven't found anything of Gabbie's.'

Mel nodded. 'Everyone just wants her found,' she said.

'It's the police who should be doing this,' Michael said. 'Not us. They're properly trained in searching for missing people.'

'They're not putting the effort in,' Deena said. 'Compared to when Erin went missing. This time we only have a few officers down on the street. They won't do a proper search, and we'll never find her on our own. The police think they can just put out Facebook appeals and be done with it, but it's not enough.'

'We should contact the local press,' Mel said. 'There's the *Gazette*.'

'It closed down last year,' Deena said. 'Online only now. But I'll email them just in case it helps.'

Mel thought of her friend, Ashley. 'I've got a friend who's a journalist in London,' she said to Deena. 'I could contact her if you like. See if we can get the national newspapers interested.'

Deena frowned for a moment, then nodded. 'Yes,' she said. 'That's a good idea. The more coverage we can get of Gabbie's case, the quicker we'll find her. Someone must know where she is.'

Mel went straight home and called Ashley, who said she'd do whatever she could to get the story into the national news.

THIRTY

Monday 30th January

Back at school on Monday, Mel could barely concentrate. She hadn't had time to do much lesson prep over the weekend, and she was relying on some very basic outlines and some worksheets she'd printed off. Her class were playing up but all she could think about was Gabbie, wondering if there was a breakthrough in the case. She kept checking the news and the street WhatsApp group whenever she got a break, but nothing seemed to be happening. She messaged Tamsin, who said it was quiet on the street, too. Finally Deena messaged to say the sighting in Brighton had amounted to nothing, but the police were sifting through hundreds more sightings from across the country. Ashley had managed to get the story into the newspapers, but it wasn't headline news.

Tuesday was the same. Mel was still completely distracted. Her mind just wasn't on the job. The parents of a boy in her class made another complaint and she was called in for another meeting with the head, but this time she just nodded politely and said she understood, without really listening. When Mel went back to Laurel Street in the evening, she felt tired and dejected. There was still no news, no hint of where Gabbie might be. The police had finished interviewing all the neighbours and they were no longer a presence on the street. The next day would be Mel's birthday, but she went to bed feeling flat. She fell into a fitful sleep, dreaming of three little girls playing happily in the woods, and then woke up with a start. Now she was the only one left.

'Hey,' Luke said, kissing Mel awake in the morning. 'I've made you a birthday breakfast in bed.'

Mel turned over groggily, opening one eye. 'Did you turn off my alarm for me?'

'Yeah, but I've woken you up at the same time. It's 6.30. Don't worry, you're not running late.' He leant down and kissed her deeply, his breath fresh. 'Happy Birthday.'

Mel forced herself up in bed. 'Thank you,' she said, smiling as he placed a tray with buttered toast, a boiled egg and a chocolate croissant on her lap. He put her steaming hot mug of coffee on the bedside table.

When she'd finished her breakfast, Luke brought Lily in to see her, carrying a small present, wrapped in animal-print wrapping paper. 'Lily chose the paper,' Luke explained.

'I love it,' Mel said, kissing her daughter on the head. Lily helped her take off the paper, revealing a mug that read *Best Mum in the World*.

'Thank you so much,' she said, kissing Lily again, and then Luke. Mel hadn't thought much about her birthday. She wanted a low-key day this year. She didn't want to celebrate when Gabbie was missing.

. . .

When she got home from school that evening, Luke presented her with a bouquet of flowers and said he was taking her out to the local pub where they'd first met.

'Your mother's agreed to babysit,' he said with a smile. 'It's all sorted.'

'Oh,' Mel said, uncertainly. She hadn't felt comfortable enough to let her mother babysit before.

'Don't worry,' Luke said. 'Lily will be fine without you. And we'll only be up the road in the village. It will be easy to come back if there are any problems. We need to go out and enjoy some time together, just the two of us.'

'I'm not sure,' Mel said. 'What about Gabbie?' It didn't feel right while she was still missing.

'Come on,' Luke said. 'The whole world can't stop because Gabbie's left Stuart.'

Mel frowned. Gabbie hadn't just left Stuart. She was missing. But then she relented. 'OK, then. That would be great.' The stress of Gabbie's disappearance had been getting to her. But like Erin, Gabbie might never be found. Luke was right; she couldn't let life stop completely.

At the pub, they saw that the table they had sat at the night they met was free, and Luke slid into the booth.

'This is where I first saw you,' he said, 'sitting here on your own.'

'I'm glad you did,' Mel said. 'And very glad you came and said hello.'

'Who'd have thought we'd end up living so close to where we first met?'

'I guess sometimes life goes full circle.' Mel thought of their move back into her grandmother's house, her mother, Joe, Tamsin. Everything felt so overwhelming. Everything was coming back.

'I'm sorry I've been a bit distant, lately,' Luke said. 'I've had a lot on my mind. I wasn't sure what to do about my dad and Lily. I couldn't figure out the right thing.'

'What did you decide in the end? Are you going to introduce him to Lily? I could come too, and meet him.' Mel knew she'd prefer to be there if Luke was going to introduce Lily to someone new. Especially someone who'd hurt him and his mother the way his father had.

'No, I decided not to. I thought about it and I can't trust him. He really wants to meet her, but I've said no. I'm hoping he'll leave me alone.'

Mel reached out and touched his hand. 'Well done. It can be hard to say that, to reject a parent.' She'd done it lots of times with her mother when she was an alcoholic. It had hurt every time, but she had known it was for the best.

'It hurts, but it's the right thing to do. I can't forgive him for what he did in my childhood. I'm happier now I've made the decision.'

'That's good. Maybe we can get our relationship back to normal now.' Mel reached for his hand. It felt like a relief to acknowledge that things were difficult between them at the moment.

'Yeah, I hope so. I'm sorry. I've been working too hard. I've been so stressed, I've just been powering myself into work. And I felt guilty about Gabbie – the kiss. I didn't know how to reconnect with you.'

'We can reconnect now,' Mel said. 'Put all that in the past. Focus on us. Our family with Lily.'

'That's what I want,' Luke said, gazing intently at Mel. 'I don't want to be anything like my father. I want a happy family. And I'll do anything to make that happen.'

That night, Mel lay beside Luke in bed.

'How are you feeling?' he asked her, gazing at her intently. 'About Gabbie?'

'Worried,' Mel said. 'The police seem to have practically given up.'

'You know, I might have been the last person to see her,' he said, his voice emotionless. 'When we were in the pool house. She must have left in the night, after she saw me. She told me she'd leave him. So it all made sense.'

'But what do you think now?'

'I honestly think she'll turn up one day like nothing's happened.'

Mel paused for a moment. What Luke was saying didn't make sense. Unless he knew something else. 'Why do you think that?' she asked. 'Have you heard from her? Has she been in contact with you?'

'No, I haven't heard from her.' He squeezed Mel's hand under the covers. 'Really, you don't need to worry about that.'

'But you're convinced she's alive?'

'Yeah, why wouldn't she be? I think she just lost her phone that night and hasn't bothered to get in contact with anyone.'

Mel was silent, her mind whirring. Surely it couldn't be as simple as that? Beside her, Luke quickly fell into a deep sleep, his breathing steady and even.

As Mel lay there, Lily started crying, a small, feeble cry, and Mel was grateful for the excuse to get up and go to her. She sat with her in her arms for a long time, appreciating the warmth of her small body. She was getting almost too big to lie comfortably in her arms, her long limbs sticking out. It felt like the time was already flying by, that she was gradually becoming her own person. The changes were so slow they were almost indiscernible, and yet so quick it seemed Lily had grown up and started to walk and talk in the blink of an eye.

'I love you,' Mel whispered to Lily. Her crying had stopped, but Mel could feel her nappy sagging under its own weight and she knew she needed to change her. She put her down on the floor and opened the nappy drawer. They were completely out of nappies.

They kept some spare ones in Luke's wardrobe in the bedroom, where he stored his clothes. She put Lily back in her cot to stop her crawling away and tiptoed back into the master bedroom, then pulled the nappies from the bottom of the wardrobe. As she did, a small piece of paper came out and floated up into the air. She thought it was an old receipt and took it with her to throw away.

But when she got back to Lily's bedroom, she saw it wasn't a receipt. It was a note, in the same handwriting as the note that had been pinned to their door when they first moved in. The note that said they didn't belong here.

Mel swallowed, a horrible feeling of dread washing over her. Why was it in the bottom of Luke's wardrobe?

She read the small handwriting.

I know who you are.

Mel frowned. Luke must have hidden the note from her to stop her seeing it, so she didn't get upset. But what did it mean? All the neighbours knew who she was. After all, she used to live here with her grandmother.

She gasped as the realisation hit her. Everyone did know who she was. It wasn't her the note was targeted at. It must be Luke. He must have hidden it because it was directed at him.

I know who you are.

Mel had no idea what it meant. As far as she knew, Luke wasn't hiding anything. He was straightforward, exactly who he said he was. A handyman originally from Scotland. He had always been open and honest with her, and with all his friends.

In London, he'd been known for being likeable and friendly. What could the note mean?

But someone in Laurel Street thought they knew who he was. And whatever it was they thought they knew, it was something he wanted to hide from Mel. Mel didn't know what was going on, but one thing was certain: Luke was keeping something from her.

Mel changed Lily's nappy and then held her in her arms until her breathing slowed and she fell asleep. She placed her daughter gently down in the cot, kissed her cheek and then went back to her bedroom.

She got under the duvet beside Luke and looked over at him, sleeping so calmly. Ever since Gabbie had gone missing he'd been like a different person. He didn't seem concerned about what had happened to her at all. Mel rolled over in the bed, to face away from him. Maybe there was a reason he wasn't bothered. Maybe he already knew what had happened to her.

Mel had to know what was going on. She got out of bed and went round to Luke's bedside table. She took his mobile phone from the side and tapped in her birthday as the code.

Wrong pin.

He had changed the code. Why? Had he been expecting her to check again?

Mel got back into the bed and lay staring at the man sleeping beside her. She wondered what secrets he might be keeping. Only one thing was certain. She didn't really know the man she had married at all.

THIRTY-ONE

Thursday 2nd February

The next day, Mel was up early and off to school, and she didn't get the chance to speak to Luke. She'd put the note back where she found it, after taking a photo of it on her phone. She needed to figure out what it meant, who Luke was. She'd never had any cause to suspect him of being anyone except who he said he was.

He'd never spoken much about his past, but it had been enough. She knew he'd grown up with his mother in Scotland and she'd died a few years ago. Over the years he'd spoken about how much he missed her, how she'd always been there to guide him. Money had been tight, but she'd managed to bring him up single-handedly. He'd moved to Scotland when he was five after she'd split up with his father. Once he'd finished school he'd become a handyman, then when his mother died he'd moved to England.

He'd been twenty-seven by then. Maybe there was something he'd done in his past life that he'd been running away from. She supposed he could have any kind of secret. A criminal past, a secret child. Her mind spun with the possibilities. She only knew the man he was now, the man he'd been since he moved to England. She didn't know who he was before.

She wondered when he had received the note. Had it been before or after the note pinned to their door? She hadn't told him about that. She'd thought the *You don't belong here* was directed more at her than Luke, implying that she'd never be good enough or rich enough to fit in. But maybe it had been sent after the note that said they knew who Luke was. Maybe it was Luke they thought didn't belong here.

As Mel had left for school that morning with Lily in the car, Luke had been going off to work for Stuart again. She thought of how he was willing to work for Stuart all hours of the day, how he was happy to shovel snow for him in the freezing cold. Luke had always turned down the awkward jobs like this before. But now he'd do anything for Stuart. Was Stuart blackmailing him? Did he feel he had to do all the work for him to stop him telling Luke's secret? It would explain a lot. But whatever Luke was keeping from her couldn't be that bad. Luke was a good, kind man. It was probably something minor he'd done that he felt guilty about. And Stuart was taking advantage of him.

Stuart seemed to be at the root of so many of the problems in the neighbourhood. She thought about what Tamsin had said about him possibly being violent towards Gabbie. They'd had such an idyllic life from the outside looking in, but under the surface there was something much darker.

Mel had intended to ask Luke about the note when she got home, but he was working late for Stuart. That night, after Mel had put Lily to bed, her mother cooked a vegetarian lasagne, making sure Mel knew how much effort she was putting in, trying out a new recipe.

Mel was setting the table when Luke got back. He went upstairs to get changed and her mother poured Mel a glass of red wine. 'It goes with the lasagne,' she said. 'I bought it specially.'

'Oh,' Mel said, surprised. 'It's a school night, I can't have too much.' She wasn't sure why her mother was suddenly serving wine, when she'd stopped drinking herself. Mel and Luke had been careful not to drink in front of her since she'd moved in.

Angela seemed to read her mind. 'Oh, don't worry, I can watch you drinking. It's one of the things I need to get used to. Kind of a test for me. If I can sit at a table while other people are drinking and not drink myself, then I'll know I can go out in the evenings again.'

'Are you sure you're ready for this?' Mel asked. 'It seems like a big step.'

'I'll know soon enough,' Mel's mum said. Mel could see her eyes were already fixated on the open bottle she'd left in the middle of the table. Angela quickly turned away from it and got the lasagne out of the oven and started cutting it into portions.

Mel felt uncomfortable, sitting at the table while her mother took charge. She was whisked back to her childhood, when she'd never been sure what her mother was going to do next, when she'd always felt on edge, adrenaline pumping, ready for the next disaster.

Luke came in and sat down. 'Oh, wine?' he said, raising his eyebrows at Mel.

'Mum bought it. It goes with the lasagne.'

'Don't mind if I do, then.' Luke poured himself a glass as Mel watched him. He seemed exactly the same man as he'd been yesterday. Not like someone keeping a secret from his wife.

Once the lasagne was on the table, they all dug in, congratulating Angela on a delicious meal.

'It's the least I could do,' her mother said. 'You've welcomed me into your family.'

Mel swallowed a mouthful of food. She'd had to let her mother live there. She owned half the house. 'It's lovely to have you here,' she said. She noticed her mother was still looking at the wine. She kept taking sips of her water, finishing one glass and immediately pouring another.

'I'm jealous of you,' her mother said. 'Having all this. A beautiful daughter. A husband that hasn't left you. Living in a nice house. You've got it made.'

'Thanks, Mum.'

'This is the life I deserved, but I choose the wrong men. Your father was a loser. And then I had a string of losers after him. I wish I hadn't been punished for my choices. Those men tore my life apart.'

'You've put all that behind you, Mum,' Mel said. 'You've done well.' She felt exhausted from everything that was going on, and she knew that she was going to have to spend the rest of the evening marking maths exercise books. She wasn't sure she had the energy for this conversation.

'Yeah. That's all down to me, isn't it? I realised I had to do it myself. Stand on my own two feet. There wasn't anyone else to do it, was there? Just me on my own.'

'Well done,' Mel repeated. She felt like a mother congratulating her child. It was the wrong way round.

'Your granny influenced you, didn't she? She told you that I'd chosen the wrong men, that I should have made more sensible choices, chosen someone more loyal. She told you to make different choices. And you did. You chose Luke.'

Mel reached for Luke's hand under the table. 'I did,' she said simply. The note from last night flashed through her mind.

'But are you really happy? Without the adventure? Was it really right to cut me off, just because I liked a drink?'

So this was what the evening was going to be about. It felt like her mother had been waiting to say this since she moved in.

'It wasn't that. You were never interested in anything I did. You never loved me. You shipped me off to Granny's and forgot about me.'

'Ah, memory's a funny thing,' her mother said. 'I guess people don't really remember what they were like as children. You were a difficult child, nothing like Lily. It was hard to look after you.'

'I was just a kid, Mum. You sent me to Gran's when I was eleven.'

'There are different types of kids,' Angela said. 'Some are hard work. You cried from the moment you were born. It wouldn't stop. It drove me insane. And your father was never around. Six whole months of continuous crying. It was hard to like you, let alone love you.'

Mel thought of the overwhelming love she'd had for Lily. Suddenly she remembered that it hadn't been instant when she'd been born, like she had expected. At first the baby had seemed alien and disconnected from her. The love had taken a few days to kick in, but once it was there it overwhelmed her. The feeling had been so intense. Had her mother never felt like that?

'All babies cry, Mum.'

'Maybe. Maybe I just wasn't cut out to be a mother. But even your grandmother said you were difficult. And as a child you were so naughty. Always breaking things, always falling out with friends at school, always shouting back at me. You were hard work.'

Luke squeezed Mel's hand under the table. 'You couldn't tell that now, could you?' he said, trying to lighten the tone. 'She's turned out alright.'

'Yeah,' Angela said. 'I would never have thought it. If someone had asked me when you were little, I'd have said you'd probably become a petty criminal.' She laughed, but no one else did.

'Granny didn't think I was hard work,' Mel said, defending herself. 'She always said I was good.'

Angela laughed. 'Yeah, that's what she told you. When I gave you over to her, she thought she could do a better job. She thought she could do this kind of reverse psychology thing. That if she told you that you were good all the time, maybe you'd become good.'

Mel took another spoonful of lasagne. She didn't know what to say.

Her mother continued. 'Of course, your grandmother changed her tune, too. She'd always known you were a difficult child. But when I started drinking more, she started to blame me. She said that my drinking made you unsettled and difficult. That it was my fault. But it was the other way round. You were such an awful child. You drove me to drink. Everything would have turned out differently if you hadn't driven me to drink, if you'd been a good child, like Lily. You don't know how lucky you are.'

Mel blinked back tears. Her mother had always had this underlying cruel streak.

'Angela – that's enough,' Luke said.

'It's only the truth,' her mother said, as Mel got up and left the table, Luke following quickly behind her.

THIRTY-TWO

Friday 3rd February

The next day was another busy day at school, and Mel hardly had time to think about her mother. The one thing she was sure of was that she didn't want to see her, and she didn't want her looking after Lily. She was entitled to live with them because she owned half the house, but Mel didn't have to see or speak to her. She hadn't realised the level of hatred her mother felt for her, how she blamed Mel entirely for her alcoholism. But she was hard to avoid when she was living in the room across the corridor.

Luke had tried to comfort her last night after her mother's outburst, but it hadn't been enough. She'd moved away from his embrace. She knew he was hiding something, too, and she felt completely alone.

Her class played up that morning. She was on break duty, and as she supervised the kids a fight broke out which she didn't see the start of. She sent both the girls to the head teacher, and her whole class was in a foul mood until lunchtime, when she finally got some time alone.

She checked her phone as she ate her lunch, ready to scroll for any news or mentions of Gabbie. She had a message from Ashley, and she opened it excitedly. She'd been disappointed with how little press coverage Ashley had managed to get so far, but it had been building over the last few days, with more and more interest from the tabloids.

> The police aren't getting much traction and want more publicity for the case. They're releasing the note that Gabbie left for Stuart to the papers. They think it will increase interest and might create more leads. Thought I'd let you know first.

There was a photo of the note attached.

The writing was neat, as if someone had put a lot of effort into writing each letter carefully. Gabbie had been very drunk, Mel remembered, and would have struggled to concentrate on what she was doing. Some words were crossed out and corrected, as if she wasn't quite thinking straight.

Stuart,
I'm leaving you – at last! I hope you are happy with Roz. You two deserve each other! I'm off to something better.
Gabbie

Mel messaged Ashley back.

> Great – hopefully that will get the papers interested. Wonder what she meant by 'something better'?

'Something better' could mean anything, Mel thought. Gabbie might have known exactly where she was going, or she might have just wanted to sound like she had a plan when she didn't. Mel read the note through again. The writing looked familiar, and she supposed she must remember it from school. It was a long time since she and Gabbie had written any notes to each other.

Then something clicked in her brain. She'd seen the neat writing more recently. She went into her photos on her phone and found the picture of the note that Luke had hidden in the cupboard.

I know who you are.

The writing was the same. Mel's head spun. Gabbie couldn't have written the note to Luke. That didn't make sense. But the same person had written both notes. Mel swallowed. *Stuart*. Had he forged Gabbie's leaving note?

She messaged Ashley again.

> I don't think that's Gabbie's writing.

This time Ashley replied instantly.

> What? Why?

> I'm sure it's Stuart's. How do the police know it's definitely her writing? Did they check properly?

> I don't know. I'll call them and ask. Leave it with me. Gosh, if it's Stuart's that will sell papers!

Mel couldn't concentrate at all for the rest of the day. In the afternoon she managed to find a video on YouTube on forest ecosystems which they'd been studying in class, and she put it on for fifteen minutes while she tried to clear her head. She pulled her phone out of her handbag and quickly checked it again while the video played. There was a message from Deena and she held her breath as it opened.

It was only a complaint about how slowly the police investigation was progressing.

Nothing from Ashley.

Mel tried to focus on her students, but it was almost impossible. She counted down the minutes until the end of the day, then left as soon as she could. While she was driving to pick up Lily from nursery her phone beeped and her fingers itched to check the message, but she made herself wait until she'd pulled into the car park.

Mel saw the message was from Ashley and unlocked her phone to read it.

> Spoke to the police and the writing is definitely Gabbie's. They checked with her mother. Going to run the story with the letter this evening. Should get a lot of interest.

Mel's whole body went cold as she read the message again. If it was Gabbie's writing, then Gabbie must have sent the notes to her and Luke. It had been Gabbie who wanted to tell them they didn't belong there, Gabbie who knew who Luke was. She was supposed to be her friend, but she had been hiding something from her. Something about Luke. Mel thought of how close Gabbie and Luke had been, the chats over coffee, the work he'd done at her house. Had she already known Luke before he'd met Mel? The notes had seemed like threats, an attempt to get at Luke. Did they have something to do with her disappearance?

THIRTY-THREE

Mel was home earlier than usual, her mind spinning with thoughts of Luke and Gabbie. Had he known that the notes were from her? And what had Gabbie meant when she said she knew who he was? Mel had thought she knew Luke so well, that they were soulmates, but now she realised she'd only seen the Luke she wanted to see.

When she turned into her road there was no sign of any police cars, and she felt a stabbing disappointment. The police had clearly lost interest in the case. She thought of Gabbie the evening of the party, in her tiny dress, shivering in the cold, hardly able to feel it because of the alcohol coursing through her system. She would have been an easy victim for someone that night. After all, everyone had heard her threatening to leave Stuart. It would have been easy to dispose of her body before anyone even questioned where she'd gone.

Mel pulled into her drive, took Lily out of the car seat and went into the house.

Her mother was kneeling by the tumble dryer, shoving clothes into a plastic bag. Mel had been avoiding her since her outburst last night. She didn't want to speak to her or see her.

The washing she was pulling out of the dryer smelt slightly damp. The tumble dryer never worked very well with a load that size.

'Maybe you should put it in one more time?' Mel said. 'Or hang it up to finish drying? That would be better, to save energy.'

'It's fine,' her mother said quickly, shoving a pair of brown cargo trousers into the bag. They looked far too big for her and Mel had never seen her wearing them.

'Why not use the washing basket? Why put them in that bag?'

'I'm taking them straight to my room, I'll hang them up there.'

Mel stared at her mother. She was lying about something. 'Those aren't your trousers, are they?'

Angela blushed, and shoved more washing into the plastic bag. She stood up to go upstairs.

'Whose trousers are they, Mum? Have you had a man here?' Mel felt the bitter sting of disappointment. She had thought her mum had signed off men for good now she was sober. She didn't want her bringing anyone back to the house. Not with Lily here. But what right did Mel have to tell her that? She was living here with Luke. Her mum was entitled to treat the house as her home, too.

'I haven't had any man here,' Angela said quickly. 'These are for a friend.'

'What friend? Who do you know round here that doesn't have his own washing machine?' Mel's brow crinkled and then she stepped back as the realisation hit her. There was only one person it could be. 'Is it Joe?' she said breathlessly.

'It's none of your business.'

'Yes, it is. Is it Joe? You know exactly what that man's like.'

'He needed his washing doing,' her mother said. 'He hasn't got the facilities to do it himself. And he's not who you think he is. He's been kind to me. I feel awful about everything everybody said about him.'

Mel stared at her mother in disbelief. She hadn't really changed. She was always fooled by men.

'How could you befriend him? What's wrong with you?'

'It was the night of the party. When you weren't here to let me in. I was all alone and it was freezing cold. I only had my motorbike, no shelter at all. I didn't have anywhere to go. No money, nothing. So I went to the old storage hut to see if I could shelter there. When I got there, Joe was already there. He woke up when I opened the door. He made me a hot cup of tea on his camping stove and then gave me his bed for the night and slept on the floor. He was kind to me.'

'He was sleeping there?'

'Yeah. He had been for a while, I think. He's been living there. He still is. That's why I said I'd wash his clothes.'

'You told me that he hadn't been there when we saw the bed in the hut.'

Angela shrugged. 'I lied. I knew how you'd react. It was clear you had something against him.'

Mel took deep breaths, trying to contain her anger. 'Gabbie's missing, Mum! And Joe is a suspect. If he's living rough in the storage hut, near where she disappeared, then the police need to know.'

'They already know,' Angela said. 'They've spoken to him.'

'I need to speak to him too,' Mel said. 'Tell him to get out of Laurel Street and leave us alone.'

'What's he ever done to you?'

'You know what he's done. He was watching me. And Gabbie. He was watching her before she disappeared.'

'And you think he had something to do with it?'

'Yes... no...' Mel put her head in her hands. 'I don't know,' she said. 'But I don't like him hanging around here. If he's as nice as you say he is, then will he leave if I ask him to?'

'I don't know,' her mother said. 'I'm not sure if he has anywhere to go. I've got his washing here. Why don't you come with me and speak to him?'

Mel swallowed, and looked down at Lily. She couldn't take her with her. Not when she wasn't sure what Joe wanted. What if he'd hurt Gabbie? What if he wanted to punish Mel?

'I'll leave Lily with Deena,' she said.

'Sure,' her mother said. 'We can walk down together. Just the two of us.'

They walked across the green field where the horses grazed in silence, getting further away from the warm light of the houses on the street. Mel wrapped her coat round her tightly, shivering in her work skirt and tights.

It was dark already. The moonlight guided them, but Mel wished she'd brought a torch. It would be harder to see once they left the field and went into the woods, the canopy of trees reducing the light further.

A part of her wanted to reach out and hold her mother's hand, to feel its warmth, to feel that there was someone in the world who loved her unconditionally and would protect her. But her mother had never offered her that. She'd disliked her even as a child. Mel had looked after her more than she'd looked after Mel.

Mel's breath made circles in the cold air and she thought of Erin as they entered the woods. The last time she'd seen her was here in these woods. She'd been so unhappy, always talking about running away. And Mel hadn't been happy with her mother either. She thought of the three little girls. Childhood was supposed to be innocent, but theirs hadn't been. Had Gabbie been unhappy too? She didn't think so. But who knew what went on behind closed doors.

Gabbie hadn't been happy recently. Just like Erin, she'd

wanted to run away. It was this place. With its picture-perfect cottages and acres of space. It did something to people. Mel had stayed away a long time herself, moving to London.

But Joe had come back. Despite what the place had done to him. The media had torn him apart after Mel and Gabbie had told the police that they'd seen him the night Erin disappeared. They'd painted him as a murderer, a paedophile. But had he been? Mel had never known for sure. All she knew was that when she was around him, she felt a fear deep in her bones. But it hadn't always been like that. As children they hadn't been scared of him. He'd always been around, and she'd just accepted that. They all had. Had they been impossibly naive? Or had there been nothing to fear?

Her mother thought he was a good guy, but then she was hardly a good judge of character. All of Laurel Street had liked him when he was the maintenance man. Everyone had been looking for someone to blame once Erin disappeared. And it had been the media that had turned them against him with their smear campaign. The pictures of him with scraggly, dirty hair and old, holey clothes and the headlines:

DID THIS MAN TAKE ERIN?

WHY DID THEY LET THIS MAN NEAR THE GIRLS?

HOW DID THEY NOT KNOW?

They entered the dark woods and had only gone a few steps when they heard voices. They stopped in their tracks, and it was her mother who reached for Mel's hand. Mel's heart beat faster as she caught the raised voices on the wind.

'You need to leave, get out of here.' She'd know that voice anywhere. It was Luke's.

The reply was muffled and inaudible.

'You can't be here anymore. You're scaring my wife. She doesn't want to see you. I don't want to see you. And you can't see Lily.'

'Please, Luke. It's all I want in the world.' Mel could just about catch Joe's words on the wind.

Why would he want to see Lily? Mel shivered as she thought of all the times he'd followed her. Was that about Lily? Had he taken Erin, and now he wanted another child?

'It's just Luke,' she whispered to her mother. 'Let's go over.'

She felt a surge of gratitude towards Luke. Despite all his flaws, he was sticking up for her, his wife. Maybe she could trust him after all.

They approached the hut, dry twigs cracking under their feet.

The men turned silent. 'Who's there?' Luke called out.

'It's me,' Mel said, as they caught sight of the hut and the two men beside it.

'And me,' her mother said. 'I brought your washing, Joe.'

The men stood in front of the hut, face to face, Joe's cheeks flushed from the cold. Mel wondered how he kept warm during the winter nights in that cold hut. No amount of blankets could fend off the smothering chill in the air.

Her mother reached out and handed the plastic bag of clothes to Joe.

'Thank you,' he said. He looked at Mel. 'But I'm leaving. Your husband thinks it's for the best.'

'It is,' Mel said, looking him in the eyes despite her fear. 'I hate you following me. It's like when we were children.'

'I was only looking out for you.'

'I don't believe that.'

Joe nodded. 'Believe what you want to believe. I think everyone does. People believe the most convenient thing for them. The thing that helps them sleep at night. I was easy to blame. But you know I wouldn't have hurt Erin.'

Mel put her hands to her temples. Her head was hurting as her memories flooded back. That night. Erin. The screams. She tried to push them away, back into the dark recesses of her mind where they belonged.

'He's going now,' Luke said. He looked at Joe. 'Aren't you?'

'I only came back because I wanted to see you all. Please, Luke. I just want to see Lily.'

'Why does he want to see Lily?' Mel asked, baffled. What could he want from her daughter?

Luke sighed and came closer to Mel. He put his hand on her shoulder. And suddenly she could see it. Luke's profile next to Joe's. The shape of his nose, the slightly exaggerated jut of his chin, the wide forehead. Luke was clean-shaven, whereas Joe had a long beard, and Luke's skin was a few shades darker than Joe's. But it was there, as clear as anything. Their resemblance.

'I'm so sorry,' Luke said. 'But there's something I haven't told you. Joe's my father.'

THIRTY-FOUR

Saturday 4th February

Mel dragged herself out of bed before anyone else was up. Last night Luke had slept on the floor of Lily's room and she'd slept alone in their huge bed. It had been an intense evening after she'd found out about Joe, and Mel had been too exhausted to clear up the kitchen the night before. But now she had to, before anyone else came down and saw the mess. She picked up a dustpan and brush and started to sweep the pieces of smashed plates up from the floor, scooping them into the bin. Her arm ached from where she had fallen and she was sure it would come up in a bruise later, but for now she had to focus on clearing up.

Tears welled up in her eyes when she thought about the previous night. How on earth had things got so out of control? She and Luke had never argued like that before. She'd felt so betrayed, had hardly been able to look at him. He'd always known his connection to Laurel Street, his connection to Mel. But he'd never thought to tell her that Joe was his father. He'd only ever talked about his father in vague terms, never mentioning his name.

Gabbie must have known. The note she'd sent. *I know who you are.* That's what she'd meant. She knew Luke was Joe's son. Mel thought of all the times they'd been together; the work Gabbie had insisted he do on her house, the time she'd seen them drinking coffee in Gabbie's kitchen. Had they been talking about Joe? Sharing the secret Luke was keeping from Mel?

She had never felt so distant from her husband. He'd been angry with her too, and they had taken everything out on each other.

Mel wiped a tear from her eye with the back of her hand. She didn't know what had happened to her and Luke. It felt like their marriage was disintegrating. She remembered Gabbie's words on the green, when they'd been drinking together. She'd said that you couldn't judge someone on what they said in anger.

'Hi.' Mel jumped at the sound of her mother's voice from the doorway.

'Oh, hi,' Mel said, forcing a smile. 'You're up early. I thought I'd get some clearing up done before I get Lily up and the day gets away from me. I should have done it last night, really.'

Angela went over to the counter and started picking up the shards of broken glass and wrapping them in kitchen roll.

'You don't need to do that.'

'I heard your argument last night,' her mother said softly.

'It was nothing serious.'

'Really?' Her mum raised her eyebrows, surveying the broken plates and glass around the kitchen. Mel wished she hadn't come to live with them, wasn't witnessing the ups and downs of their lives. She made such an effort to make her life look perfect. But it was all falling apart.

'Was it about Joe?' her mother asked.

'Yeah, I can't believe Luke didn't tell me. Our whole marriage has been a lie.' Mel felt the weight of it all. She'd married a man she didn't even know.

'You can understand why he didn't want to tell you. And it could be a good thing that Joe's his father. Honestly, Joe's a good guy.'

'Mum, please.'

'Come on, you know he was just the scapegoat for Erin.'

Mel put her hand to her head. She wished her mother didn't live here, that she could be left alone.

'Let me clear up,' Angela said.

She reached out to touch Mel, and Mel winced away from her, shielding her bruised arm.

'Oh,' Angela said, frowning. 'Did Luke hurt you?'

'No, of course not!' Mel said sharply.

'It's OK,' her mum said. 'You can tell me. I know what it's like to keep up appearances. To pretend everything's OK when it isn't.'

'I know, Mum. But I'm not like you.'

'I can help you, Mel. If you need to leave him.'

'I don't want to leave him,' Mel said. Although a part of her wasn't sure. He'd lied to her about who he was. Her head hurt. She'd had more than a few glasses of wine last night. She wasn't used to drinking that much. But she'd needed them to calm down, to come to terms with what Luke had told her. She thought of her mother drinking throughout her childhood, thought of Gabbie, roaming the street at night with her bottle of wine. Was Mel heading the same way?

'Anyone who hurts you is definitely not right for you,' Angela said gently. She was too close to Mel, right in her face. Mel's body tensed. She poured herself a glass of water from the kitchen tap, trying to calm down.

'I'm not like you, Mum. Everything's fine.'

'No, you're not like me. You've made much better decisions in your life than I ever did. But that doesn't mean you have to stick in a marriage if you're not happy.'

'I am happy,' Mel said, fighting back tears. No one except for Luke had ever really cared whether she was happy before. She wasn't sure why her mother was being so nice now, after everything she'd said the other evening. 'It was just a little row,' Mel said, looking at the plates on the floor. 'I guess we both overreacted, smashed a few plates.' She tried to laugh. 'We were both tired.'

'You have a scratch on your forehead,' her mother said, reaching up to gently touch it. Mel winced. It must have been from when the wine glass had smashed against the kitchen counter beside her so hard that a tiny shard of glass had hit her face.

Angela got a bit of damp kitchen roll and cleaned the graze. 'I heard the shouting,' she said, looking into Mel's eyes. 'And the plates smashing. Are you sure you're OK? Are you coping?'

'I'm fine,' Mel said. 'Last night everything got the better of us. There are so many horrible things happening at the moment. With Gabbie's disappearance. And it's bringing everything back about Erin. And now Joe being back, and Luke confessing that Joe's his father. It's just... a bit much. Honestly, normally we hardly ever argue.'

'Once is enough,' Angela said. 'I should have asked your father to leave long before I did. And the next man. And the one after. I let things drift on, thinking if I just changed, then he would love me. I was always trying to change to please them. Nothing ever worked.'

'It's not like that,' Mel said forcefully. 'And I need Luke. We have Lily together.'

'Look,' Angela said, wrapping her arms round Mel. 'I know

I've been out of your life for a long time. I have no right to get involved. Your marriage is none of my business. But you'd tell me if there was anything seriously wrong, wouldn't you?'

'Of course,' Mel said, tears filling her eyes. For the first time in a long time, she felt her mother might be on her side.

THIRTY-FIVE

'You've cleared up the kitchen?' Luke said, when he came downstairs an hour later.

'Yeah,' Mel said.

'Thanks.'

'No problem.'

'I'm sorry about last night,' Luke said, stepping towards her. 'How's your arm?'

'It still hurts a bit. I fell quite badly.'

'Do you need me to take you to the doctor?'

Mel shook her head. 'No, it's OK.'

Luke poured himself a bowl of cereal and ate it in silence. Lily was in the highchair, attacking a yogurt with a spoon and spreading it over the tray. Mel and Luke watched in silence, all their anger and emotion spent in their argument last night.

'We need to talk,' Luke said.

'I think we did enough of that yesterday,' Mel said. She didn't want to go over the same argument they'd had the evening before.

'I need to explain things to you properly,' he said. 'Neither of us was rational last night. We let our emotions get the better of us. And I understand why you would be upset about Joe. We need to talk without drinking. We should go out for a walk, with Lily. How about we go down to the village? We could take Lily to feed the ducks and talk things through there.'

Mel felt the bruise on her arm, remembered the plates and glasses smashing. 'I suppose so.' It would be good to get out of the house. Maybe with a change of scene they'd be able to communicate without shouting. The duck pond would be a safe space, with lots of people around. Things wouldn't get out of control there like they had last night.

As Luke drove them down to the village, Mel pointed out the cows and sheep in the fields to Lily and she giggled happily in the back of the car. When they arrived, Mel looked across at the beautiful old church, where they held the memorial for Erin every year, and felt a stab of sadness.

Luke got Lily out of the car, while Mel unfolded the pushchair. Lily refused to go in it and she walked along, gripping Mel's hand tightly, until Luke put her on his shoulders. She loved being high up and she smiled down at Mel. Mel felt the winter sun on her face and had a fleeting moment of happiness.

At the duck pond, Luke got Lily down and poured some seeds from a packet into her hands. Lily laughed delightedly as she threw them towards the pond. A lot of them landed on the footpath and the ducks got closer and closer. Luke bent down to her level and helped her to throw further, into the water. Mel felt her heart tug. They looked so good together. Anyone looking in from the outside would think they were the perfect family. She didn't want to leave Luke, not even after everything he'd said and done. She wanted to be that perfect family, to make their marriage work.

After they'd finished all the seeds, Luke put Lily in the

pushchair and they walked round the church. Lily was soon asleep, tired from the morning's activities.

'Why don't we go to the pub for lunch?' Luke said. 'We can talk there.'

'I'm not drinking,' Mel said. She still felt shaky from last night.

'I don't think either of us should drink,' Luke said.

'OK,' Mel said, and they wandered over and went inside.

She'd met Luke at this pub after the memorial three years ago. He was there because he was working in the area. It had seemed like just a coincidence at the time, a romantic twist of fate, that meant they had been in the same place at the same time. But maybe it hadn't been.

They found a table with space next to it to fit the pushchair. Luke went to the bar and ordered them both burgers, then came back with the drinks.

'Why were you here, staying in this village, when we first met?' she asked, as Luke put a pint of cold Coca-Cola in front of her.

Luke sighed. 'I was working here. Doing up a house down the road. But I chose to come here after my mother died, because I was curious about my father. When I was little, we lived about three miles from here, in the village of Burton. After Mum left my dad when I was five and we moved to Scotland, she didn't talk about him much. And when she did, she just said he was a bad man. He'd hurt people, and I couldn't be near him or he'd hurt me too. I knew something of Erin's disappearance, but not much. I remembered seeing my dad's picture on the front pages of the papers, but I'd been too young to read the headlines. I'd looked it all up when I was a teenager, read the old newspaper articles online. I wanted to come here, to the village, to understand what he'd done, to see the impact of it. And somewhere in the back of my mind I hoped to find out it wasn't as bad as I thought, or that he hadn't done anything.'

'Were you at the memorial that day?'

'Yeah. I went along. I saw the effects of Erin's disappearance, how distraught Tamsin still was after so many years, how the whole community had been affected. And afterwards I hung around on the edges of conversations, trying to get a bit more information about my father.'

Mel took a sip of her drink. She understood that desire to know your own father, even if your mother had told you he wasn't worth knowing. She had tried several times to track hers down, and when she'd eventually found him, he hadn't wanted anything to do with her. But sometimes, she still longed for him.

'I left straight after the memorial,' Mel said. Throughout the service, she'd felt a pressure in her chest, a desperate desire to stand up and walk out. She always felt like she had to come every year, like she couldn't abandon Erin. 'I couldn't bear how sad it made me feel. I went to the pub because I wanted to have a drink on my own.'

'You did a speech about her that year, do you remember?'

'Yeah,' Mel said, blushing. She had written a couple of paragraphs about the fun she and Erin had had together, how she'd never forget her friend. How their friendship had meant the world to her. She'd felt guilty as she'd read the words. Only some of them had been true. She had loved Erin, but sometimes she'd hated her too. The friendships between ten-year-old girls were far too complex for eulogies.

'I listened to your speech. And then after the service I saw you sneak away, go into the pub across the road.'

'You followed me?'

'Kind of. I spoke to a few people first, tried to gather information. But it felt like you had the key. You'd been Erin's best friend. You would know all about my father, whether the things they said were true. So I came to the pub.'

Mel looked into his brown eyes and saw the emotion

churning behind them. 'I thought it was a chance meeting,' she said. 'Fate.'

'Yeah, well it was, in a way. I didn't make up my feelings for you.'

She couldn't remember everything she'd said to him that evening. She was emotional after the memorial and it had felt good to have someone to let it all out to, someone who listened. She had splurged all her feelings, told him about Erin, about Joe, about how Erin had never been found.

A waitress came and put their burgers in front of them. Luke lifted his up and took a small bite.

'You just wanted the information about Erin and your father from me,' Mel said.

'Yes, at first. But you soon told me all I needed to know. You told me how he used to follow you and the two other girls, and you told me how he used to take Erin to his hut. It confirmed what my mother had told me about him. That he was sick and that I needed to stay away from him. That was all I needed to know.'

Mel felt slightly faint. She hadn't realised that her words had had such an impact on Luke, that he had remained estranged from his father because of them. But it was probably for the best.

'Why didn't you tell me he was your father?'

Luke frowned. 'I was ashamed. And if I'd told you, you would have hated me, just like you hated him.'

'But it was such a huge thing to keep from me. For all this time. Didn't you ever think of telling me?'

Luke grimaced. 'Sometimes I felt guilty. Especially late at night. But I didn't think it would be good for either of us if you knew. And after a while, the fact that I'd lied to you was bigger than the lie itself. I knew you'd be angry about the lying as well as me being Joe's son. I wasn't sure if you'd forgive me.'

'So you kept it up?'

'Yeah. Remember, I was estranged from Joe. I didn't want anything to do with him, after what mum said he'd done. He wrecked my family, tore us apart. After Erin disappeared, the press were always hounding him, taking pictures of him, of our house. Those are some of my earliest memories. I was only little, but I remember how intrusive it was, how much it frightened me. And then my mother had to move all the way up to Scotland to escape him. I had to leave my home and everything that was familiar to me. And I no longer had a father.' Luke paused for a second. 'But of course, I was lucky. It's nowhere near as bad as what he must have done to Erin.'

Mel felt ill, and she took a huge gulp of her Coke. Luke really believed that Joe was guilty. He always had. He was on her side.

'I'm sorry I didn't tell you the truth,' Luke said. 'But that's the only thing I've lied about. You can trust me, honestly.'

Mel didn't answer, thinking of Gabbie; the kiss between them, the notes she'd sent him. She took a bite of her burger. Could she really trust him?

Just then, her phone rang.

Tamsin.

She answered it. Tamsin was breathless on the other end. 'They've arrested him,' she said quickly.

'Who? Joe?' Mel said. She looked at Luke. How would he feel about this?

'No, not Joe. Stuart,' Tamsin said hurriedly. 'The police are on the street now. There's lots of them. They've taken Stuart away in a police car.'

THIRTY-SIX

'What's happened?' Luke asked.

'Stuart's been arrested. We need to get back.'

'Arrested? Why?'

'Why do you think? They must think he had something to do with Gabbie's disappearance.'

Luke went pale. 'You mean, they think he murdered her?'

Mel put her hands to her head. 'I don't know.' She really didn't want to think that. But what else could it mean? 'Let's just get back,' she said.

'He wouldn't have hurt her,' Luke said, shaking his head vigorously. 'I know he wouldn't.'

Mel glared at Luke. 'Don't be so naive. The police have arrested him, Luke! There must be a good reason.'

'I just can't believe this,' Luke said.

Mel didn't have any appetite to eat the rest of her burger, but Luke finished his quickly and they left the pub.

When they got back to Laurel Street, a line of police cars were parked on the grass verge. Behind them was a media van. Finally. Since Ashley had got hold of Gabbie's leaving note, the press coverage had increased dramatically, but this was the first time she'd seen them on the street. There was a reporter on the green talking into a microphone, with Gabbie's house in the background of her shot.

Mel thought of Roz, how angry she'd be about the police cars tearing up the grass. That would be the least of her worries now Stuart had been arrested. Mel shivered. As much as she was pleased that there was progress being made on the case, she knew what this might mean for the chances of Gabbie being found alive.

Tamsin had sounded distraught on the phone. This must be bringing back memories of Erin's disappearance, how the police and media had invaded Laurel Street. She would need someone with her, to help her get through. Deena would have the police with her to support her, but Tamsin would be all on her own.

'Can you look after Lily this afternoon?' Mel asked Luke, as he drove slowly past the parked cars.

'Yeah, of course, why?'

'I need to go over and see Tamsin. I don't think she's taking this well. Can you drop me here?'

'No problem. You do what you need to do.'

Mel started to open the car door, but Luke reached over and held her arm.

'What?' she asked.

'I know this will be hard on you too,' he said. 'Not just Tamsin. Just remember you've got me and Lily. We love you.'

'I know,' Mel said, forcing a smile. 'I love you too.'

As soon as she got out of the car, she saw the reporter jogging towards her from the green. Mel put her head down and hurried towards Tamsin's house, but the reporter caught up with her.

'*Did you know Gabbie? Are you a neighbour? Were you a friend?*'

The reporter hurled questions at her.

Mel got to Tamsin's door and rang the buzzer.

'It's Mel,' she said. 'Can I come in?'

'*Mel?*' The reporter started saying as the door unlatched and Mel pushed it open. 'Mel, do you have time to talk to me later?'

The reporter stuffed her card into Mel's hand, as Mel went inside and shut the door firmly behind her. She went up the stairs, to where Tamsin was waiting on the top floor.

Mel put her arms round her. 'Are you alright?' she asked.

'Just about coping. The police arrived at Stuart's this morning and took him away.'

'He was arrested?'

'I think so. Although maybe they were just questioning him. They left Roz here. She's still in the house. They were interviewing her earlier. Now she's waiting in the kitchen with another officer.' Tamsin led Mel over to the window of her studio and they looked down into Gabbie's kitchen. Mel could see Roz sitting with a cup of coffee in front of her, her shoulders slumped.

'Wow,' Mel said. 'They're finally taking it seriously.'

'Yeah, they really are. Apparently a dog walker found one of Gabbie's earrings, on the footpath near the stables. It was from the pair she was wearing the night of the party.'

'Maybe it just fell out,' Mel said. She thought of when she and Gabbie had taken the horses out in the middle of the night. 'Maybe she went to say goodbye to the horses before she left.'

'I just hope she's still alive,' Tamsin said. 'It's been two weeks since she went missing. I pray that she ran away, that she's out there somewhere, choosing to not make contact for whatever reason.'

'But then why would they arrest Stuart?'

Tamsin sighed and sank into the chaise longue. 'You're right, of course. Stuart must have something to do with it.'

Below them, the police were searching the outbuildings again. Mel spotted more police walking around the perimeter of the house and then unlocking the pool house. Her mind flashed back to the night of the party, to Luke and Gabbie in the pool house. What if the police found something there? What if they thought Luke was responsible?

'I have to go and find Luke,' she said. She needed to talk to him about what had happened with Gabbie and the notes she'd sent. She needed to understand what had been going through his mind the night she disappeared.

THIRTY-SEVEN

Mel went downstairs and let herself out the front door. Now the road was even fuller, with media vans parked all the way along the tiny street, reporters out in force, standing by the edges of the fields and telling Gabbie's story to people in homes across the country.

As she went past Gabbie's house there was a sudden scrum as the reporters rushed towards her. She didn't want to be interviewed or be on TV, so she walked on, head down, trying to avoid the questions being hurled at her. She remembered Gabbie's interview after the memorial. Was that when all this had begun?

But then as quickly as the reporters had swarmed around her, they seemed to move on, the pack attracted elsewhere. It took a moment for Mel to realise that the door to Stuart's house had opened and Roz had come out.

Roz looked completely bewildered and scared as the flash-bulbs clicked. She brushed a hand through her tangled, curly hair, her face smudged with mascara from crying. Struggling to find a gap in the crowd, she tried to barge past the reporters. She seemed like a diminutive figure to Mel now, not the rude, intimidating woman Mel knew.

Roz pushed her way through and started to run, the cameras following. Tears were streaming down her face. For a moment, Mel took pity on her. She reached out and grabbed her hand.

'Come with me,' she said. Mel's house was a bit nearer than Roz's; she could get inside quicker. They got to Mel's door and she fumbled with the lock and then they stumbled inside, Roz shutting the door behind them.

'Thank you!' Roz said, her eyes puffy.

'It's no problem. Do you want a cup of tea?'

'Yes please.'

Mel remembered she needed to find Luke. 'Hello!' she called out. 'I'm back.' She looked round the downstairs rooms but she couldn't see him or Lily anywhere.

'Hello?' she called out again. She turned to Roz. She was already regretting letting her into her house, but she could hardly ask her to leave when she was so upset. And Mel could see the shadows of reporters outside. 'Let me check upstairs for Luke and Lily, then I'll make you that tea.'

Luke wasn't upstairs either, and Mel messaged him to see where he was, then after she'd made the drinks, she sat down with Roz on the sofa. 'Are you alright?' she asked. 'It must have been a terrible shock, Stuart being arrested.'

'He hasn't been arrested. At least I don't think so.' She lowered her eyes. 'He's just been taken in for questioning.'

'OK.'

'He didn't do it, you know. He didn't hurt Gabbie. I know everyone thinks he did, but he didn't.'

Mel thought of her poor friend, drunk and confused that night. Something had happened to her. 'What do you think happened?'

'I think she's just left him, doesn't want anything to do with him.'

'You can understand why. He got together with you.' Mel wasn't going to let Roz off too easily.

Roz sighed. 'I know I'm always going to be the bad guy in this, but you don't realise what their relationship was like. She was so volatile and difficult. Drunk. Unpredictable. He never knew where he was with her.'

'That's not fair,' Mel said, sticking up for her friend. 'He was cheating on her. He made her feel insecure about herself.'

'Stuart's not a bad guy,' Roz said. 'Honestly.'

Mel thought of her friend. Gabbie *had* been unpredictable. She'd kissed Luke and sent him those notes. Even though she and Mel went way back, she hadn't known her as well as she'd thought she had.

'I'd better get back to my house,' Roz said, downing the rest of her tea. 'Sorry I've kept you.'

'Will you be OK, going past the reporters?'

'I'll survive,' Roz said, going over to the door and putting on her coat. 'Thanks, Mel. You're the first person who's been kind to me in weeks.'

When Roz left, Mel reached for her phone and saw that Luke had messaged her. He'd taken Lily to the playground in a village a few miles away. They wouldn't be back for a while. Mel decided to go back to Tamsin's house and watch what was going on from there. She would have to talk to Luke later.

Before she went to Tamsin's she wondered if she should check on Deena. The poor woman must be going through hell. Ignoring the reporters, Mel walked towards Deena's house. There were even more journalists there, standing watching the house and chatting. The curtains in the house were drawn to keep out their prying eyes. They were like vultures, feeding on the grief of ordinary people.

Mel hesitated. She didn't want to go and knock on the door and force Deena to open it. The press would be all over her. Mel could see there was a police car on the drive and another car too. It looked familiar, and Mel realised it was Deena's sister's car.

What Deena was going through was so private and personal. She didn't need another person there. Mel would leave it to her sister and the police to comfort Deena. She turned and walked the other way, back towards Tamsin's house.

THIRTY-EIGHT

Mel rang Tamsin's buzzer and then went upstairs. In the studio Tamsin was still looking out at Gabbie's house. There were even more police now, and they were finally searching properly, spreading out over the fields. She wondered if they'd go as far as the woods, as far as Joe's storage hut. Her mother had said they had interviewed him, but had they searched the hut?

Mel squeezed her hands together as she watched the search. She realised her palms were sweating. She couldn't stop thinking about what she'd said to the police. She'd lied completely unintentionally, saying that the last time she'd seen Gabbie was at the party, when in truth, the last time she'd seen her was at the pool house with Luke. She should have corrected herself straight away, but she hadn't. Since then she'd found the notes from Gabbie to Luke. Surely she should tell the police about those. Maybe Luke had told them himself, although she doubted it.

Mel wished she had just told the police about the kiss and made things simpler for herself. She must have been subconsciously trying to protect Luke, to ignore the fact that he could have hurt Gabbie. He'd had the opportunity. He'd been alone with her.

'I saw you get caught by the media,' Tamsin said, interrupting her thoughts. 'Are you alright?'

'It was Roz they wanted more than me. Did you see?'

'It's only what she deserves,' Tamsin said, bitterly. 'I don't know why she came out by the front door. Surely she should have gone out the back?'

'I don't think she was expecting the media to be waiting for her,' Mel said.

Tamsin leant forward towards the window, looking down on the road. 'It brings it back, doesn't it?' Tamsin said. 'All the media, all wanting a piece of you.' There were tears in her eyes. When Erin had gone missing, the press had been outside Tamsin's house for weeks.

'They always wanted to see me crying,' Tamsin continued. 'They wanted to see a distressed mother. It was brutal. But I needed the press more than they needed me. I had to make sure everyone knew what Erin looked like, in case a member of the public spotted her. I needed to keep the story in the public eye. It was bad when the reporters were here, but worse when they went away. They'd lost interest then, given up hope for Erin.'

Mel reached out and squeezed Tamsin's hand.

'Roz was silly to run,' Tamsin continued. 'Hasn't she ever watched the news? People never run. They carry on with their normal lives as if the press aren't there. They try to look as ordinary as possible. Running makes them look guilty.'

'There are already articles up about her,' Mel said, scrolling through her phone. 'Look at this.' She held up her phone to show Tamsin.

SICK NEW GIRLFRIEND OF MURDER SUSPECT STUART JACOBS MOVED INTO MISSING WIFE'S HOME WITHIN DAYS

The story was accompanied by a video of Roz running away, her hair dishevelled, tears running down her face.

'They're so cruel,' Mel said. They were always looking for a scapegoat.

'Oh my goodness,' Tamsin said suddenly. 'Look what's happening. There are even more police.'

Another police car was pulling up outside Gabbie's house. They both watched in silence as an officer got out of the front. Then he opened the back door and Stuart appeared.

Mel gasped. 'He's been released,' she said.

'But why?'

'They can't have enough evidence,' Mel said. 'He will have just been helping them with their enquiries.'

'But he did it,' Tamsin said. 'Didn't he?' She stood up from the chaise longue and glared out of the window.

'I don't know,' Mel said. She really had no idea anymore. Outside, teams of police officers were searching the fields. 'I guess if they find her then they'll arrest him again.'

'Her body, you mean?' Tamsin said darkly, pacing up and down.

'Don't say that.'

'I can't just sit and watch him go back to his big house without her, pretending he hasn't done anything. I need to go and see him. He can't get away with this.' Her voice wobbled as she headed towards the door.

'No, Tamsin,' Mel said, standing in front of her and blocking the door. 'Don't be silly. You can't go marching over and threatening him.'

'What else can I do? He hurt her, I know he did.'

'How do you know?'

'Because it's like history repeating itself. I made this mistake once before, with Erin.'

'What mistake?'

'I didn't look at the person right in front of me. My husband.'

'Erin's stepdad?'

'Yeah. He hit me. I told you that. But I didn't tell the police at first, I didn't think it was relevant. I told them we had a happy marriage.'

'It's OK,' Mel said. She thought uncomfortably of the things she hadn't told the police about Luke. 'I doubt it made a difference. No one thought he took Erin.'

'I know,' Tamsin said. 'But by the time I told them about him hitting me, he'd had enough time to cover his tracks. If it was him, that is.'

'I don't think it was. The police would have been on to him. They always look at the family first, don't they?'

'Maybe,' Tamsin said. 'But I just feel so guilty. I keep imagining the worst. If it was my ex, then he got away with it because I let him.'

'I'm sure it wasn't him,' Mel said gently.

'But Erin was planning to run away. She'd packed a rucksack. You remember, don't you? I always told myself she was just childishly acting out, but maybe it was him she was trying to get away from. And if she hadn't been planning to run away, then perhaps she wouldn't have disappeared that night.'

'There were three of us in those woods,' Mel said, shivering as she remembered the cold air on her face, the twigs cracking beneath her feet. 'It could have been any of us who went missing.'

'What do you think happened?' Tamsin said. 'Honestly?'

'I used to think she'd run away, but now, well, I think Joe had something to do with it,' Mel said.

Tamsin nodded. 'He targeted her because she was unhappy at home. And that was my fault.'

'Come back to the studio and sit down,' Mel said, taking Tamsin's hand.

They sat in silence in the studio, looking out on to the street. The police were in the woods now. Mel could see a line of fluorescent jackets at the edge.

Mel thought of Luke, with Lily at the playground. He wouldn't know about the search.

She thought of what Tamsin had just said about her ex, how she wished she'd told the police about their unhappy relationship at the time. She felt a stab of worry. She should have told the police about the notes to Luke. And the kiss in the pool house. A tear ran down her cheek and she wiped it away quickly.

Tamsin was staring down at the woods. 'What if they find her?' she whispered.

'Gabbie?' Mel asked.

'No, Erin. What if she's still down there, in the wood?'

'She's not there,' Mel said. 'They searched at the time.'

'They could have missed something.'

'They're looking for Gabbie.' Mel thought once again of Luke, of the police. She should have told them everything.

'You know, sometimes I still think I hear Erin at night, crying out for me. I go all the way down to her room, but she's never there. She still haunts me.'

'I'm sorry,' Mel said, her words muffled.

Tamsin turned her head sharply to look at her. 'Why are you crying, Mel?'

Mel felt a wave of emotion wash over her as she thought of Gabbie, of Erin, of Luke. She cried harder, wiping the tears away with the back of her hand.

'I'm sorry if I upset you,' Tamsin said, squeezing her tear-stained hand. 'You've always been there for me. I forget sometimes that you lost a friend, too. Erin and now Gabbie. Two friends.'

'It's not that,' Mel said. She felt the need to unburden herself. Lately it felt like she was always making mistakes.

'What is it?'

'It's Luke. I didn't tell the police everything about Luke. The night of the party Gabbie kissed him, in the pool house. And Gabbie might have been blackmailing him. She'd been sending him notes, saying she knew who he was.'

Tamsin frowned. 'What does that mean?'

Mel sighed. She'd started now; she might as well tell the whole story. 'He's Joe's son.'

'What?' Tamsin ran her hand through her hair. 'I had forgotten Joe had a son. He often talked about him, that was one of the reasons I trusted him so much with Erin.'

'Of course. You weren't to know what he was really like.'

'So Luke must have been living with Joe when Erin went missing?'

'Yes, they lived three miles away, in Burton. He was only five years old. After she went missing, he moved away with his mother.'

'But you haven't told the police any of this?'

'No, but I should have, shouldn't I?'

Tamsin nodded seriously. 'Of course you should have. If Luke has nothing to hide, then it won't be a problem. But if he did have something to do with Gabbie's disappearance, then time is of the essence.'

'I'm sure he didn't,' Mel said shakily. 'But I'll go and tell the police everything. I know I have to. I'll go now.'

THIRTY-NINE

When Mel walked over to Gabbie's house, she saw that a lot of the press had moved to the woods, trying to film as much of the search as possible. The reporter who remained by one of the vans no longer seemed interested in talking to Mel. Someone else must have obligingly supplied them with their interview. There was a fizzing tension in the air among the police and the remaining press, and Mel knew it was because they were expecting something. They thought that there would soon be a body.

Mel approached a police officer standing near the house. She stumbled over her words, as she told him that she'd remembered something she hadn't told the police and she needed to talk to them again. She was sure he would know she was lying, that she had chosen not to tell them and was now coming clean.

The officer took her details and then went to get a colleague from inside. He was gone a while, and Mel had a huge desire to run back home, curl up under the covers and pretend none of this was happening. What if she was about to drop Luke in it?

A police detective came out, and introduced himself.

'Can we talk somewhere private?' Mel asked, not wanting

to have the conversation in her own house, in case Luke interrupted them.

'I'll take you to the station,' the detective said. 'Lots of privacy there.' Mel froze, remembering being interviewed there as a child – the cold sterile room in the police station, the adult faces staring down at her.

'OK,' she said meekly, and followed the detective to the car. As she climbed inside, a reporter took a photo and Mel worried about how quickly it would be put online. She glanced up at Tamsin's house and saw her watching from her window.

At the station, she was led to an interview room.

'So,' the detective said. 'You have something else you wanted to tell us?'

'Yes, I – well, I forgot to mention something when you first spoke to me. I was a bit overwhelmed then. I wasn't thinking straight.'

The detective nodded for her to continue.

'The last time I saw Gabbie wasn't at the party. I saw her in the pool house after the party.'

'Right. And what happened there?'

'I went to look for her when she was upset after her argument with Stuart, but I couldn't find her. Then I heard voices from the pool house.'

'She was with someone?'

'Yes,' Mel hesitated, feeling like she was on the edge of a precipice, about to jump. 'She was with my husband, Luke.' She took a deep breath. 'They were talking and... and then she kissed him.'

The detective remained expressionless. 'OK. What happened next?'

'Nothing,' Mel said, confused. 'I had to go. The babysitter was finishing up. I went back to Tamsin's house to see my daughter, Lily.'

'Did you see them leaving the pool house?'

'No.'

'And where were you the rest of the night?'

'I slept at Tamsin's house. On the first floor. With Lily.'

'And can anyone vouch for that?'

Mel felt a rising panic. It hadn't occurred to her that the police might suspect her, that they'd see the kiss as a motive for her hurting Gabbie. 'Well, no. I mean, the babysitter saw me come back. But I was on my own overnight.'

'And Luke. Where was he?'

'He slept at our cottage that night.'

'On his own?'

'Yes.' Mel thought of how he hadn't been at home when she'd got back in the morning, how he'd been out in his van. She didn't know for certain that he'd slept at the cottage.

The police detective went over the questions again, asking her more details about exactly what she'd seen between Gabbie and Luke, how she'd reacted, how she'd felt towards Gabbie.

'And why didn't you tell us this before?' the detective asked.

'I just... didn't think of it at the time.'

'You forgot? Didn't you think it would be relevant? It's the last sighting of Gabbie. Were you protecting your husband?'

Mel didn't know what to say.

The detective frowned. 'You should have told us straight away. Is there anything else you need to tell us?'

Mel sighed and picked at her cuticles. 'Actually, there is. I only found this out recently, but I think Gabbie may have been blackmailing Luke.'

The interview went on and on, with the detective asking her question after question. By the end of it, Mel's head hurt and she desperately wanted to get home.

'I'm going to need to see the notes that Gabbie sent to Luke,' the detective said, finally. 'I can come with you now to get them. And then we're going to interview your husband at the station.'

· · ·

Two police officers accompanied Mel home, steering the car past the media vans that lined the street, before pulling up in front of Mel's cottage.

When Mel came through the door with the two officers, Luke's face paled.

'Is everything alright? Have the police found something?' he asked Mel.

Mel could barely look at him. 'I need to show them something,' she said.

'What?' Luke asked, baffled.

One of the officers turned to Luke. 'And we'd like to talk to you at the station. We need more details about your relationship with Gabbie.'

Luke shot Mel a look. *What have you said to them?* his eyes silently asked.

FORTY

Luke wasn't back until the evening, long after Mel had put Lily to bed. As the hours had ticked on, she'd been worried that he wasn't coming back at all, that the police had arrested him.

When Luke finally came home, Mel was sitting at the kitchen table alone with a glass of wine. Angela had gone out somewhere on her motorbike, saying she was meeting up with an old friend from the village. Mel had promised herself she wasn't going to drink today, but she'd given in and opened a bottle as soon as Lily was asleep. It had been a long day. It felt like their trip to the duck pond with Lily had been a lifetime ago, but it had only been that morning.

Luke looked weary as he walked through the door.

'Are you OK?' she asked.

'I've been better. You could have told me you were going to tell the police all that. You could have warned me.'

'I'm sorry. I just... well, I started to feel guilty about not telling the police in the first place.'

Luke frowned. 'I should have been the one to tell them. You've made me look suspicious.'

'Why didn't you tell them?' she asked.

Luke shrugged. 'The same reason as you, I suppose. I was on my own that evening, at the cottage. I can't prove where I was. I was worried they'd think I had something to do with Gabbie's disappearance.'

Mel looked at her husband. She needed to know the truth. 'How long had Gabbie known you were Joe's son? Is that what the notes she sent you were about?'

Luke nodded. 'Yeah. She found out soon after we moved in. I'd always wanted to know more about my father, and when she gave that interview on TV, after the memorial, I thought she might be able to tell me more about Joe. I'd found out all I could from you when we first met, but I thought Gabbie might have some missing pieces of the puzzle. I went round to see her the next day while you were at the supermarket with Lily and Stuart was at work. I told her I was worried about the effect of Erin's disappearance on you and asked her lots of questions. To be honest, she wasn't particularly helpful. She just said the same thing you'd told me about Joe following you all. I thought I might get more out of her, that she might have seen something different, but she hadn't.'

'And she figured out you were Joe's son? Because of all the questions?'

'Yeah, although she didn't tell me she'd worked it out. Not at first. She sent me those notes anonymously. The first one appeared when you were out, on your first day of school. It said *"You don't belong here."* I didn't think it was referring to me specifically then, I thought it was just some snob on the street targeting both of us. I tore it down from the door and meant to put it in the bin, but it blew away. Then my phone rang and I got distracted and went inside and forgot to go back and find it.'

'I saw it that afternoon,' Mel said. 'Between the flowerpots.'

'I didn't tell you about it because I thought it would upset you. I thought it was aimed at both of us, and I knew how happy you were to be back on the street. I didn't want the note to ruin that for you.'

'It did upset me,' Mel said, remembering how the note had unsettled her. 'I thought it was meant for me.'

'The second note came a few days later, again while you were at school. This time it was clear it was for me. Whoever sent it knew I was Joe's son and I was worried they would tell you. I realised Gabbie had sent it when I was round her house doing some work and I saw the shopping list she'd left on the kitchen counter. I recognised the writing and confronted her.'

'What did she say?'

'That she'd remembered that Joe had a son about my age and she'd put two and two together. She was angry with me for lying to you. She said I was just like my father, a liar, and she wanted me to tell you the truth. I explained that I hadn't seen my father since I was five and that if I told you, you might not forgive me. I could lose you and Lily. She relented a bit. At first she said she wouldn't tell you, but later she wavered, saying that a good friend would tell you. It felt like a threat.'

'She was manipulating you,' Mel said. She thought of all the times she'd seen Gabbie before she'd disappeared. They'd got drunk and ridden the horses, they'd chatted in the pool house. But not once had Gabbie given any indication that Luke might be hiding something from Mel. Instead she'd used the knowledge she had to control him.

'Yeah, I suppose so,' Luke said. 'I felt under a lot of pressure to be at her beck and call, in case she told you the truth. Even the night of the party. That was why I went with her to the pool house. She asked me to look at something that needed fixing and I was worried what she would do if I said no. So I went along. She'd always been a bit flirty with me, but I'd managed to make it clear that I wasn't interested. But she was worse than usual that evening. By the time we were at the pool house she had made up her mind to leave Stuart. I thought that was the right thing to do and I said so. But she thought I was coming on to her. She was so drunk, and then she kissed me. I'm sorry I couldn't explain properly before. I shouldn't have let it get to that point.'

'How did you feel after she kissed you?' Mel had a sinking feeling in her chest. If Gabbie had been threatening to tell her Luke's secret, then he had a reason for wanting her out of the picture. And the opportunity, as he was alone with her. She'd never seen either of them leaving the pool house.

'I felt angry, irritated, confused. Honestly, it happened in an instant. The next day, when we thought she'd left Stuart and the street, I was relieved. I wanted her out of my hair.'

'I see.' Had he just wanted that, or had he been willing to do something about it?

'And when Stuart asked me to do lots of work for him, I didn't feel I could say no either. I was sure Gabbie would have told him who I was. And I knew how the whole road felt about my father. You hated him too. I thought you would split up with me if you found out. So I did anything Stuart said. All the little odd jobs for him.'

Mel thought of how often Luke had been round at Stuart's house, how little time he'd had for her or Lily. He'd been scared that Stuart would reveal his secret.

Stuart had always needed work doing, even the morning after his wife had gone missing. Mel shivered. Something must have happened to Gabbie that night. And if someone had hurt her, they would have had to clear up the evidence and hide her body. The police were zoning in on Stuart. Was it a coincidence that Stuart had asked Luke to unblock a drain by the pool house the next morning? Had Luke inadvertently been helping him cover up her murder?

FORTY-ONE

When Mel woke up in the morning her eyes were puffy and her head ached. She'd slept fitfully, everything that had happened the day before playing over and over in her mind. When Luke had tried to cuddle her in the night, she'd rolled away, wanting her own space. The things he had kept from her had spun through her head: the fact that Joe was his father, Gabbie threatening that she'd tell Mel. If she hadn't overheard him talking to Joe by the hut, she still wouldn't know anything. She wondered if he'd ever have told her.

While everyone was still asleep and the house was silent, Mel got up and went down to the kitchen to make herself a cup of tea. She was so behind on her lesson planning and marking that she felt she should use this time alone to get on with it. It was a welcome distraction from her thoughts.

She managed forty-five minutes of marking before Lily woke up and started crying. Luke brought her downstairs and they all had breakfast together.

'Have you got work today?' Mel said to Luke.

He shook his head. 'It's Sunday. I've kept it clear. I haven't got anything unless there's an emergency call-out.'

They heard a car on the street and Mel automatically got up and went to the window. A media van. No doubt there would be more. The police were going to continue the search of the area today. Mel closed the curtains. She didn't want to be there when that happened. She wanted to get away from it all.

'Let's go out somewhere today, take Lily somewhere fun,' she said.

'Good idea,' Luke said, putting another slice of bread into the toaster. 'Let's make the most of the weekend.'

'There's a children's farm about ten miles away. It's got a tractor ride, a maze, and kids can feed some of the animals.'

'Sounds perfect,' Luke said.

Mel felt a combination of guilt and relief as they drove past the police cars and media vans and out of Laurel Street. She felt bad about being away from Tamsin and Deena in case they needed her, but she'd had to get away from the street. Angela had felt the same, and she was now sitting in the back of the car with Lily, chatting to her and pointing at things out of the window. Mel hadn't been sure if she really wanted her mother to come with them, but she was helping to relieve the tense atmosphere between her and Luke. Mel knew she'd have to work on the trust in her marriage if it was going to be a success. Ultimately she knew Luke was a good guy, but he'd lied to her about so many things. She hoped there wasn't anything else he was keeping from her.

At the farm, Lily was in her element. She loved feeding the animals, particularly the goats, and she laughed as their wet tongues ran over her hand to get the food. It felt good to be out in the fresh air, away from home. Mel knew that the search around Laurel Street would be progressing, but she stopped herself from checking the news until they got back in the car to make their way home. There was nothing new from the police, but public interest in the case had really picked up, and the online news articles had become more detailed, with maps of Laurel Street and profiles of Gabbie and Stuart. Social media was alive with theories about what had happened.

Mel kept scanning through account after account. And then she saw it. The picture of her being transported away in the police car to be interviewed. She remembered the camera in her face. The picture online was grainy and she could see why it hadn't been used in the main news articles. But someone must have published it somewhere, because now there was a TikTok video entitled *Who is Gabbie's 'friend' Mel?* Mel swallowed back bile as she watched the video. A teenager, a self-styled amateur detective, was asking questions about her, pointing the finger. *Who is Mel?* he asked. *Is it a coincidence both her friends have gone missing? Erin went missing twenty-five years ago when she was playing with Mel and Gabbie. Then when Mel moves back to Laurel Street, Gabbie goes missing too. If I was the police, I'd be taking a good look at Mel...*

'Are you OK?' Luke asked, interrupting her thoughts. 'Any updates on Gabbie?'

'I'm fine,' Mel replied, feeling faint. 'It doesn't look like the police have found anything today. There's nothing on the news.'

They were back late, and after putting Lily to bed then eating dinner, they settled down to watch the news with Angela. Gabbie's disappearance was the headline story, and Mel felt her whole body tense up as she watched the footage of the search taking place around Laurel Street.

Police have spent today searching around the location where Gabrielle Jacobs was last seen. She disappeared two weeks ago and is believed to have been carrying a pale blue rucksack. One of the things concerning locals is the similarity between this case and the case of Erin Radley, a girl who went missing in the same area twenty-five years ago. Just a month ago Gabrielle herself gave an interview about Erin's disappearance.

The studio cut to a clip of Gabbie's interview and Mel watched with her hand over her mouth as Gabbie talked about Erin, her eyebrows raised and her expression sorrowful, but still very much alive. Mel felt a tear running down her cheek, and brushed it away.

Mel thought of Tamsin, watching this alone, remembering Erin.

The report went back to the studio.

Neighbours have become increasingly concerned about missing Gabrielle. We interviewed some today.

It cut back to their street, outside Gabbie's house, and an interview with Mr and Mrs Dawson, the parents of Freya in Mel's class. They said how sad the whole thing was, and how Gabbie had always seemed like a happy member of the community.

The segment finished and moved on to tensions in the Middle East, and Mel switched the television off.

'I'm nipping over to see Tamsin,' she announced. 'She's going to be so upset that they've brought Erin up again.'

'You were with her most of the day yesterday,' Luke said, unable to keep the frustration out of his voice.

'She needed me,' Mel said. 'I'm worried about her.' Tamsin had seemed so erratic and on edge yesterday.

'It's late, after ten,' Luke said. 'Are you sure she'll appreciate it? She might not have even seen the broadcast.'

'I just need to check she's alright,' Mel insisted.

When she arrived at Tamsin's house, Mel noticed that there was one police car still parked outside Gabbie's, but the rest were gone. She supposed they'd be back in the morning, along with the media. Luckily, Mel would be far away from it all, at school.

There was no answer when Mel pressed the buzzer, so she stepped back a bit and looked up at the house. The light was on in the top-floor art studio, and she could see Tamsin's shadow at the window. Mel waved, but Tamsin didn't see her – she was too fixated on Gabbie's house across the street. Mel noticed there was also a light on in one of the lower rooms of Tamsin's mansion. Erin's room. Mel remembered what Tamsin had said about hearing cries in the night, how she would go down to Erin's room, thinking her daughter was crying out for her.

Mel pressed the buzzer again, and it was a moment before Tamsin answered.

'Yes?'

'It's me, Mel. I wanted to check how you were.'

'Oh, Mel. I'm OK. Why don't you come up?'

Once she got upstairs, Mel saw that Tamsin was already ready for bed, in a long grey nightdress which looked like it had seen better days. Her long auburn hair lay loose over her shoulders.

'I'm so sorry. I didn't mean to disturb you.'

'It's alright. I was about to go to bed. But I doubt I'll sleep. I haven't slept properly for weeks.' Tamsin laughed bitterly. 'No, that's not true. I haven't slept properly since Erin disappeared.'

'I won't stay long. I just wanted to check in on you. Did you see the BBC news?'

Tamsin nodded.

'I thought it might have upset you, them bringing up Erin like that.'

'I guess it's good they remember at all, that someone's still thinking about her. I've been trying to get her case back on the TV for years. But no one really cares after all this time. It's taken Gabbie disappearing for them to take an interest.'

'Yeah. They love to draw links between cases,' Mel said. 'Look for patterns that aren't there.' She thought of the TikTok video she'd seen earlier which had suggested Mel herself had been involved in Gabbie's disappearance. She felt herself tense. Surely no one would believe that she had something to do with it?

'Oh, I think there probably is a link,' Tamsin said. 'Don't you?'

Mel put her head in her hands, trying to think. Joe had been around at the time of both disappearances and she'd been sure he had been connected to both. But recently her certainty had started to fade, and she didn't know anymore. And then there was Stuart, who had never known Erin, but had wanted his wife out of the picture to be with Roz.

'But what about Stuart?' she asked.

'I've been thinking about this all day, going over everything again and again in my mind. I'm not so convinced it's him anymore. Yes, he's been a complete bastard to Gabbie. But I don't think he's stupid enough to kill his own wife. He would have known he'd be the first person the police would look at.'

'Right,' Mel said.

'He is horrible, though. Look at him down there.' Tamsin walked across her studio and pointed out of the window. 'Lying on his sofa watching TV without a care in the world. But just because he didn't care about her at all, doesn't mean he killed her. I think the BBC is right – Gabbie's disappearance is linked to Erin's. After all, the two of them were such firm friends. With you as well, of course.'

Mel shifted uncomfortably. 'Yeah. I can hardly believe what's happened. I miss them both.'

'I bet you do. Very difficult to lose two friends. Very unlucky.' Mel thought she heard an edge to Tamsin's voice and she stepped back a bit, wondering if she'd seen anything about Mel online.

'I'm sure it's linked,' Tamsin continued. 'The last few days I've been sleeping downstairs in Erin's room. I want to feel more connected to her. I've been feeling her presence more and more. It's like she's inside me these days, desperate to tell me something.'

'Like what?' Mel said, concerned. It sounded like Tamsin was losing her grip on reality.

'I don't know. I've spoken to the police, told them I think the two disappearances are connected. Maybe Gabbie found out what really happened to Erin and someone wanted to keep her quiet.'

Mel put her hand gently on Tamsin's arm. 'What did the police say?'

'They said they'd look into it. They're going to have another look at the files from Erin's case.'

Mel clasped her hands together, feeling faint. She didn't want the police to start looking into Erin's disappearance again. There were some things only she and Gabbie knew about the night Erin disappeared. Things they'd agreed never to tell the police.

FORTY-TWO

Mel was exhausted the next day at school, but she was relieved to be away from the tension in Laurel Street. In her breaks she kept checking the news on her phone for updates about Gabbie. There wasn't any new information, just speculation on Twitter and TikTok. Mel didn't have time to go too far down the rabbit hole of social media, but she could see that all the neighbours on the street were the subject of gossip: her, Tamsin, even Gabbie's parents. Everyone seemed to want to 'solve' the case. Mel tried to ignore the gossip and focus on the legitimate news sites. She checked every newspaper site again and again. *Refresh. Refresh. Refresh.*

But there was no update on the police search.

She thought back to her fight with Luke on Friday night. She'd been angry with him for lying about Joe being his father. So much had happened since then.

Remembering the plates and glasses that had been smashed in their kitchen, she felt a rush of guilt. She needed to make things up to him. After school, she picked Lily up and drove over to the shopping centre. As she browsed the displays of crockery, she told herself it was normal for couples to fight, normal even for a few plates to get smashed. If she replaced them with a brand-new set, then that could be her way of saying sorry.

She found some blue and white plates with a sale label on them and picked up the nearest one and inspected it. She quite liked the design, and she decided to buy them. She hadn't meant to smash the plates and glasses; she'd just lost her temper and hit out at the nearest available target. She'd had too much to drink after she'd found out that Joe was Luke's father and she'd got out of control. She'd been so drunk that she'd fallen and bruised her arm. She swallowed down the guilty feelings. It was already in the past. And she always tried to live in the present. There was no point dwelling on things she couldn't change.

When Mel got home, Luke was cooking pasta for everyone in the kitchen.

'You're back late,' he said, without turning round.

'I bought these,' Mel said, putting down a heavy box of plates beside him. 'There's more in the car. I bought the whole set.'

'Oh,' Luke said, turning now and studying the box. 'Thank you. They're a nice design. Good choice.'

'Thanks. I'm sorry I smashed them in the first place.'

'It's OK,' he said, although Mel wasn't really sure he meant it.

After Mel had put Lily to bed, Luke served up the dinner and Mel sat down beside her mother.

'What's going on with the police?' Angela asked, as they tucked into their spaghetti.

'They're still searching the local area. They're in the woods.'

Mel shivered as she remembered them searching for Erin so many years ago.

Luke's phone rang and he frowned as he looked at the number, then went out of the room to answer it. He shut the door of the kitchen behind him. Mel strained her ears to hear his side of the conversation, but she couldn't make anything out.

'Do you know why they're searching the woods?' her mother whispered anxiously.

'They found one of Gabbie's earrings, and now they think she never left the area that night.'

'They don't think it's anything to do with Joe, do they? After what you said to them?'

Mel looked towards the door through which Luke had just left. They hadn't talked about Joe since their discussion at the pub, and Mel wasn't sure if Joe had moved out of the storage hut like Luke had asked him to.

'I don't know,' Mel said.

'I hope they don't try and pin it on him again,' Angela said. 'That wouldn't be right. He didn't deserve what the media put him through when Erin disappeared.'

Mel sighed. 'Even if he didn't hurt Erin, he was a man in his thirties who befriended a ten-year-old girl. Can't you see that's wrong?'

Angela shook her head. 'I knew him well back then. He was only trying to help. Do you really think it's the right thing to do, to stop him seeing his son and his grandchild?'

'Yes, Mum. I do,' Mel said. But she wasn't sure of anything anymore. Nothing was what it seemed.

Luke came back into the room, his face pale, his phone in his hand.

'I'm so sorry, Mel. That was my dad. He wants to come round and say goodbye. Right now. We asked him to leave so he's leaving. He'll be round any minute.'

Mel and Angela looked at each other. Why was Joe

suddenly upping and leaving when the police were searching the woods? Did he have something to hide? 'They don't think he hurt Gabbie, do they?' Mel asked quickly.

'No, nothing like that. He just thinks it's time to go. He knows we don't want him here, that he can't be a part of our family.'

'I don't think you should push him away,' Angela said. 'He's your flesh and blood.'

They were interrupted by the doorbell, and Luke and Mel went to answer it.

Joe was at the door, as dishevelled as ever, his grey hair all over the place.

'Hi,' he said politely. 'Can I come in?'

Luke hesitated a moment and Joe continued. 'I need to speak to you, Luke. And Mel. And it might take a while. It's time to tell the truth. I want to tell you what really happened to Erin.'

FORTY-THREE

'What?' Luke said, staring at his father. 'You know what happened to Erin?'

Mel's brain was racing, realisation dawning. What everyone had suspected all along was true. Joe was responsible for Erin's disappearance. Her heart pounded and she wiped her sweaty palms on her jeans.

'Can I come in?' Joe repeated. 'I need to explain.'

'OK,' Luke said, looking at Mel and holding the door open. 'Come in.' Joe smelt damp and earthy, like he hadn't showered for days. Luke led him through to the kitchen, and Mel followed behind nervously. Why did Luke think it was a good idea to let Joe into the house? She was glad Lily was safe upstairs, away from him.

Angela was finishing off her dinner in the kitchen and she looked up in surprise at Joe. 'What are you doing here?'

'I need to speak to Luke and Mel,' he said. 'In private.'

She nodded, and squeezed his shoulder as she walked by. 'I've told them I think you should have access to Lily,' she said.

He nodded, and waited for her to leave. Mel could see tears in his eyes.

Joe sat down heavily on one of the kitchen chairs, and Mel and Luke sat opposite him.

'This story is just for the two of you,' Joe began. 'You're my only family, even if you don't want me to be part of yours.'

'What's going on, Dad?' Luke asked.

'I'm going to the police after I leave here,' Joe said. 'I'm going to tell them what really happened to Erin. I should have done it a long time ago.'

Mel put her hands to her temples, her mind crowded with flashbacks. Of her. Of Gabbie. Of Erin. The laughter, then the screams, then finally the silence.

'OK, Dad,' Luke said. 'Go on.'

'OK. Well, first I need to explain my relationship with Erin. We were friends, her and I. And I know what you're thinking. That a friendship between a grown man and a child isn't appropriate.' He met Mel's eyes and then continued. 'But Erin needed me. She was desperately unhappy. She talked about running away all the time. And I listened. The thing was, I thought she had a point. Her stepdad hit her. Did you know that, Mel?'

Mel nodded. 'I can see that now, but I didn't realise it at the time. When I was a kid, I saw bruises on her arms and her wrists. And she hated her stepfather, she was always talking about running away. But I was ten and back then I didn't put two and two together.' Mel felt tears form in her eyes. She'd been far too young to understand.

'I thought I could help her,' Joe continued. 'I was just trying to figure out how to do it. I knew I needed to speak to social services but I wasn't sure if the abuse was bad enough, or if he'd be able to talk his way out of it. I didn't want to report it and then have her left with parents who were angry with her for telling someone. So I was still working out what to do. In the meantime I tried to look out for her. I followed her. And you and Gabbie too, Mel.'

'I remember,' Mel said softly.

'So that's the context. And now on to the night of the New Year's Eve party. I want you to know what really happened.'

Mel gripped the table so hard her knuckles turned white. She didn't feel ready to hear the truth, to learn what happened to Erin. Luke reached for her hand and squeezed it.

'I'd heard the three of you planning the party, so I knew all the details. You were going to have a midnight feast in the woods, sing and dance, then go home. I didn't think it was a good idea, but I could hardly stop you. But I could watch over you instead. The thing I didn't realise was that Erin was planning to run away that night, that she'd packed a bag.'

Mel remembered the tiny rucksack Erin had packed. It contained one set of spare clothes and some of her toys. That was all. She'd thought Erin was crazy for wanting to run away from her big house, full of the toys she'd got for Christmas. She'd thought Erin was just saying she would run away for attention.

'So the night she disappeared, I watched you all in the woods. When I heard Erin tell you she was going to run away, I started to worry. She'd told me her plans so many times. I knew she'd walk through the woods towards the farm, try and find shelter there. She had no idea what she was doing, or what danger she'd be in out there on her own. I was concerned about her. I thought I needed to find someone, tell them. So I started walking back to Laurel Street. I was going to tell your grandmother, Mel, ask her advice. I was halfway back when I heard screaming.'

Joe met Mel's eyes, his bright blue eyes intense. Mel felt as if she might throw up. She remembered the screams echoing round the woods.

'I was ten minutes away by then, but I ran back. I wasn't long, but when I came back Erin was lying on the floor, completely still. She wasn't breathing. I performed mouth-to-mouth, chest compressions. I think I must have broken one of her ribs doing them. But nothing I did brought her back. She was dead.'

'She was dead?' Mel whispered. It couldn't be true. Erin couldn't have died that night. It didn't make any sense. She had disappeared. There hadn't been a body in the woods. The police had searched and searched.

'Yeah,' Joe said simply, a tear running down his cheek. 'She was already dead.'

A surge of emotion rose up in Mel. Finally she knew for certain. Any hope she had left was extinguished. She couldn't hold it together anymore. She felt her stomach swirl and shift, and vomit rise up in her throat. She ran to the toilet, gripped the seat with one hand, held back her hair with the other and let everything come out of her.

Luke appeared behind her, helping her hold back her hair.

'Are you alright?' he asked.

'I don't know,' Mel said. She could hardly process what Joe had just said. Erin had been dead all these years.

'It must be a big shock,' Luke said, stroking her hair.

Mel nodded mutely.

'I think he has more to say,' Luke said. 'We need to hear him out.' Luke led Mel back through to the kitchen, and she sat down reluctantly. She didn't think she could bear to hear any more.

Joe was at the table, wiping tears from his eyes.

'Dad,' Luke said gently. 'What happened next? Where's her body?'

'I was devastated,' Joe said. 'I loved her almost like my own child. I had promised to protect her. And I had failed. I was holding her tiny body in my arms and I didn't know what to do.'

They waited as Joe composed himself and then continued. 'I already knew that people's opinions of me had begun to change. People had started to comment on the amount of time I spent with Erin. The previous week, a neighbour had told me to stay away from her, and there were rumours that I might be the man flashing at children in the woods. I was about to carry Erin back home to Tamsin and explain how I'd found her. But then I realised that no one would believe that I'd found her dead. They'd think I'd killed her.'

'What did you do?' Mel asked. She felt numb, unable to take in everything that had been said.

'I carried her through the woods into the village, and buried her in the graveyard. There was a recent grave in the church-yard, dug just before Christmas. A distant relative of Tamsin's had been buried there. The grave hadn't settled yet and the soil was still in a mound on top, without a headstone. So I dug until I hit the coffin, then wrapped Erin in my coat and buried her on top of it, with her rucksack.' Joe fought back tears. 'I thought that way, if Tamsin was visiting the grave of her relative, then she'd be close to Erin too. I didn't know that she'd choose to hold a memorial at that church every year. That she'd be so close to Erin, but not know she was there.'

'How could you do that? What about Tamsin?' Luke asked. 'She hasn't known if her daughter was dead or alive.'

'I know,' Joe said sadly. 'I didn't mean to hurt her. A part of me regretted it over the years, wished I had just taken her to Tamsin that night. Maybe the police would have believed me when I said I found her. I don't know.'

'You committed another crime instead. By burying the body.'

Joe put his head in his hands. 'I know. But I really wasn't thinking straight. I was devastated by Erin's death. I couldn't believe she was gone. And I was so worried about being sent to prison for murder. I just did what I could to protect myself. Even the next day, I questioned myself. I nearly went to the police and confessed. But by that point people were already accusing me. And I knew that if I confessed to burying her body... well, they'd only draw one conclusion, wouldn't they? I had to stick to the plan.'

'You didn't have to, Dad. You could have told the truth.'

Joe shook his head. 'No, I couldn't. Not back then. I had my own family to think of. You, Luke. I didn't want to lose you.'

'But you lost me anyway.'

'I did,' Joe said. 'Your mother believed every bad thing the papers said about me. Used it as an excuse to take you away to Scotland. But now there's nothing left to lose. You don't want to have a relationship with me, and you won't let me see Lily. Now it's time for me to confess to my part in what happened to Erin. When I leave here, I'll go and tell the police where her body is.' He looked at Mel, and then at Luke. 'It just seems like the right thing to do.'

FORTY-FOUR

Mel stared at Joe, memories flooding back into her mind, all the things she had blocked out for so many years. The dark woods, her hands tingling with the freezing cold, the bag of chocolate she'd bought for the midnight feast rustling. Erin there with her little backpack, ready to run away from her parents.

They'd gorged themselves on crisps, chocolate and sweets, then talked and laughed and told ghost stories. Erin had told the others how she hated her mum and stepdad, how awful her life was, how her only option was to run away. It made Mel furious. Erin didn't know how lucky she was. She couldn't leave her and Gabbie.

But Erin was determined.

'I'm leaving,' she said again, after they'd packed away the remaining food. 'Tonight. I'll say goodbye to you here.'

'Don't be silly,' Gabbie replied.

'I'm not silly!' Erin said. 'You have no idea what my life's like. You'd leave too if you were me.'

'But we'll miss you.' Gabbie pulled Erin back by the strap of her rucksack.

'Come on, you can't leave us,' Mel implored, taking the other strap.

Erin tried to run, but they pulled her back by her backpack until suddenly Mel got bored and let go, and Erin fell face down into the dirt.

Mel saw her chance, and jumped on top of her. 'Hold her down,' she shouted at Gabbie. 'Don't let her go.' They giggled.

Mel sat on her head, and Gabbie sat on her back, as Erin wriggled and fidgeted beneath them.

'You can't leave us,' Mel said. 'Or you'll be punished.' It had just been a game, a joke. Gabbie and Mel had both laughed.

Erin continued to fidget, her head moving slightly underneath Mel. But she didn't say anything, and Mel would not let her up. For once she had the upper hand over her friend. She was in control.

But then Erin had stopped moving. And Mel and Gabbie hadn't noticed immediately, because they were so busy laughing at their attempts to keep Erin from running away.

'She's not moving,' Gabbie said after a while.

'She's just pretending,' Mel said, not giving up her position on Erin's head. 'As soon as we get off her, she'll make a run for it.'

'Erin?' Gabbie said tentatively.

Erin didn't respond.

'Why's she not replying?'

'She's just pretending!' Mel insisted. But something was taking her over now, some kind of primal fear. She looked down at Erin's head below her, and saw her face was still pressed into the dirt, not turned to the side as she had thought.

'Erin?' she said, easing herself off her head.

'Don't get off her, she'll get away!' Gabbie shouted, but she sounded unsure, as if she didn't really think that anymore.

'She's not moving,' Mel whispered.

She moved Erin's head to the side. She could see her lips

and nose were covered with mud. Her face was scraped from where she'd tried to move it to the side.

'I don't think she's breathing,' Mel said.

Gabbie knelt down beside her. 'What's wrong with her?'

'I don't know.' Mel was half-expecting Erin to open her eyes and say 'gotcha', but she didn't. A horrible feeling was developing in Mel's stomach, a whirring awfulness that she couldn't control.

She rolled Erin over and pointed her head towards the sky but it flopped back down to the side.

Then she noticed the spider, making its way up her hair and onto her face. Erin was terrified of spiders, but she still didn't move.

Gabbie started screaming, loud, hysterical screams.

'Calm down,' Mel said to her friend urgently. 'That's not helping.' She started shaking Erin. 'Wake up! Wake up!'

There was no response.

'Oh my god,' Gabbie cried. 'What's happened to her? What have we done?'

'We need to get help,' Mel said.

'We can't go to my mum,' Gabbie said immediately. 'She's at the party with Erin's mum. She'll kill me for being out in the woods at night.'

'We can go to mine,' Mel said, although her mother would be cross too, but more because Mel would be interrupting her drinking than because Mel was in the woods late at night.

They'd run off together as fast as they could, tripping and stumbling as if someone was chasing them. They didn't stop until they reached Mel's mother's house.

By the time they got there twenty minutes later, they were no longer really sure what had happened. It all felt like a dream, like they might have imagined the whole thing.

Mel's mother was passed out asleep on the sofa, one arm dangling over the edge.

'Mum! Mum!' Mel shook her awake.

'What?' her mother asked groggily.

'We were in the woods. Erin's hurt. She's not moving.' Mel's words came out in a rush.

Her mother rolled over, then sat up, frowning. She looked at her watch.

'It's the middle of the night,' she said. She took Mel in her arms and hugged her for a moment. She didn't seem to notice Mel was in her coat, or that Gabbie was standing beside her. 'You must have had a bad dream,' she said. 'Get back to bed.'

'It wasn't a dream,' Mel said desperately. 'We need help.'

'We were in the woods,' Gabbie whispered. 'Erin...'

'Gabbie?' Her mother noticed her for the first time, then looked from one to the other. 'What happened?' she asked.

'Erin wanted to run away, and we tried to stop her. We sat on her, and...' Gabbie looked at Mel for confirmation.

'We sat on her and after a while she wasn't moving anymore...'

'She just wouldn't move,' Gabbie said, getting hysterical now. 'She wouldn't move at all.'

Mel's mum stood up and tried to steady herself. She was still dressed, but now she put on her coat and boots.

'You stay here,' she said. 'I'll go down to the woods and look for her. Where was she when you left?'

'She was in the clearing,' Mel said.

It seemed like a lifetime before Mel's mother returned, but when she did she smiled at them softly.

'Is Erin alright?' Mel asked, desperately.

Her mother ran her hand through her hair. 'She's fine, Mel. She wasn't there when I got to the woods. I searched everywhere, but she wasn't there. She must have gone home.'

'Oh,' Mel said, suddenly feeling elated, like something

awful had nearly happened and she'd somehow avoided it. It was all fine. Erin had been fine. She must have just been pretending to be dead.

Her mother turned to Gabbie. 'You need to get back home,' she said. 'Run back now, as fast as you can. Get into your bed and go to sleep.'

When the morning had come and Erin was missing, Mel had assumed she had got up and run away, just like she'd said she would. But as the days went by, Erin didn't return like Mel and Gabbie expected. Nobody heard from her. They both remembered seeing Joe in the woods that night. They had told the police. So when the rumours started about Joe taking Erin, they made perfect sense. As the months passed, Mel's memory of that night had started to fade and become woolly at the edges. She could no longer remember the details. How long had they really sat on Erin for? Erin hadn't been there when her mother went back to the woods. Either she had run away or someone else had taken her. She'd started to think it must have been Joe. Mel hadn't thought her disappearance had anything to do with her or Gabbie. She'd been wrong.

FORTY-FIVE

Tuesday 7th February

The next day, Mel woke up with a hollow feeling in the pit of her stomach. She threw up as soon as she got up, but she dragged herself to school regardless. It was easier than being at home, where she had to face up to what she had done. It had been her and Gabbie who had killed Erin. And somehow she had managed to put what had happened completely out of her mind for years, not letting herself think about those moments in the woods before Erin went missing.

Her mother had told her that Erin must have run off, and it was so easy to believe because it was what she wanted to believe. But Gabbie and Mel had agreed not to mention to the police how they'd held Erin down. They had known what they'd done was wrong, and a part of them had felt guilty about it, even though they didn't think they had hurt her.

If Joe hadn't come along and chosen to bury her, then she didn't know what would have happened to them. Ten was the age of criminal responsibility; they could have been locked away.

How could she ever face Tamsin now? She had always felt guilty about leaving Erin in the woods, but now things were far worse. She was responsible. Mel and Gabbie had taken Erin's life.

At school, the other staff members had started to ask her about the case.

'Any update?' Mr Gresham said in the staffroom.

She shook her head 'no' and hurried off. But she knew that soon Erin would be headline news. Joe had confessed to burying Erin, but the news hadn't been released yet and Mel was dreading him being targeted by the media again, accused of being a murderer.

After lunch, her phone didn't stop ringing. She could hear it vibrating in her bag under her desk. Eventually, while her students sat down to do a maths worksheet, she checked it. She had ten missed calls from Tamsin and a text message.

> They've found Erin. Can you come over?

Mel blinked back tears. She couldn't face seeing Tamsin. Not now.

That evening, she watched the news with Luke.

The body of Erin Radley, a ten-year-old girl who went missing twenty-five years ago, has been found today.

Her mother reached for Mel's hand and gripped it tightly.

Mel's phone was ringing again on the table, its blue light illuminating the room, despite being on silent. She looked down. *Tamsin.* Again. She couldn't bring herself to answer it.

The news camera cut to an overhead shot of the church graveyard, a crime tent over one of the graves and a team in white around it. Mel felt tears rolling down her cheeks. All those years, Tamsin had spoken at the memorial, begging for anyone to come forward with more information, praying that Erin came back. She had been there all along, in the graveyard outside.

The news report continued.

A man has been arrested on suspicion of murder. It is thought he used to work as a maintenance man in the area.

'Mum was right about Dad,' Luke said softly. 'He wasn't a good man.'

'He didn't kill her though, did he?' Mel said. 'He told us she was already dead when he found her.'

'Do you really believe that?'

'Yes,' Mel said. 'I do.' She understood why he'd buried Erin. He'd been an easy target for the police and the media. If he'd taken her body back to Tamsin, he would almost certainly have been arrested for murder.

'I don't think he's telling the truth,' Luke said bitterly. 'He's been lying all these years.'

Mel frowned at Luke, her head pounding. She felt so guilty. It was her fault he believed his father had murdered Erin. She wanted to confess to him, to tell him the truth about what had happened. But if she did, then she'd have to go to the police. And if she was arrested and tried for her crime, she might go to prison. She'd miss out on Lily's childhood.

'I'm going to bed,' Luke said at last, getting up from the sofa. 'I need to sleep. A lot's happened today.' Mel got up and he hugged her tightly. 'Are you sure you're alright?' he asked.

'Yes,' Mel said, although she was anything but.

'It must be so awful for you. Knowing she's dead. But at least you've finally got closure.'

Mel nodded. She thought of Erin, who she had imagined doing a million different things as an adult, but whose life had ended at ten years old. And then she thought of Gabbie, imagined that perhaps she had run away, that she was living a new life with a new boyfriend. She prayed that Gabbie's ending would be different, more like the one in her imagination.

FORTY-SIX

That night Mel couldn't sleep. Memories of Erin flashed through her head: the two of them playing on the climbing frame in the school playground; her contagious laugh as she told a joke; Erin climbing a tree in the middle of the woods and pretending to be the figurehead of a ship. Mel could remember the feel of Erin's curly hair on her face when they put their heads together, her slightly sweaty smell, the softness of the cashmere jumpers Tamsin made her wear in winter.

Luke was lying in bed beside her but Mel had never felt so alone. Luke didn't know the real her, he didn't know she was responsible for Erin's death. And she felt that she didn't know herself anymore either. All these years and she had never realised it had been her fault. Mel got up and padded over to Lily's room, to be close to her daughter, the only person in the world who she knew loved her unconditionally.

Mel thought of Tamsin as she watched her daughter sleep, her chest gently rising and falling. Tamsin still had Erin's room set up exactly as it had been when she disappeared, as if she was waiting for her to return. But what would she do with it now? How would she face the fact that she wasn't coming back?

Mel looked guiltily at her phone, at all the messages from Tamsin. She knew she should call her, but she couldn't face it. Anything she said would be insincere. But she'd have to reply to her messages tomorrow. It was unbearably cruel to ignore her when the worst possible thing had happened to her.

Mel leant over into the cot and kissed Lily lightly on the cheek.

'Everything alright?' a voice said softly from the doorway.

Mel jumped and turned to see her mother.

'I feel awful about Erin,' Mel said. 'Joe's been arrested, but he said she was dead when he found her. Which means, well, Gabbie and I... well, we must have killed her.' Her voice was a whisper now. She didn't want Luke to wake up and overhear.

'Not on purpose,' her mother said, stroking her arm.

'I sat on her head. I didn't want her to leave. I felt so determined, so powerful. I thought I could stop her. We must have suffocated her.'

'You don't need to think about that now. I thought you'd forgotten.'

'I had forgotten, because I didn't realise it was important. I thought Joe had killed her, or that she'd run away.'

'So now you know,' her mother said calmly.

'I have to tell Tamsin. I have to confess. All these years she's longed for some kind of closure, to know what really happened. She still doesn't know. She'll think Joe did it. I have to tell her the truth. It wasn't a violent death. It was an accident.'

'You can't tell her,' Angela said.

'I have to.'

'Think about Lily. Think about your future. Ten is the age of criminal responsibility. You committed a crime.'

Mel frowned, a hazy memory sliding back into view. 'I remember you saying something like that before, about us being ten. You said you wished we were a year younger. You whispered it to yourself when you thought I wasn't listening.' She remembered her mother, her voice strained, looking into the mirror as she whispered it, after she'd come back from the woods that night. Mel had thought she'd been drunk. 'Did you know what we'd done?'

Angela sighed, reaching out and touching Mel's arm. 'I tried to hide it from you, to protect you and Gabbie.'

'What do you mean?'

'I told you that Erin wasn't there when I went back to the woods. But that wasn't true. When I got there, she was dead. Joe was already there. He was in tears. He'd tried to resuscitate her, but he hadn't succeeded. He'd picked her up to carry her back to Tamsin's to explain how he'd found her.'

'You stopped him?'

'Yes. I explained what had happened, what you and Gabbie had done. I trusted him. You see... he and I... for a while we were in a relationship. It was just a casual thing, really, but to be honest I should have chosen him over the deadbeat I was with at the time. We were both outsiders on Laurel Street, and he understood me. He was so kind, so thoughtful. I'd never met anyone who'd treated me so well.'

'Oh,' Mel said. She'd never guessed her mother had been seeing Joe. 'What did you tell him?'

'I told him it was a game gone wrong. That you and Gabbie and Erin had been playing and by mistake you'd suffocated her. He believed me. He'd seen you all playing together, he knew you wouldn't have done it on purpose. He thought we should go back and tell Tamsin it was an accident, explain exactly what had happened.'

'Why didn't you?'

'It wasn't an option. You and Gabbie were ten – the age of criminal responsibility. You could have been prosecuted. I didn't want you going to a Young Offender Institution. It felt like everything was my fault, like I shouldn't have let you out in those woods in the first place.'

'What did he say?'

'At first he still thought we should take Erin back to Tamsin. But I convinced him we couldn't. I told him that if he took her back to Tamsin then I wouldn't back his story. I wouldn't tell the police what you and Gabbie had told me about what really happened. And I'd ask you to keep quiet, too. If he went back to Laurel Street carrying Erin's body, then everyone would think he was a murderer, including the police. Erin was already dead. It was best for everyone for her body to be removed. It would be best for you and Gabbie. And best for him as well.'

Mel thought of Joe's confession the other night. He hadn't told her and Luke that he knew that Mel and Gabbie had killed Erin by accident. He had protected Mel. He must love Luke so much in order to do that. He was still taking the blame, trying to protect her and Luke and Lily from the fallout.

'How could you do that, Mum? How could you threaten him in that way?'

'Why do you think, Mel?' Her mum's voice was louder now, angry, and Mel was aware of Luke sleeping in the next room. 'I did it for you. I didn't want to hurt Joe. I think I may have even been falling in love with him. But you were more important to me, Mel. I had to protect you. I helped prepare you and Gabbie for speaking to the police, told you not to tell the police about you restraining Erin. You both agreed not to say anything.'

'You were protecting me?' Mel could hardly believe what she was hearing.

'Yes, Mel, that's exactly what I was doing. Because, despite what you say, I *am* a good mother. I do look out for you. If I hadn't told Joe to bury the body you would have ended up locked away.'

'You hid the truth all these years?'

'It was horrible for me. It tore me apart. I felt so guilty about Joe, especially when the whole of Laurel Street turned against him and the newspapers started to attack him. I felt sure they would find Erin's body and he'd be charged with murder any day. I couldn't cope with my role in it all. I ended up drinking more and more. And you know what happened next.'

'You lost me,' Mel said. 'You gave me to Granny to look after.'

Angela nodded. 'I'd got to the point where I couldn't do anything else. I couldn't look after you anymore. What you and Gabbie did took my whole life away from me. I gave up everything for you. And yet you were still so ungrateful. When I came back from Spain, you didn't even want me in your home.'

'I never realised you'd done all that for me,' Mel said. She felt tears prick her eyes. Her mother had loved her, in her own way.

'I know,' Angela said. 'I never wanted you to realise. I wanted you to live your life freely, without guilt. Instead I carried the guilt for you. But you can't ruin everything now. You can't tell Tamsin what really happened. You can't give yourself up. No one needs to know what you did. Not when I sacrificed everything for you.'

FORTY-SEVEN

Wednesday 8th February

Mel woke up early the next morning after a fitful sleep. She knew what she had to do. Despite everything her mother had said, she had to tell the truth. She'd been running from it for so many years, hiding what she'd done even from herself. She'd worked so hard to be a good granddaughter, a good wife, a good neighbour. But that wasn't enough. She would go straight to the police after school and tell them what had happened the night Erin disappeared.

As she drove to the nursery, her phone beeped with message after message. When she opened the street WhatsApp group a stream of conversation greeted her. Everyone had seen the news last night and knew that Erin's body had been found and that Joe had been arrested for murder. It confirmed what they had always believed.

Mel welled up as she thought of Joe locked up in a cell overnight, being interrogated by the police. She should be there as well as him. She should take her fair share of the blame.

A text message came through from Deena.

I think Joe took Gabbie too.

Mel swallowed. Things were already getting out of hand. She couldn't leave it until after school to go to the police. She had to go right now. She couldn't let Joe take the blame any longer. She dropped Lily off at nursery, said a tearful goodbye, called in sick to school and drove straight to the police station.

Three hours later, Mel was back at home. She'd been terrified at the station, worried the police would arrest her straight away and put her in a cell. But she knew confessing was the right thing to do.

The police had asked question after question, and Mel had answered them to the best of her ability. They'd wanted to understand every detail of Erin's last moments, and tears had run down Mel's face as she'd explained how she'd sat on Erin, how she'd never intended to kill her, but they'd been mucking about and it had gone wrong.

The police had wanted to know why she hadn't told them before, and she'd explained that she'd assumed Erin had run away, as her body had disappeared. She wasn't sure they believed her, but they had let her go after three hours, telling her they would investigate further. She was worried that they would charge her. Not for murder, but manslaughter. Mel had googled the maximum sentence for manslaughter on her way home. It was life imprisonment.

Mel couldn't face going back to school and finishing her day. She only wanted to see Lily, to hold her daughter in her arms. If she went to prison, she would lose her. So she drove to the nursery and picked her up after lunch, then took her home to play with her toys.

Mel was going to have to go and see Tamsin later, to tell her her side of the story, before the police did. But for the moment, she just wanted her daughter.

When she got home, Luke was in the kitchen, making himself a cup of tea.

'Mel?' he said. 'Are you OK? Why aren't you at school?'

Mel sighed. It was now or never. She doubted very much Luke would forgive her for what she'd done. But she already felt lighter after confessing to the police. Now it was time to tell her husband.

'Sit down,' she said. 'We need to talk.'

Mel put Lily in her highchair and placed a few toys on the tray for her to play with.

Then she explained what had happened the night Erin died, how it had all been an accident, and Luke listened intently.

'You mean, Dad wasn't lying?' he asked, finally. 'He did find Erin dead?'

'Yeah, she would have already been dead when he got there.'

'But I don't understand,' he said. 'Why didn't you tell the police what had happened at the time?'

Mel shook her head, remembering how scared she'd felt, how easily she'd been convinced by her mother that Erin had run away.

'Erin wasn't there anymore. She'd disappeared. It didn't seem possible she had been dead when we left. I thought she'd recovered and run away.'

'But you didn't tell the police about sitting on her? About her not moving?'

Mel shook her head. 'I felt ashamed and confused by what I'd done. And Mum told me not to.' A memory came back to her: her mother looking deep into her eyes. '*If the police come, you mustn't tell them that you sat on Erin. You mustn't tell them she wasn't moving. Just tell them about the midnight feast. Do you understand?'* Her mother had shaken Mel lightly, and Mel had said that of course she understood, that she wouldn't say anything. And she hadn't. She'd never mentioned it, no matter how many questions the police asked. Neither had Gabbie. And then somehow she'd just blocked those moments out of her mind, forgotten they had happened completely.

'She told you to lie to the police?'

Mel put her head in her hands. 'Not to lie. Just to omit some bits.'

Luke stood up and gripped the table hard. 'But if you'd told the truth then Dad wouldn't have been accused.'

'He buried the body, Luke. They would have still thought he was guilty.'

'But that's the bit I don't understand. Why did he bury the body? Surely that was more suspicious?'

Mel sighed. She hadn't told the police about her mum's role in the burial, but she knew she had to tell Luke. She didn't want there to be any secrets between them.

'Mum persuaded him to bury the body. She'd seen that Erin was dead. He was going to take her back to Tamsin. But Mum convinced him that everyone would think he killed her.'

'But she knew he hadn't.'

'She said she wouldn't stick up for him,' Mel said, sadly. However misguided it had been, she knew her mum had done that for her. 'She would have let him go to prison.'

'I need to speak to Angela,' Luke said, rushing out of the room. 'Right now.'

Mel picked Lily up from her highchair and followed him up the stairs. He burst through the door of Angela's room without knocking.

'What's going on?' Angela asked. She was standing by the bed folding her laundry.

Mel didn't know where to start. 'Luke knows the truth, what happened to Erin.'

'How could you do that, Angela?' he said. 'How could you let my father be blamed for so many years? How could you persuade him to bury her body?'

Angela shrugged. 'I did what I had to do. To protect Mel.'

'You need to get out of my home,' Luke said. 'I can't stand to look at you.'

Angela looked at him and then at Mel. 'Are you going to let him speak to me like that? In my own home? After everything I've done for you?'

'Surely you can understand why he's upset, Mum?' Mel heard her voice rising in anger. 'He's thought his father did something unspeakable all these years. He was estranged from him because of it. But I've gone to the police now, told them the truth, put things right.'

'What?' Angela's face paled. 'Are they going to charge you?'

'I don't know. They're going to investigate.'

Angela started laughing, a bitter, angry laugh. 'You shouldn't have told them anything. Me and Joe protected you. What was the point if you were just going to tell the police what happened?'

'We should have told the truth in the first place.'

Angela put her hands to her temples. She looked at Luke. 'I'll do what you want,' she said. 'I'll leave. Go back to Spain. I'll go as soon as I can. I know when I'm not welcome.'

FORTY-EIGHT

Luke and Mel went back downstairs in silence, Mel carrying Lily.

'I'm so sorry, Luke,' Mel said. She reached out to him, but he pulled away.

'I don't know what to think, Mel. This is such a huge thing you did. It changes everything. I need some time to think about it all.'

Mel understood. 'I have to go and see Tamsin,' she said. 'I need to tell her what I told the police. She needs to hear it from me.'

'Yes,' Luke said. 'You must go now.'

Mel swallowed. She couldn't bear the thought of telling Tamsin, but she knew she had to. She'd started to put her shoes on, when a flurry of messages came through on the street's WhatsApp group.

> Joe's been released. He's been spotted in Burton.

> I can't believe they let him out. He murdered a little girl. What were they thinking?

> The police are useless. There's no justice anymore.

Mel imagined these messages coming through one after the other on Tamsin's phone. How could she cope with that? It was her daughter they were talking about.

The messages kept coming.

> Where's he staying? We should pay him a visit.

> A B&B in Burton. Someone I know saw him arrive.

> We should go down. Take justice into our own hands.

> It's up to us to punish him. The police won't do anything!

> If we all turn up, he'll have to confront the hurt he's caused.

> I'm in!

> Me too!

> He has to answer to us.

> Yes!

> When shall we go down there?

> Now?

> Yeah, this is important. We need to show our solidarity. Show him that he can't carry on as if he hasn't done anything.

> I'm in.

> Meet at 5 p.m. outside the B&B?

> See you at 5.

> We'll be there.

Mel swallowed.

'Luke,' she said. 'Look at this.' She held up the phone towards him. 'We have to go down there and help Joe.'

She couldn't let them hurt him. He had protected Mel all these years, but now it was time for them to protect him.

Mel and Luke bundled Lily into her car seat and then raced over to Burton.

By the time they got to the B&B where Joe was staying there was already a crowd gathered outside, standing in small huddles, whispering. Nearly the whole street had turned up: Tamsin, Gabbie's parents, the parents from her school, everyone who had been at the party. There were others too, large men Mel didn't recognise. Someone must have let them know what was happening, told them to come down to intimidate Joe.

Mel went over to Deena, who was standing at the back. 'What's happened?' she asked her.

'Nothing yet.' With a jolt, Mel noticed Tamsin standing beside Deena.

'Oh Tamsin,' she said, struggling to find the words.

'I had to come,' Tamsin said sadly. 'Justice will never happen with the police in charge. I'm lucky to have friends who will do it for me.'

'It's not a good idea,' Mel said. 'Everyone needs to calm down, before this gets out of hand.'

'Don't talk to me about calming down. I've lost my daughter.'

'I know,' Mel said. 'But it's not Joe's fault.' She wanted to tell Tamsin that it was all her fault, but she found she couldn't get the words out. All these years Tamsin had trusted her, confided in her.

'Are you sure he's in there?' someone asked.

Mel turned to see a man from the crowd opening the door

of the B&B and a few of them storming inside. Mel handed Lily to Deena. 'Would you mind holding her a minute?'

Deena took the little girl into her arms and cooed at her, while Mel rushed after the others into the B&B. They were already past the reception desk and Luke was holding out his arms, trying to stop them going up the stairs. The receptionist was calling the police.

'Get out of my way!' one of the men shouted at Luke.

Luke stood his ground.

'He's the son!' another said. 'Just push him aside.' And with that, they barged past Luke and thundered up the stairs.

Mel went back to the doorway, and tried to reason with the rest of the group, to stop more of them piling inside. This was getting out of hand. 'We need to calm down,' she said. 'Think things through rationally. The police are coming. You don't want to end up arrested too.'

'He killed a little girl!' Someone shouted. 'He's going to get what he deserves.'

Just then, someone shouted from the back of the crowd and pointed down the street.

Mel saw a man walking down the pavement, hunched over, carrying a Tesco bag with his shopping. His grey beard was instantly recognisable.

'There he is!' The crowd surged towards him, surrounding him. Joe put his shopping bag down and held his hands up, perplexed.

'Murderer!' someone shouted. Mel saw the glint of a knife.

'Stop!' she shouted. She tried to stand in their way, to get closer to Joe. 'He didn't kill Erin.'

Luke had heard the commotion outside and had run out of the B&B. Everyone was outside now and he was in the middle of the scrum. 'Leave him alone!' he shouted.

'He killed her!' another voice shouted. 'Let's give him the justice he deserves.'

'No!' Mel said. 'He didn't kill her. Her death was an accident.' Mel felt a huge release as she said it.

'Of course that's what he'd say. But he murdered her.'

'No, it was an accident,' Mel insisted. She took a deep breath as the crowd fell silent. 'I was there.'

'What?' Now the crowd was turning on Mel. She saw Deena's face, but couldn't look her in the eye. Mel was glad she couldn't see Tamsin. She didn't want to see her reaction to what she was about to say. It would devastate her.

'It was a game gone wrong. Gabbie and I... we were trying to stop her running away. She fell to the floor and we sat on her. She couldn't breathe... She suffocated.'

'I don't believe you!' someone shouted.

'Why would she make it up?' Luke said. 'Why would she lie about something like this?' She stared into her husband's eyes, saw the pain etched across his face.

The mob turned towards them, surrounding Mel and Luke.

'But why didn't you say anything back then?' someone asked angrily. Out of the corner of her eye, Mel saw Joe sneak away behind the crowd and go inside the B&B.

A man grabbed Mel's arm. 'Why did you let Tamsin believe her daughter was missing?'

'Why didn't you just tell the truth?'

She couldn't answer any of the questions. 'I need to go,' she said. She searched the crowd until she found Deena, and barged through to reach her, ignoring the barrage of questions being thrown at her. 'Where's Lily?' she asked.

'You liar!' Deena spat. 'Gabbie wouldn't have hurt Erin.'

'Where's Lily?' Mel shouted desperately.

Deena frowned. 'I gave her to Tamsin to hold when everyone was going inside the B&B,' she said.

'Tamsin?' Mel looked around, but Tamsin was nowhere to be seen. And Lily was gone.

FORTY-NINE

'Where's Tamsin gone?' Mel shouted urgently, her heart pounding. 'Where's Lily?' She hadn't seen Tamsin's reaction to her confession, but she knew she would feel completely betrayed. Tamsin had wanted justice served for Erin. Now she knew it was all Mel's fault. Would Tamsin hurt Lily?

'She left,' Michael said. 'She went towards the car park.'

'Did she have Lily?'

'I didn't see.'

'She was carrying a child,' a man Mel didn't recognise said.

'Did she say where she was going?' Luke asked.

'She muttered something about needing to get back home. That this was no place for a child, with everyone shouting.'

'Let's go,' Luke said. 'I can phone the police on the way.'

'OK,' Mel said. She couldn't think clearly. All she knew was that she had to get to Tamsin's house, to get Lily back. They ran back to her car, and Luke jumped into the passenger seat. Mel looked anxiously at Lily's car seat behind her as she put the key in the ignition. She couldn't believe she was driving off without her daughter.

Luke called the police from the car. 'They'll be with us as soon as they can,' he said when he hung up the phone.

When they arrived at Tamsin's house ten minutes later, Mel rang the buzzer but there was no answer. She pressed it again and again.

'What if she's not here?' Luke said, looking at Mel desperately. 'I can't see her car.'

'She always parks in the garage,' Mel said.

She got out her phone and tried to call Tamsin, but she didn't answer. It just rang and rang.

'I'm sure she's here,' Mel said. Tamsin's studio was dark, but she could see light coming from the first floor, from Erin's room. She must be in there.

'Tamsin!' Mel shouted. 'Tamsin!' But there was no reply.

'We need to get inside,' she said to Luke. She remembered how, when she and Erin where young, Erin had used to go in and out through the window in the basement to meet the other girls at night. The window didn't lock and the hinge had been broken, so it opened inwards as well as outwards with just a little push.

'We can get in round the back,' Mel said. Luke followed Mel to the back of the house, out of sight of the street. Mel found the window and pushed it hard. It gave way as easily as it always had. Tamsin hadn't done much maintenance on the house since Erin disappeared.

Mel wasn't as thin or agile as she used to be, but she managed to slide down into the basement. As she did, she fell over something on the floor.

'Ow!'

'Are you OK?' Luke shouted.

'I tripped and hurt my ankle.'

Luke climbed through the window after her. 'Is it alright?' he asked.

'Yeah,' Mel said, wincing as she put weight on it. I'll be fine. We need to get Lily.'

Luke shone his phone torch around the room. On the floor was a rucksack, that Mel must have tripped over. Luke's torch darted over it, then stopped at the stairs. 'There are the stairs up into the house,' he said. 'Let's go!'

'Luke – wait!'

Mel grabbed his phone from him and shone the torch back onto the bag.

It was a light blue rucksack.

She'd known it looked familiar.

It was Gabbie's. The rucksack she had run away with.

Except she couldn't have run away with it. Because it looked like it had been in Tamsin's basement all along.

FIFTY

'What are you doing, Mel?' Luke shouted. 'We have to find Lily!'

Fear constricted Mel's throat. She could hardly get the words out. 'Luke – look. It's Gabbie's rucksack.'

'Why's that here? Oh my god...'

Mel was already dialling 999 on Luke's phone. The phone cut off. No reception.

'I can't get through to the police.'

'Mel – don't worry about that now. They're on their way anyway. We have to find Lily.'

Luke was right. They rushed through the cold basement and up the stairs.

Mel suddenly realised that the door might be locked and they wouldn't be able to get into the house. But when Luke turned the handle it gave immediately, and she found herself in Tamsin's huge, ornate hallway.

They ran up the stairs to the first floor, to Erin's room, and Mel pushed open the door.

Her mouth dropped open as she stared round the room. It had been ripped apart. Tamsin had taken a knife to the duvet and pillow, tearing the stuffing out of them and spreading it round the room. The books from the bookshelf had been pulled out and thrown all over the floor, falling open at random pages.

'She's crazy, isn't she?' Luke whispered. 'The grief drove her mad.'

'Let's check upstairs for Lily,' Mel said. 'She must be here somewhere.'

Mel ran up the stairs to the art studio and flicked on the light. Luke came in behind her.

'Tamsin?' she called out. The studio was fuller and more cluttered than ever, crowded with unfinished sketches and paintings. All the new ones were of Erin. A smiling little girl. A screaming little girl. A broken little girl. In some of them the likeness was realistic, but in others Erin's features were twisted out of shape in grotesque expressions of horror. Some were half-sketched, only her hair or her eyes or the jut of her chin. Others were drawn but only half-painted, the shock of the red of her dress the only colour.

Mel checked the living room, the bathroom, the kitchen. She kept expecting Tamsin to jump out or grab her from behind, but she didn't.

She picked up her phone again to ring the police. She knew there was reception in the studio.

When she looked at her phone, she saw she had a message from Deena.

> Tamsin is in the churchyard with Lily. You should come straight away.

FIFTY-ONE

As Mel drove over to the churchyard, her heart pounded. She kept thinking of how violently Tamsin had destroyed Erin's room. It looked like she had been in some kind of frenzy.

'Tamsin's killed Gabbie, hasn't she?' Luke said, quietly. 'Gabbie's rucksack is in her house. There's no other explanation.'

Mel frowned as she sped down the country road. 'I don't know... it just doesn't seem like her.' She couldn't get her head round the idea. But then she thought of how traumatised Tamsin was by Erin's disappearance. 'But maybe she knew about Gabbie's role in Erin's death. Maybe it was a kind of revenge.'

'How would she have known?' Luke asked. 'You and Gabbie didn't even realise you were responsible.'

Mel remembered Tamsin and Gabbie on the sofa at Tamsin's party, talking animatedly. Had Gabbie confessed what she'd done then? Had she wanted to clear her conscience before she left Laurel Street for good? 'I think Gabbie always felt guilty about leaving Erin alone. Maybe she just gave Tamsin a bit more information about what we'd done that night, and

Tamsin put two and two together. Gabbie must have told her at the party. Then Tamsin must have snuck away later to confront her when no one was watching.'

Mel thought of all the times she and Tamsin had watched the police investigation from Tamsin's studio, how quick Tamsin had been to suggest Stuart had had something to do with Gabbie's disappearance. Tamsin had known what had happened all along.

'Now she has Lily,' Mel said, panicking. 'What will she do to her?' They had to get to the churchyard quickly. Mel took a corner a little too fast and skidded slightly across the road.

'I'll call the police again,' Luke said. 'Tell them what we found. And that Tamsin's in the churchyard.' He rang the police as Mel drove into the village, pulling up haphazardly in front of the entrance to the church, her wheels spinning on the grass verge.

There were two figures in the graveyard, and Mel instantly recognised Tamsin's long, fiery hair. Mel and Luke jumped out of the car and ran over to her and Deena. The police tent that had been covering the grave was gone now and Erin's body had been removed, the grave refilled with soil.

Tamsin held Lily in her arms, and she was staring down at the grave, tears running down her face. Deena had her hand on her shoulder. 'She's here now,' she said. 'Mel's here. You can give Lily back.'

'Hello, Lily,' Mel said softly, and her daughter reached out her arms to her.

'No, you don't,' Tamsin shouted at her, her eyes wild. 'You don't deserve her. You don't deserve anything.'

'Come on, Tamsin,' Luke said.

'I'm so sorry about Erin,' Mel said, her words muffled by her tears. 'I didn't mean to hurt her. I never thought we'd killed her. I thought she was alive when we left. I thought she'd run away.'

'Well, you did kill her. You suffocated her!' Tamsin said, angrily. 'And now you think you can care for a child? Your daughter? That's not how it works. They don't let murderers look after children.'

The words hit Mel like a punch to the chest. She wasn't a murderer. She never meant to hurt Erin.

'She didn't mean to do it,' Luke said. 'She was only a child.' He tried to take Lily from Tamsin's arms, but she pulled her away, and Mel could see that Luke didn't want to physically wrestle his child from her.

'I'm so sorry for what happened,' Mel said. She desperately wanted to make things better, but she knew there was nothing she could say that would change anything.

'I still thought there was a chance they'd find her alive,' Tamsin said. 'But now I know the truth you always must have known, in your heart.'

'I didn't know!' Mel insisted. But she wondered if deep inside she had. She remembered the guilt she'd always felt around Tamsin, the way she'd desperately wanted to please her, to help her recover from Erin's disappearance.

Mel reached out to her daughter. 'Just give Lily back to me. Then we can talk.'

Tamsin stepped back, pulling Lily away from Mel and gripping her tighter. 'But we've done a lot of talking, haven't we, Mel? Over the years. You've always been there for me. Attended every memorial. I always thought you were the one who came closest to understanding what I was going through. After all, you'd lost your best friend. But you were the one who killed her. Well, you had me fooled.'

'I'm sorry,' Mel said to Tamsin. 'I really am. Please forgive me.'

'I loved her,' Tamsin said. 'I know she wanted to run away from me, but I loved her, I really did. I tried my best for her.'

'You did,' Deena said gently. 'We all try our best for our children.'

Tamsin spun round and turned on Deena. 'You tried your best for Gabbie, did you? You didn't do a very good job. She was as guilty as Mel.'

Luke took advantage of Tamsin being distracted by Deena. He lunged forward and grabbed Lily from her arms, pulling her away before Tamsin realised what was happening. He held his daughter close, kissing her on the head again and again. Mel took her from his arms and hugged her tightly.

Tamsin barely glanced up, completely focused on Deena, who was staring at Tamsin angrily. 'You shouldn't speak about my daughter like that,' Deena said. 'She's still missing.'

'I know how that feels,' Tamsin said bitterly. 'My daughter was completely innocent when she went missing. Unlike Gabbie. Maybe Gabbie's disappearance is karma. Maybe she's got what she deserved.'

Mel looked at Tamsin, thinking of Gabbie's rucksack in her basement. 'You killed Gabbie, didn't you?' she said to Tamsin.

'What?' Deena said, shell-shocked.

'Tamsin has Gabbie's rucksack,' Mel said. She turned to Tamsin. 'You killed her because you found out what she did the night Erin disappeared. She must have told you at the party. I saw you two, as thick as thieves on the sofa. And then after her argument with Stuart, you saw your opportunity to sneak out and kill her.'

'What are you talking about?' Tamsin said. 'You're the one who killed someone, not me.'

'Why's Gabbie's rucksack in your basement, Tamsin?'

Tamsin frowned. 'It isn't. Why would it be?'

Deena had heard enough. She threw herself at Tamsin,

pummelling her fists into her. 'What did you do to Gabbie?' she screamed.

'I didn't do anything! I didn't touch Gabbie!' Tamsin sank down into the dirt by the grave and sobbed, as Luke pulled Deena off her.

FIFTY-TWO

The police came while Tamsin was on the ground and they led her away, into a police car, to take her to the station to interview her. They took statements from Mel and Luke and they described exactly what they'd found in Tamsin's basement.

By the time Mel and Luke got back to Laurel Street, Tamsin's house had already been cordoned off and a team of police officers were searching it. Now they were sure that Gabbie had never left the local area. They had extended their search beyond the woods and into the surrounding farmland and fields, the media following their every move.

Mel was just glad to be home. Luke lit the fire and put Lily to bed, and then they sat on the sofa together. They were completely drained, as they tried to digest what had happened that day. Mel could hardly believe that Tamsin had Gabbie's rucksack, that she must have hurt Gabbie, most likely killed her. The chances of finding Gabbie alive now seemed vanishingly small. But Mel still held onto a glimmer of hope that she had simply run away. They hadn't found a body.

Above them, they could hear Angela in her room, opening

and closing cupboard doors. She came downstairs to the kitchen to get her washing from the machine.

'I'm doing what you want,' she said bitterly as she returned with the laundry basket. 'I'm going back to Spain. I'll be out of your way soon.'

'I think that's for the best,' Luke said evenly.

Mel didn't know what to say. She was too tired to deal with her mother.

'I just need to borrow some money for the plane fare,' Angela said.

'Aren't you riding there on your bike?' Mel asked. 'The same way you came?'

'No. That was exhausting last time. And I've decided to ditch the bike. I won't need it once I'm there. You can have it. You can sell it to cover the money you're going to lend me.'

'I didn't say I'd lend you money, Mum.'

'Come on, Mel. Otherwise I can't leave. There's a plane tomorrow morning. If you lend me £200, I can be on it.'

'OK,' Luke said, looking at Mel. 'I'll lend you the money. If you promise you'll get the flight tomorrow. Can you tell me the details?'

Her mother smiled. 'Of course. It's the 9.45 a.m. Ryanair flight.'

Luke searched for it on his phone and then showed Mel the screen. The flight was just under £200.

'I'll transfer the money now and then you can book it.' He clicked a few buttons on his phone. 'It should be in your account.'

'Thanks,' Angela said. 'I'll go upstairs and book it.'

When her mother had left, Luke turned to Mel. 'We'll have our home back,' he said.

Mel nodded. 'Do you really want to stay here?' she asked. 'After everything?'

'I don't know,' he replied. 'So much has happened. I feel like I don't know you anymore. Did you want to stay?'

'I'm not sure I can. This place is so full of bad memories. I'm still praying that Gabbie will be found safe and well.' Mel sighed, swallowing back a rush of emotion. 'But it seems so unlikely now. And even if she is, I'm not sure this is the right place for me anymore.' Mel wondered if she'd been drawn back to the street because she felt guilty, because she had unfinished business. Now she had told the truth, she didn't feel the compulsion to stay here.

'We'll have to talk about it later,' Luke said.

'Yeah,' she said. 'I hope we can work things out together.'

Luke shifted away from her on the sofa. 'Things haven't been good between us for a while,' he said. 'We've both kept secrets. It's too early to talk about our future together right now.'

Mel felt deflated. Her phone beeped and she checked it without thinking. It was a news alert.

She went pale. A body had been found two miles away from Laurel Street. Dumped in a cesspit on the farm the other side of the woods.

Her breath stuck in her throat; she could hardly breathe.

Gabbie.

FIFTY-THREE

'She was here all along,' Luke whispered, staring at the phone alert over her shoulder.

Mel felt tears streaming down her face. Until this moment she'd had some hope that Gabbie would be found alive. Tamsin had been so adamant she hadn't hurt her. But it wasn't to be. Gabbie was dead. The news was reporting that she'd died the night of the party.

Luke wrapped his arms around her, hugging her tightly. 'I can't believe it,' he said. 'I'm so sorry.'

Mel pulled away from his embrace, and Luke got up and started to pace up and down. 'I just can't get my head round this,' he said. 'I need to get out for a bit, get away from this place, clear my mind. Do you want to bring Lily and come with me?'

Mel shook her head. She couldn't go outside and face the press on Laurel Street. She wanted to stay inside by the fire, away from everyone else, and pretend that it hadn't happened. 'I'm OK here,' she said. 'But you go.'

. . .

After Luke left, Mel went into her mother's bedroom. She was packing her few possessions into the holdall that she'd brought with her when she first arrived.

Mel showed her the news headline wordlessly.

Her mother burst into tears. 'Oh my god,' she said. 'They found her.'

'In a cesspit,' Mel said. 'Someone put her in a cesspit. How could they?'

'It's this place,' Angela said bitterly. 'This road, it's poisonous. The things it makes people do. I need a drink.'

'No, Mum. Don't be silly. You can't start drinking again, not now.'

Angela laughed. 'Not even now? What does the article say? Do they have a suspect?'

Mel shook her head. It seemed so unlikely that Tamsin would have killed Gabbie and taken her all the way to the farm to dispose of her body. Mel read the article again. 'It doesn't say anything about a suspect. But it says there was a glove in the cesspit with the body. They're hoping to be able to identify who it belonged to.'

'A glove? Right. Let's have that drink, Mel.' Angela went past Mel and down the stairs. In the kitchen, she took out a bottle of wine from the fridge and poured herself a large glass. She downed it in one and poured another. 'That's better,' she said.

'Mum, don't do that,' Mel said, trying to grab the glass from her. 'Please.'

'Believe me, it's better than not drinking. I won't be here for much longer.'

'But you can't start drinking and then go back to Spain. It will be like it always was. You'll spiral again.'

'I don't mean Spain,' Angela said. 'I don't have time to go to Spain. They'll catch me before then.'

'They'll catch you?'

'Don't be so dense, Mel. You know exactly what I mean. The glove the police found. It's mine.'

'What? You knew where Gabbie was?' Just like she'd known where Erin was. Mel's head hurt. She stared at her mother in disbelief. 'What happened to her?'

'What do you think happened? I killed her,' Angela said, knocking back her glass of wine. 'And the ironic thing is, I was stone-cold sober. I always thought it was the wine that was the problem. But it's not. It's me.'

'Mum.' Mel thought of Gabbie, who'd been so full of life, with so much ahead of her. 'Why?'

'It was her fault, really... She was the one who was drunk and obnoxious. I bumped into her that night, when she was running away. I tried to help her. But no one ever appreciates my help, do they? Neither of you did when you were kids. And it's exactly the same now you're adults.'

'What do you mean, you were trying to help her?'

Angela sighed. 'I might as well tell you. I'm going to go down for a long time for this. Why don't you have a drink with me?' She took another wine glass from the cupboard.

Mel shook her head. 'Just tell me, Mum.'

'That night, I came to see you, to stay with you. I arrived late. I'd been riding for two days from Spain. I was exhausted. So when Tamsin told me I couldn't see you, I was angry. But it didn't matter. I had a key for your house. But when I tried to get in, I realised you had changed the locks. I tried to pick the lock but couldn't, so I walked round the backs of the houses looking for an unlocked outbuilding where I could shelter for the night. I didn't have much luck. Then I remembered the farmhouse. There were sheds there that I could shelter in, just for one night, until the morning. The bridle path along the edge of the woods leads there. So I took the bike down.'

Mel's breath caught in her throat. If only Tamsin had told

Mel that her mother had come to see her at the party, none of this would have happened.

'And when I was there, I saw Gabbie. She'd ridden her horse down there. She said she'd left Stuart, that she'd written him a note. She was leaving Laurel Street for good. But she wanted one final ride on her horse before she went. She was going to take it back to the stables and then leave. I felt sorry for her, and I said I could help her escape. I could give her a lift to the station on the bike. I was all ready to help her.'

'What happened?' Mel asked in a whisper.

'She laughed at me. When I said I could help, she laughed. She said why would she want help from an alcoholic like me? She said that I was the worst kind of mother, and if she ever got to be a mother she didn't want to turn out anything like me.'

'Oh, Mum,' Mel said. She felt a flicker of sympathy for her.

'I told her I was a good mother, that I'd done everything for you and for her too. How I'd arranged for Erin's body to be taken away to protect you both. And you know what happened? She just laughed and said she didn't believe me. That I'd made it all up. It was then I felt the fury. I wasn't myself. It was like I was taken over by someone else. I grabbed a shovel from beside the farm shed and I hit her over the head as hard as I could. I couldn't help myself. All my rage came out. All the anger I felt over what happened. Carrying the guilt all those years. Turning to drink. Losing you to my mother. It's sad, isn't it, that I went through all those things for you? For you and Gabbie. And as I thought all of this, I hit her harder and harder and harder.'

'I can't believe you did that,' Mel said. She felt sick at the thought of her mother battering Gabbie with shovel, imagining her screaming out in pain.

'Then I panicked,' her mother continued. 'I knew the farm well. I used to do Saturday work there as a girl. And I was right by the cesspit. I used the shovel to lever up the manhole cover, and I managed to drag Gabbie in. She was always so slim, and she hardly weighed anything. It was easier than I thought. I washed my hands under the farm tap and then I took Gabbie's horse and rode it back to the stables. By the time I got back, I was thinking clearly. I knew I'd made a huge mistake, that I could easily be caught when everyone realised Gabbie was missing. But when I got to the stables I saw that Gabbie had left her packed rucksack there. I remembered the note Gabbie said she'd written to Stuart. If I got rid of her rucksack, everyone would think she'd run away like she planned and no one would come looking for her. Luckily the party had finished and there was no one about. But I still needed to be quick. I needed to put her bag where no one would find it. Then I remembered the broken basement window at Tamsin's house that you and Erin sometimes used to get in and out when you were young. I prayed Tamsin hadn't bothered to fix it. I went behind the houses and approached the house from the back. It was risky, but there was no other way. I put the rucksack through the window of Tamsin's basement. I knew Tamsin never went down there. It would be a long time before it was found.'

Mel stared at her mother, hardly able to take in what she had told her. She had killed Gabbie.

'Did you think you could get away with it?' she asked. 'Is that why you were taking the early-morning flight to Spain?'

'I hoped to be out of the country by the time she was found,' Angela said. 'I was going to disappear. Maybe there's still time. They haven't come for me yet. You'd help me, wouldn't you?'

'You can't just leave, Mum. Not after what you've done. It's not right.'

Angela laughed. 'Really? All those years I spent covering for you, and you won't do me the same favour?'

'It's different, Mum. Erin's death was an accident. We didn't mean to kill her.'

'And I didn't mean to kill Gabbie. I just lost my temper. She provoked me.'

'Don't be ridiculous. That's no excuse.' Her mother was never able to take responsibility for her actions, always finding someone else to blame. 'They're going to find you, Mum. It will look better if you go to them first.'

Her mother sighed. 'You're right,' she said. 'They'll find me. I'll go to the police, but let me have one more drink first. Then I'll kiss Lily goodbye and we can take one final walk down Laurel Street together.'

EPILOGUE

6 MONTHS LATER

'It's time to say goodbye to Laurel Street,' Mel said softly to her daughter as she strapped her into her pushchair. All their things were packed up neatly in boxes in the living room and Luke would be round later with his van to help them move.

Mel was glad to be leaving. The investigation into Erin's death had hung over her for months, but finally the police had rung and told her it wasn't in the public interest to charge her with anything. They believed Erin's death was a childhood accident. She had wept with relief and then immediately put her home on the market.

Before they left, Mel wanted to take Lily along the street one last time. The sun streamed down on them as they made their way to the green, the grass parched yellow from a hot, dry August. Mel got Lily out of the pushchair and let her walk around on the grass. The swing still hung from the old oak tree, and Lily was still too young for it. Now she would never get to try it. Next to the tree, there were ashes from a recent neighbourhood barbecue, hosted by the couple who had moved into Deena's old house.

Behind the green, Tamsin's beautiful Gothic mansion was

covered in scaffolding. She had sold it to developers for a knock-down price, and the builders had already dug up the old fountain and turned it to rubble. Soon the building would be high-end flats. Tamsin had moved away as soon as she could, to a house by the sea on the south coast.

Mel hadn't spoken to her since Erin's belated funeral. Tamsin had finally put her to rest in a different plot in the churchyard where her body had been found. Mel had offered her condolences, but Tamsin had blanked her. Once she'd returned from the funeral service, Tamsin didn't leave her house again until she moved out for good. She was completely reclusive, only answering the door to supermarket deliveries. Mel had rung her buzzer so many times. She'd wanted to explain and apologise. But Tamsin had never answered.

Now Mel looked over at Gabbie's house. She could see Roz through the window, cooking. Stuart was standing beside her, drinking a glass of wine. They looked the image of the perfect couple.

'Come on, Lily,' Mel said. 'Let's go.'

Mel wheeled the pushchair down the bridle path beside Gabbie's house, to the stables. Stuart owned the horses now, and no one rode them anymore. Mel held Lily up so she could stroke the horse's mane and thought of Gabbie. She'd always been happiest when she'd been riding, and Deena and Michael had scattered her ashes along the bridle path and in the fields behind Laurel Street. They had moved away too, and were now living in a nearby village.

As Mel returned home, she thought of her final walk with her mother down Laurel Street, before Angela had confessed to the police that she'd murdered Gabbie. It had been chilly back then, but her mother had appreciated the fresh air on her face. She'd told Mel she was proud of her and reached out to hold her hand, but Mel had pulled away. She couldn't forgive her mother for what she'd done to Gabbie. Angela was in prison now, awaiting her trial for murder, but Mel hadn't visited.

When Mel got home, she saw Luke's van was already on the drive, and that he was waiting beside it, ready to help them move.

'Lily!' he said, rushing over to his daughter with a beaming smile, unstrapping her from the pushchair and spinning her round.

'Hi, Luke,' Mel said. 'How are you?'

'Good,' he said, with the easy grin she'd once fallen in love with. 'Are you all ready? I'll help you get the stuff into the van.'

'Thanks.' Since their split, Mel and Luke had managed to keep on good terms, but sometimes Mel felt a pang of longing for the relationship they used to have, the people they used to be. Luke had moved out soon after Gabbie's body was found. There had been too many secrets between them, and as hard as they'd tried, they'd seemed to be always arguing. They'd decided to take a break from each other, and that break had extended and extended. Mel still wasn't sure it was what she wanted, but she had found herself able to cope better than she had expected on her own, and teaching kept her busy.

'How's Joe?' Mel asked.

'He's good. There's a date for his trial – it's in three months' time.' The police were charging Joe with the unlawful burial of a body, but he was out on bail and Luke was letting him have supervised visits with Lily.

'Stuart's finished his new pool,' Luke said conversationally as they went inside the cottage.

'That's good,' Mel said. She knew that Luke had been working tirelessly to help him and Roz complete the project. The money he'd earnt was paying the rent on the small one-bed flat he was renting in Burton.

'It looks really beautiful,' he said. 'The glass roof lets the sunshine through. It's been returned to its former glory.'

Mel thought of how excited Gabbie had been about the pool, and felt a twinge of sadness. Roz had made the pool project her own, and there had been no expense spared. Roz and Stuart had a baby on the way, and they seemed to be the only ones who were happy to remain in Laurel Street in the shadow of Erin's and Gabbie's deaths.

Two hours later, Luke had disassembled all the furniture Mel was keeping and loaded it into the van, along with the rest of Mel's belongings. A house clearance company was coming later to take away the rest of the furniture. She didn't need so much for the small flat she was moving to.

Mel put the last box into Luke's van and then went back inside the house for one final look round, to check they hadn't left anything behind. Running upstairs to have a last scan of the bedrooms, she stopped at the window and looked out over the fields and down to the woods. She closed her eyes, remembering. In the back of her mind she could almost hear the sound of laughter, three little girls heading down to the woods for a midnight feast.

She opened her eyes and the sounds were gone and the sun was on her face. She was the only one left. After everything that had happened, Mel knew that she was the lucky one. She was the one who had the chance to start again.

A LETTER FROM RUTH

Dear reader,

I want to say a huge thank you for choosing to read *The Party on Laurel Street*. If you enjoyed it, and want to keep up to date with all my latest releases, just sign up at the following link. Your email address will never be shared and you can unsubscribe at any time.

www.bookouture.com/ruth-heald

I hope you loved *The Party on Laurel Street*, and if you did, I would be very grateful if you could write a review. I can't wait to hear what you think, and it makes such a difference helping new readers to discover one of my books for the first time.

I love hearing from my readers – you can get in touch on my Facebook page, through Twitter, Goodreads or my website.

With best wishes,

Ruth Heald

KEEP IN TOUCH WITH RUTH

www.ruthheald.com

 facebook.com/rjhealdauthor
twitter.com/RJ_Heald

ACKNOWLEDGEMENTS

Firstly, thanks, as always, to my wonderful family, who keep me sane while I'm writing and make sure I go out for some fresh air when I'm up against a tight deadline. This book has been particularly hard work, and I'm very grateful for their continued support and encouragement.

The Party on Laurel Street is the result of many people's labours. Thanks to my editor, Laura Deacon, for her expertise and for providing guidance, encouragement and patience when this book wasn't going the way I had hoped. My copy editor, Laura Gerrard, and proofreader, Jenny Page, have helped to fine-tune the prose. Thank you to Tamsin Kennard for narrating my audiobook, and to Lisa Brewster for designing the cover. Thanks to the marketing and publicity teams for helping my books to reach my readers. And to everyone in the wider Bookouture team, for being part of what makes Bookouture so special and for helping my books succeed.

Once again, I'm grateful to my beta readers, Charity Davies and Ruth Jones, who have given invaluable feedback and helped me to refine my ideas. Graham Bartlett provided incredibly useful advice on the mechanics of missing person investigations. And I'm always appreciative of the wonderfully supportive writing community, particularly The Savvy Writers' Snug.

Finally, and most importantly, many thanks to you, my readers.